Also by Robert Wilson

Barnum:
An American Life

Mathew Brady:
Portraits of a Nation

The Explorer King:
Adventure, Science, and the Great Diamond Hoax—
Clarence King in the Old West

Praise for *The Love You Take: A Novel*

"An … insightful novel about love and aging."

—*Kirkus Reviews*

" … And in the end *The Love You Take* comes unexpectedly: things get complicated, confusing, are you thinking clearly, or has your brain been hijacked? Robert Wilson's energetic, funny, sad, extremely relatable book about transitioning into adulthood is played against the serious backdrop of Vietnam and its aftereffects. Remember friends? Their couches, so often helpfully available? Hearty Burgundy? Singing along with Mick Jagger on the car radio, when those songs first came out? Alas, our country's on a very different road trip now, but this novel is a reminder that we don't leave the past behind, or need to; eventually, lovingly, we focus on the way forward."

—Ann Beattie, author of *The New Yorker Stories* and
Chilly Scenes of Winter

"*The Love You Take* is a novel of rare beauty. Wilson's clarity of expression gives us a perfectly transparent window into the lives of these characters and the times in which they lived. As I read, I kept being reminded of another great American realist, Richard Yates. I was entranced by this book."

—Steve Yarbrough, author of *Stay Gone Days* and
The Unmade World

"*The Love You Take* is a memorable and provocative exploration of life's timeless moral dilemmas—political stands, personal ambitions, faithfulness in love—those compelling universal lessons that Robert Wilson has successfully pulled into a vivid time and place."

—Jill McCorkle, author of, most recently, *Old Crimes: and
Other Stories* and *Life After Life*

"A front runner in this year's fiction list should be Robert Wilson's *The Love You Take*. Hard to believe it's a first novel, so convincing is the interior life and motivation of young Andy Watson and the pod of familiars who follow him through adventure and misadventure in 1970s America. The pleasures of Wilson's close observation keep pages turning. And, as Andy steers between the love of two beautiful women, toward shipwreck or safe harbor, the pages begin to turn themselves."

—John Rolfe Gardiner, author of, most recently, *North of Ordinary: New Tales* and *Newport Rising*

"This wise and witty—and often downright funny—chronicle of a young man's coming of age in the Seventies reminds us that while we may recall our lives according to where we were when catastrophe struck—Kent State, John Lennon's assassination—it is the people we knew, and the collisions we sustained with those people—some seismic, some silly, some both—that define us best. That is the news that stays news. No matter who you are, or where you are, or where and when you grew up, you'll recognize the people in this novel. You might even recognize yourself."

—Malcolm Jones, author of *Little Boy Blues*

THE LOVE
YOU TAKE

First Warbler Press Edition 2025

The Love You Take © 2025 Robert Wilson

ISBN 978-1-965684-47-4 (hardcover)
ISBN 978-1-965684-48-1 (paperback)
ISBN 978-1-965684-49-8 (ebook)

Library of Congress Control Number: 2025940148

warblerpress.com
New York, NY

THE LOVE
YOU TAKE

A Novel

ROBERT WILSON

warbler press

For Martha

PART I

CONCORD, 1970

1

ECAUSE ANDREW WATSON was a child in the Sixties, he could not be a child of them. The Berkeley Free Speech Movement, in the salad days of the decade, began before Andy's eleventh birthday, and although he was of driving, if not quite of drinking and doping age, by the summer of Woodstock, in the hazy golden final days of the decade, he had spent the summer not joining the half-a-million strong, but working on a tan. He was also working on his longtime girlfriend, Shelley, urging her to join her untanned parts with his in the sofa-like back seat of his grandfather's 1967 Chrysler Imperial. Andy's had not been a summer of love but a summer of heavy petting, and yet it was by far the heaviest to date, so he was not in any way discontented or even disappointed.

It had not bothered him, either, to have missed the news-magazine version of the decade, those marquee events involving "the frees"—speech, love, and drugs—that had so aroused the prurient interest of Manhattan's button-down-shirt weekly journalists. After all, the kids his age got their own Sixties. It lasted about five years, and it started exactly five months and five days after the real Sixties ended. His Sixties, better known as the early Seventies, began in blood, just as the real Sixties had ended, and his Sixties would sidle out, with the end of the Vietnam war, just as the real one had sidled in. Andy had long since lost any enthusiasm he might ever have had for Vietnam, had he been old enough to think much about it, and the '68 convention in Chicago had troubled him enough to make him notice for the first time that his parents' take on televised events could be so much at odds with Walter Cronkite's. But Kent State, in May of 1970, was the first large public outrage to get to him beneath the tan, so to speak. Suddenly not only were his parents wrong, not only was his country wrong, but his aspirations were wrong, his college was wrong, and even his clothes were wrong—although that was pretty easy to fix, because he proceeded to wear the same green fatigue pants and red knit shirt for twenty days in a row after Kent State. On the twenty-first day, he laundered.

He had set off for college the previous fall with sports coats and flannel slacks and even a suit, and each piece of clothing had had a small strip of cloth with his name on it sewed in. Concordia College in the beautiful valley town of Concord, Virginia, was something like a higher form of prep school, all-male, tradition-trod, honor-bound, well-endowed. Andy was a public-school boy, but he had taken easily to the casual, upper-class mediocrity of the place, the shirt-cuffs-rolled-up, jacket-over-the-shoulder look, the slouching gait, the confident and confiding way of speaking. Unlike the prep-school boys, Andy had had to study to keep up, but he did this furtively, and no one thought the worse of him for it if they caught him in the act. It was looked upon as a minor vice, like unceasing mastur-bation or an unwillingness to drink—separating him from the crowd, but not fatally.

He joined a fraternity—not without soul-searching about which one, and not without a warning that the one he'd chosen was comprised of a "bunch of potheads." Andy did not quite believe that real people he really knew really smoked pot, but the warning turned out to be prophetic. His fraternity was one of the things lost in the moral confusion if not conflagration of the month following Kent State. The national organization closed it down for wanton dope smoking and an utter indifference to paying its bills. The Concordia chapter would be reinstated only after Andy's class had graduated four, and in some cases five or six, years later.

He made friends. Not in the fraternity, particularly. After all, most of the older guys were stoned most of the time, a state that Andy did not recognize for a few months. They were friendly but zonked—not conducive to real friendship. But real friendship would turn out to be something that Concordia College offered Andy in abundance. It would take not months but years for him to recognize that. For all its narrowness, its relative isolation, its determination to fall short of real excellence, its cruel absence of female students, Concordia was a perfect medium for friendship. He would make friends for life there, and even those friendships that weren't for life were so vivid that they would give him retrospective pleasure for many years. It was no substitute for Shelley, offering herself without urging now that the field of play was not the plush back seat of the Imperial but the slightly filthy sheets of his dormitory bed. But that was weekends. Friendship was for the rest of the week, for the rest of his life.

THE DAYS LEADING up to Kent State had been unusually beautiful, even by the high standards of spring in the great western valley of Virginia. The afternoons had been so warm and clear that the campus had already turned itself inside out. Seminars moved outdoors, and in the labs the large unscreened windows of the science building had been thrust open to the sunlight and the distant views of the greening mountains. The dress code had perceptibly relaxed—ties loosely knotted at mid-chest, shirttails flapping, more and more Bermuda shorts in evidence. The campus was restless, after a cold winter, anxious to propel itself straight into the summer that those toasty spring days foretold.

For many freshmen like Andrew, the habit had developed

after supper in the dining hall to drift to one of the rooms in the student union for television watching. After the last few minutes of the comically inept local news from Roanoke—filmless reports of fires, endless footage of the tree in which a cat was invisibly stuck, the weather girl who could not quite coordinate her patter and her arm motions with the screen behind her—Cronkite would crank up the national news. Here was a brief connection with home, the longstanding ritual of turning, stomachs full, to the alarming events of the day—the faraway war, the domestic protests and even riots. Since the '68 convention, Uncle Walter himself had seemed increasingly alarmed, his voice tight, his face red, and Andrew and his friends had, like much of the rest of the nation, become attuned and susceptible to this subtle ratcheting up of the old newsman's emotions. In those days even the great Cronkite—undoubtedly the most trusted, seemingly the most rational man in America—would not tip his hand in any way. But it was the very subtlety of the signs of his deepening anger that made it so powerful, the way a certain bob of the head or emphasis on a syllable would betray the effort to remain straight-faced.

Everyone who watched, not just in the student union but throughout the land, knew what Uncle Walter did not, that this was not as be believed a question of journalistic comportment. In truth it was a long-running morality play, with Uncle Walter cast as Virtue and the former vice president as Vice. It was Tricky Dick Nixon's latest move that finally made the epic personal confrontation explicit even to Uncle himself. The old wire-service correspondent, a print guy after all, had not been able to swallow the Nixonian word "incursion" to describe the early May invasion of Cambodia. Uncle spit the word out like so much ash on his tongue, his attempt at putting verbal quotation marks around the word giving it a strange hissing emphasis, almost as though Beelzebub himself were ventriloquizing through the kindly face of this venerable dummy. With the first utterance of the word, the slouching, full-stomached crowd of students snapped to attention, bracing for moral if not mortal combat. The word did not come up just once but several times in the newscast, and each time was turned into the same unearthly epithet.

Once Cronkite had released them with his trademark banality, the boys stumbled out into a golden evening, the sun having passed beyond Hump Mountain but still brightly illuminating the puffy occasional clouds above. Andy found himself walking as he did most nights in the direction of his ill-fated fraternity house, hurrying to catch up with one of the other freshman members (the class had passed imperceptibly from pledges to what nobody called brothers). His name was Hubert, and he was a sweet, frizzy-haired, marble-tongued Savannah boy. Andy and Hubert had sat up late one September night on the steps of what was about to be known as the Old Gym, deciding whether the pot-smoking reputation of the KAs should deter them from joining up. They had actually cried, being somewhat inebriated, at the prospect that these dastardly rumors might be true, and in the end had decided, soberly they believed, to follow their instincts and go with these roadmap-eyed boys they liked so much. By Valentine's Day Hubert was roadmap-eyed himself; he got stoned every day until Easter break, and it was after that that Andy himself had fallen somewhat less heavily under the influence of the demon weed. Unlike Hubert, and ever the plodding, aspiring public-school boy at heart, Andy had continued to make his classes, except for the occasional eight-thirty ones. As it turned out, he received only knowledge for his extra effort. The school would soon be on strike and all grading suspended for the semester. Even Hubert got to pass that term.

As he caught up to Hubert, Andy said, "Nixon's really done it this time."

Hubert looked up, startled, and said something in his nearly impenetrable Coastal South accent that sounded like, "Mo-fo-go-do-ay," which Andy naturally interpreted to mean, "Yeah, that motherfucker's really going to pay." But on further reflection, and remembering Hubert's careful upbringing and exquisite manners, Andy realized his friend had meant, "Yes, mother will be dismayed." Hubert's mother, it seemed, was the only white lady in Savannah-Georgia who was against the war. Her disillusionment had grown out of a particular disappointment in the neighborhood boys, who had not only not ridden off to war on white horses as their great-great-grand-daddies had done, but had faked "every sort of disease including homosexuality" to get out of it. Little by little his mother had realized, as Hubert told it, that it was the Black boys who not only went to war but returned home covered in glory, although dead. Because Andy agreed with her general interpretation, while fully prepared himself to head for Canada, he did not wish to inquire too closely into the exact attitudes that fueled Hubert's mother's seeming right thinking.

When they reached the fraternity house, a handsome 1850s brick affair in the front yard of which the town had inexplicably allowed a post office to be built, they found the older boys sprawled in a somewhat more kinetic state than usual.

"Road trip," announced one. It was not a question but still an invitation. "Thursday Kunstler's speaking in Charlottesville. Got to make that *scene, man.*" The emphasis was meant to be ironic.

"Mark me down," Andy said.

"Mo-fo," said Hubert. Me, too.

"We will mark you down and toke you up," said Goodrich, who had a car and thus was the trip's organizer.

It seemed that William Kunstler—who had grown famous representing the Chicago Seven—those mix-and-match radicals accused of conspiring to undermine the not-very-good name of the city of Chicago during the '68 convention—had been scheduled to speak to the law school in Charlottesville this same dramatic week. Such was the restlessness even of doped-up frat boys in that warm time in early May that they were drawn even by the prospect of seeing a bottle-tanned old attorney with the irritating habit of parking his glasses far up on his head, where his deeply receded hairline marked a too-dramatic transition from too-brown skin to too-dark, too-wild hair. Kunstler might look like someone's youth-worshipping grandmother from Miami Beach, but his silken tongue, a virtually frictionless environment from which his decades-old radical clichés could tumble, had a remarkable appeal for the likes of Andrew, just emerging from the cocoon of opinionless childhood.

Hubert said something that Andrew first interpreted to mean, "Kunstler's going to make us see the light." But since Hubert was digging in the pocket of his remarkably dirty khakis, Andrew reconsidered. "Can't I make a contribution for a lid?" seemed a likelier interpretation.

"Save your coin, my frosh-faced friend," said Goodrich. "I've got pounds of the stuff in the trunk of my car." Goodrich and a few of the other KA boys had spent the previous summer in agricultural pursuits, managing to grow half an acre of what they called hemp among the two thousand or so acres of prime Mississippi bottomland his Memphis lawyer father owned. Goodrich liked to tell how proud his father had been of him and his friends, living in a former slave cabin, tending the acres of cotton, soybeans, and sorghum the old plantation land still supported. But it had not occurred to Goodrich's boasting father that the fraternity boys had early cut a deal with the kindly Black farmers who actually worked that land, so that Goodrich and friends could lavish the hour or two of energy they could muster a day on their real crop. Ever since he had returned to school, Goodrich had taken genuine pleasure in imagining those farmers sitting before their coal stoves on cold evenings getting baked on Mississippi Gold, as Goodrich called his product.

And so a carload including Andy and Hubert would make its way two days hence up the valley and over the mountain to Charlottesville. But two days hence the campus world will have changed utterly, and Kunstler the entertaining radical will be Kunstler the pied piper of the Piedmont, a man who would lead the provincial prepsters of the Old Dominion down the path of the hipper, smarter universities of the north and west.

YET IT WOULD be a university that was neither hip nor smart that would blow the lid off. Kent State, by its very banality, proved that the antiwar, anti-Nixon, pro-dope protest movement was not just a product of too much leisure and money, too many SAT points, and too little reality. To murder students at Berkeley or Antioch, Harvard or Michigan, to have attacked the advance guard—this would have been appalling but not surprising. But to strike at State U.—middle-class kids with student loans, kids whose politics just might extend to a disinclination to wade through rice paddies for *what*—that act redefined the *us* and the *them*. In a matter of one or two days the us included at least some element of every college and university in the country, perhaps excluding the service academies and other military schools. Even at the girls schools within dating distance of Concordia, such towers for belles as Sweet Briar and Hollins, the maidens doffed their dresses and donned their denims (how had a million pairs of jeans faded just so in the fanny, developed peekaboo slits at the knees, all without anyone's really noticing, and seemingly all at once?), their blue work shirts, their green fatigue jackets, and scarves of red or blue calico tied cowboy-style at the neck? In these uniforms they were ready to march, bearing roach clips even when wearing pearls. The muffled sounds of desert boots stepping lightly became a background noise on the newly dangerous landscape of the campus. The shining-faced, statue-like pose of the Kent State martyr Alison Krause just before she fell became the image of a new Jeanne d'Arc, and it burned in the brain of everyone under the age of twenty-two. In their legions these straight-haired college girls descended—with or without dates—upon University Hall in Charlottesville.

To this very day it is hard to find, from that intimate universe of college students in Virginia in the year 1970, one who does not claim to have been in University Hall that evening. And although the flying-saucer-shaped basketball arena could not possibly have accommodated all those who later made the claim, the crowd was indeed vast—a vast sea of wasted youths. Andy, Hubert, Goodrich, and two or three more upperclassmen of his acquaintance had piled into Goodrich's hemped-up Bonneville and headed for Mary Borden College—Lizzie Borden as it was inevitably called. There they more or less randomly invited several—three? four? who knew?—women along for the ride to Charlottesville.

When Andy entered the arena, it was instantly apparent that this speech would be unlike any college lecture anyone there had ever attended. The place was already nearly full, and as Andy climbed with the rest high up to where some seats remained, they passed a Breughelian tumult of excited kids. Frisbees soared far out across the spacious hall to the cheers of those in the crowd who could still follow them with their eyes. Far down on a stage that was set up on the basketball floor, a band provided raucous, nondescript rock music. Even louder than the music was the murmur of the exuberant spectators. The scent of marijuana wafted over Andy in waves. A parade of kids climbed past them to seats still higher in the building's upper reaches. Gone among their clothing was any trace of what most of these kids had worn not a month, not a week, before: khaki, madras, silk, wool—gone; boating moccasins and espadrilles—gone; dresses—gone, gone, gone.

Denim, denim, and still more denim. Army green and camouflage. The occasional Hawaiian or African print. Headgear of all sorts, from Aunt Jemima-style kerchiefs and berets to Australian bush hats and baseball caps. Headbands? There were some. Granny dresses? Yes. Tie-dyed T-shirts? Okay. Bell-bottoms? Of course.

The tumult below, and above, and all around the arena continued for what seemed to Andy both a very long time and a series of vivid moments—many of them charged by the image of a beautiful long-haired girl, cheeks red with excitement and anticipation, eyes red with need-I-say-what. The truth was not that Andy was fading in and out of consciousness, although his memories of the event would have suggested this. Finally the band stopped, and if the Frisbees did not cease to ply their lazy arcs, the sound level fell to a low babble. Onto the stage bounced a law student who, in the pre-millennial days of April, would have worn a herringbone jacket and khaki pants, but was now wearing an olive drab T-shirt and the inevitable tattered jeans. His introduction was less that than an exhortation, a whipping-up of the crowd with references to "our brothers in Chicago"—Abbie and Jerry and the rest—and to the evil but comic Judge Hoffman. Soon the crowd was roaring its approval or disapproval, and when they had reached the right pitch, the law student, who is today undoubtedly well beyond the point in his career of using those powers to derange juries, did at last introduce the celebrity of the hour.

But it was Kunstler's pleasure to quiet the unruly crowd, to pinch them back from the possibility of premature ejaculation. He adjusted his glasses just so upon his forehead. Thus the crowd was signaled that this was not a speech he would read, but one coming from someplace deep inside. He spoke a few quiet halting words—too silent for Andy to hear—and then he spoke a little louder. "News ... serious news ... very serious news has just been delivered to me through channels I trust." It was his understanding, he said importantly, that the slaughter at Kent State had not been limited to four students after all. He had it on good authority—"through underground channels," a phrase that made half the kids in the audience think involuntarily of the gurgling caves that dotted the Blue Ridge—underground channels he did not name or describe, he had information leading him to believe that the deaths at Kent State, the executions by Nixon's goons, had numbered in the dozens, and that Kent State was only the beginning of another sort of incursion. Nixon meant to silence the campuses, to kill as many longhairs as he found necessary. Nobody knew where his soldiers might strike next.

A low murmur began again among the potentially targeted. Most of the people within Andy's range of hearing were saying only "Huh? What'd he say? Why can't he speak up?" but when these questions asked softly were multiplied hundreds and thousands of times, the murmur seemed ominous rather than quizzical. As the level began to rise, it became apparent that a claque had formed or been formed directly in front of the stage, from which the odd cry of "pigs" or "murderers" emanated. This group was hairier by far than the rest of the crowd, and certainly dirtier-seeming—Andy could tell this from the fifty-yard distance that separated him from them. Somehow they didn't smack of Virginia college students.

As Kunstler prattled on, piling outrageous untruth upon ever more outrageous untruth, the claque began to utter a single word over and over again with metronomic monotony. The word made no sense at first in the context of what Kunstler was saying. His paranoid ravings would seem to call for expressions of disbelief, or at least outrage to match their outrageousness. But instead the claque yelled, *Strike!* Huh? *Strike!* Strike what? *Strike!* Strike back? *Strike!*

Soon, though, Kunstler the Old Leftie took his speech where the claque was leading it. For him if not for any of these mostly privileged, mostly, until recently, Republican kids, this was a moment whose promise had been pending for decades. *Strike!* What he had before him was not a bunch of stoned-out college kids but—a proletariat! *Strike!* Workers! *Strike!* Workers of the world! *Strike!* Unite! *Strike! Strike! Strike!*

The kids were roaring back at the stage now. Andy, Hubert (although to the uninitiated his expostulations sounded more like *Stuck!*), the Mary Borden girls, and even the entrepreneurial Goodrich, were howling the word at the top of their voices. *Strike!* For what slowly dawned on the sobering, sweating crowd was that this excitable old radical was suggesting that they, well, cut classes, and cut on a level that they'd never even contemplated before. This went far beyond Senior Skip Day in high school. *Strike!* And at such a lovely time of year. Kunstler was screaming now, "Close it down, close it down, close it down!" In his own mind, of course, the shaggy Kunstler was striking, striking at the very heart of the capitalist beast. To close down this major university, perhaps the most elite of all the public universities in the country, the cerebral cortex of the military-minded South, what a headline this would get in *The New York Times.* Even Uncle Walter would have to lead with it. Never mind that this campus had once been the dream of one of the world's great revolutionaries. Never mind that these kids, most of them, were not even enrolled here.

2

T HE NEXT DAY, the day after the Kunstler rally in Charlottesville, would be remembered as the last normal day at
Concordia in a long, long time. For Andy, this day would
seem, when he thought about it later, to be the last day of his
former life, perhaps even the last day of his childhood. By
that evening the world in which Andy had so pleasantly been
drifting, the world of back seats or dorm beds with Shelley, a
world disconnected from what appeared on the television news,
suddenly became charged with meaning. Not that everything
suddenly became meaningful; not that he knew what the meaning was. But from that time hence the world would not simply
exist for him as a medium like the ocean in which a fish swims.
It would forever more be subject to interpretation. All actions,
whether by presidents of nations or presidents of small men's
colleges, whether by one's draft board or one's French professor
or one's blind date, would be subject to political interpretation.
Anyone, from the Black barber in Concord who only rarely now
cut Andy's hair to the braless and far from brainless exchange
students from Hollins to the many professors only now finding
the courage to come out of the closet—any of these people could
be casually deemed fascist or Marxist, their most banal gestures
described as reactionary or revolutionary. Perhaps because this
need to label applied to everything—a meal in the dining hall,
a rainy day—the powder behind these charged words soon
went damp. While the need to judge was urgent, the judgments
themselves were mild. Andy and his suddenly radicalized

classmates were young and far from home, the weather was generally beautiful, and their responsibilities were few. Just how bad could anything be, even the fascists who wanted to mow the broad front lawn of the university—a reactionary impulse if ever there was one—even while Andy and his revolutionary friends were trying to occupy a blanket-sized section of it?

For on that day after the Kunstler rally, the second day after the Kent State massacre, it was not just the odd Milton seminar that was meeting out-of-doors. The word had gone out on mimeographed notices hastily composed and stealthily posted that all Concordia students should gather on the front campus that morning, on the downward-sloping expanse of grass that formed a sort of amphitheater. Its stage was a slate rectangle at the entrance to Cyrus McCormick chapel, a place built in the last century at Concordia by the great inventor himself. His reaping machine had indeed sown concord in the South, throwing out of work thousands of Black descendants of slaves, sending them north with their families to the big cities, and placing a poetically just burden on those cities more destructive, almost, than the north-south war itself. A statue of Cyrus in glowing white marble graced the entrance from one side, its arm raised in a gesture of what? Peace? Capitalist glee? The moment of discovery? As the days on the lawn would wear on, it was noticed by Andy's friends that Cy's arm pointed vaguely north. The new interpretation of the gesture was that he was hieing the Black population out of town.

Andy had first seen one of the posters soon after his return from Charlottesville. The excitement of the Kunstler rally had more than offset the effects of dedicated cannabis consumption, leaving the carful of kids in the relatively safe hands of the bug-eyed Goodrich. Adrenaline had driven them home in what seemed like minutes, and even the stop at Mary Borden to drop off the girls had been perfunctory, featuring none of the usual cajoling or wheedling intended to land the girls at Concordia for the whole night. When Andy and Hubert disembarked at their dorm, with the mildly disingenuous cries of "Peace, man!" and "Far out!" drifting after them from the Bonneville's open windows, they were still too charged up to stay put. It was not yet late in any case, not even eleven o'clock, and the dorm was half-empty. The two friends wandered back downstairs to the quadrangle, and discovered there and beyond small clumps of students in excited but amiable conversation. The boys saw the first poster on a door to the co-op.

STRIKE!
Join the free university!
Meet by Cy!
First Bell!
Stop the War!
STRIKE! STRIKE! STRIKE!!!

"This is it," Andy said. "The revolution comes to Concord."

"Stuck," Hubert said, rather mildly, it seemed to Andy.

FIRST BELL WAS pretty early for a revolution, eight in the morning, but such was the level of expectation on campus that Andy rose by seven-thirty, showered, donned his green Army fatigue pants and his red knit shirt, and wandered over to the dining hall, intent on consuming a big pre-strike breakfast. Several of his friends had already gathered at the long wooden refectory table where they usually met, and seemed by their heavily burdened trays to have shared Andy's concern that the strike might be so effective as to end for the moment the regular supply of prepaid meals. Only Hubert's tray contained no food, just several white institutional mugs of black institutional coffee. Andy could tell with one look that Hubert had been up all night, presumably having procured a tab of amphetamine after the two boys had parted just past midnight. Not only was Hubert's thin, high-cheek-boned face, normally a rusty-looking red, now sallow, but beneath his enormous lips came the steady sound of his teeth involuntarily clicking, a sure sign that he was on speed. His eyes were bloodshot even on a good day, but they looked less sleepy than usual—exhausted, perhaps, but filled with a chemical liveliness, too.

Next to Hubert, leaning into a tray displaying an assortment of breakfast meats—not just ham, bacon, and sausage but even the idiosyncratic scrapple—sat Rick the ultra-rationalist, a young man who would turn out to be spectacularly unsuited to these emotional, go-with-the-flow, fuzzy-thinking times. Argumentation was so intrinsic to Rick's personality that only he among their friends failed to see that he was destined for law school and a lifetime of litigation. Rick argued that he would surely be a philosopher-king, or at least a philosophy professor.

"Running low on chipped beef this morning, Rick?" Andy asked by way of greeting. "Perhaps I could get you a couple of Slim Jims from the co-op, just so you get enough animal protein?"

"You know I never eat no SOS, army boy. Too much flour makes me lose my edge."

Rick did have the look of a philosopher, Andy thought, or a monk. Like Hubert he was hollow cheeked, but his dark hair and bushy dark beard formed a perfect spiral around his face, bringing to mind a Russian anarchist like Kropotkin, or perhaps an Eastern Orthodox priest.

"Didn't see you at the rally last night, Rick," said Andy.

"Well, I was right there in seat 2-2-9-D. Don't know how you could have missed me."

"Rick spent the evening in the library," said the third member of the group, John Stuart Brockenbrough III, a handsome, self-possessed, and even well-dressed boy from Richmond, whom everyone called Saint John.

"Reading Hegel," Rick explained. "Appropriate, eh?"

Andy, who was an English major, had only vaguely heard of Hegel and had no idea what Rick was getting at.

"Think I'll get some food," he said. "We've got a university to close today."

As they wandered across the campus half an hour later, their stomachs were leaden with the sort of foods the revolution really ought to do away with, not just the pig meat on Rick's plate, but the scrambled eggs, grits, hashed browns, and white toast that, between them, Saint John and Andy had consumed. Even Hubert had been prevailed upon to eat something, a lowly and seemingly harmless banana (so rich in potassium, as Andy's mother liked to point out at home), but soon to be recognized as the most male chauvinist of fruit, the very symbol of what was wrong with the relations between the sexes. And think how neatly it symbolized what was wrong with American foreign policy. Banana republics, indeed. Still, Hubert seemed revived by the banana he'd consumed, either that or the four-teen teaspoons of sugar that had gone into the four or five mugs of coffee he'd drunk. Sugar and coffee—more foreign policy implications to be explored there later, as the free university would soon teach them.

But what another glorious day, the sunlight poking through the leaves of the massive oaks high overhead, taking the chill off the May morning. A heavy dew had fallen, which would have made sitting on the front lawn at this hour a problem, had there been anyone looking for a seat.

At the moment the rally consisted mostly of its organizers, six or eight people standing idly, paper coffee cups in hand, watching as two or three others fussed with a microphone, an amplifier, and four large black speakers. None of the leaders appeared to Andy to be undergraduates. One was an older law professor Andy knew from his flaming red beard, which was famous on campus, and the others were young faculty and what Andy took to be law students. The microphone faced the lawn and the audience that had not yet appeared; across and above the lawn stood the college's oldest building, Comity Hall, which once had housed the whole academy that preceded the college, but now was the campus administration building. Flanking it on either side were three or four other old brick classroom buildings of various heights; each of them had white columns that together formed a colonnade of three or four hundred feet. Normally at this time of day, moments before the first class bell rang, the brick path between the columns and the buildings would be crowded with students moving as quickly to class as an ambling gait could take them. On this morning there were not more than a handful of students peering around the columns at the somnolent activities on the lawn below them. Four big speakers blared in a way that could only sound abrasive at such an hour, but the words were the anodyne, "Test, one, two, three, four … test, one, two, three …" After a few minutes the repetition itself grew irritating, and yet no member of the college administration burst forth from Comity Hall to silence it.

Still, when the first class bell did sound, Saint John worriedly excused himself. "Professor Bear in public administration," he said by way of explanation, although none of the rest of the group had heard of this professor, nor could they really believe that there was a class at the college so named. Off John bustled to the commerce school building, at the south end of the colonnade, a building in which Andy had never once set foot.

John returned in a few minutes.

"No Bear," he said sheepishly.

"Any other brown noses like yourself show up?" asked Rick.

"Only a couple," said John, no longer doubting that the revolution was indeed at hand.

Hubert weighed in with what Andy first thought was a lame pun on Professor Bear's name: "Does a brown bear shit in the woods?" But since Hubert was reaching for the copy of the Roanoke *Times* that Rick had tucked under his arm, "Has anyone heard the news?" now seemed likelier.

"Nothing on Kunstler," said Rick. "And even the war itself doesn't make the front page. There is, however, extensive coverage of a city council meeting and a compelling photograph of an accident scene after the wrecked cars have been towed away."

The four boys were getting tired of standing, and the level of activity both behind the microphone and in front of it was beginning to pick up. The dew on the grass was still heavy enough to discourage flopping down there, so Saint John, who had the nicest pants and thus the most to gain, offered to hike back up to his room and fetch a blanket for them to share. Hubert offered to go on a coffee run, which left Andy alone with Rick for a few minutes.

"Do you suppose that anyone there," Rick began, nodding at the microphone, "has really thought about what they are doing? The school hasn't closed once since the death of Cyrus McCormick."

"Not even for Pearl Harbor? Not even for a blizzard?"

"December 7th was a Sunday," Rick patiently explained. "Monday the college was open. The biggest snowfall was twenty-eight inches in 1897. Everyone lived on campus or a short ride by horse away."

"You know this because … ?"

"I recently read *The View from Comity Hall,* by Jefferson Davis Schwartz."

"That fascist? Andy said.

"What the book lacked stylistically it made up for by its scrupulosity with the facts."

"Scrupulosity?" As an English major, Andy felt safe asking this with a certain skepticism.

"Look it up," Rick responded with a dismissive wave of the hand.

When Saint John returned with the blanket he also had in tow Susanna Agincourt, an exchange student from New Orleans by way of Hollins. Susanna's eyes were sleepy beneath the perfect circles of her wire-rimmed glasses, and her arms were clasped tightly beneath her breasts, as though she were chilly despite the knee-length L.L. Bean pea coat (possibly John's, given its size?) she'd thrown over her shoulders like a cloak.

"Coffee," she said in a zombie-like monotone. "Café. No chicory required."

Hubert returned at this very moment and drew a paper cup of it out of a paper bag. He said something that, had it not been offered as an interrogatory, Andy would have assumed was "Damn, what a mess," but given the upturn at the sentence's end and the shy, glittery-eyed smile with which he extended the cup, he'd probably said, "Damsel in distress?"

"Why thank you, gentle knight," said Susanna with a slight curtsy. "Sir Hubert of Savannah-Georgia, thanks be to you."

Meanwhile, John spread out the handsome red-plaid wool blanket and the five students arranged themselves on it, each taking a cup from Hubert's bag. The extra cup had likely been for Hubert himself, but he never flinched in giving it up, only distributing packs of sugar and powdered cream and stirrers as requested.

By now the big speakers had begun to blast out music—at the moment, it was the Rolling Stones doing "Brown Sugar"—as a clarion call to the campus at large. More people had straggled down the hill, and other blankets bearing students began to dot the hillside in an aimless pattern. The group behind the microphone had also grown larger, and a lot of earnest-seeming conversations had begun. Perhaps they were deciding the order of attack. The sun was now high enough to bathe the lawn in gentle sunlight, and the dew began to steam up from the still-plentiful empty spaces on the grass.

After a while it dawned on Andy that the discussions behind the microphone must have had to do with who would speak first. Perhaps the day of revolution had arrived at last, a day of potential comity such as even those who had built Comity Hall up yonder had never hoped to see. Now everyone on campus— from the freshest freshman (if there were any of those left) to the most cynical young faculty members (those who knew that, given their Ivy educations and ABDs from prestigious grad schools, Concord was merely a layover, a place of rural quietude where they could finish those dissertations) to the senior faculty (GI Bill PhDs from Plains states who were now for all their lack of distinction turning distinguished looking and would live out their days hereabouts)—everyone would at last be equal, equal, equal. Perhaps this day had finally arrived, but not one of those among its self-appointed harkeners wanted to go first, not until a sufficient crowd had gathered. Such was the day's momentousness that the faculty could no longer worry about casting pearls before swine, however many of the teachers tended to wrinkle their noses at the porcine qualities they observed in so many of their students.

No, now was a time for elevated oratory, for the likes of a Patrick Henry or even a Cicero, and each of the dozen or so ill-dressed men beneath the raised right arm of Cy's statue, each believed that his would be the speech remembered down the long years of the post-revolutionary order.

So it was something of a surprise when one small man neither young nor old burst out of the group and grasped the microphone. He was not ill-dressed at all but rather natty in a lightweight gray suit, white button-down shirt and a tie not fashionably wide or offensively thin, a just-so streak of yellow down his shirt front that evidently (given his willingness to start the revolution off) was unmatched by a similar streak down his back. Who was this dainty figure, Andy wondered, waiting for the crowd to settle, exhibiting that air of authoritative impatience of the professor at his lectern? Just then Saint John uttered with reverence and wonder the unlikely appellation, "Professor Bear!"

"That's Bear?" asked Rick in a voice that carried, followed by a loud snort. "That's BEAR?" he asked again incredulously.

The professor seemed not to hear. Still he waited for the crowd, which by now had grown to maybe four-score and twenty, waiting with that cool confidence that struck such fear in the scholarly hearts of Public Administration 202.

"Citizens of the world," he at last began, perhaps too grandly, it seemed to several of those sprawled there on Saint John's blanket, if not to John himself. "A great wrong has been perpetrated by the leaders of our nation on a sovereign empire far away."

"Holy shit," said Rick in his usual deafening whisper. "He thinks Cambodia still has an emperor."

"No, he doesn't," Andy felt compelled to respond, not knowing what his objection would be but anxious to save John the embarrassment of his mentor's being caught by Rick on this point. "'Sovereign empire far away' is in quotation marks. It's an allusion."

"Yeah, to what, you English freak?" Rick asked.

"Shakespeare," Andy replied confidently. "One of the histories."

Rick gave him a disbelieving look but Andy stared him down.

"World order depends," Bear was saying, "on the fundamental recognition of international borders. For our own government," and there were definite quotation marks around that word, "to ignore and transgress these borders ..."

Here Bear paused meaningfully, whether to emphasize his point or to search for the perfect phrase his audience knew not, "To ignore and transgress these borders is a violation of ..."

With the second pause, even those gathered on the blanket really did give Bear their full attention.

"... is a violation of PUBLIC ADMINISTRATION!"

At those words Saint John leaped to his well-shod feet and yelled an apparently heartfelt "Right on!" His sudden movement caused Susanna to let loose a scream and upend her coffee. Fortunately the pea coat had been well waterproofed and the still-hot liquid dribbled harmlessly onto the grass beside the blanket.

Professor Bear seemed encouraged by the commotion that his opening salvo had produced, but instead of raising the level of his rhetoric it seemed to calm the diminutive orator. The timbre and cadence of his speech became more, well, professorial. No further yells of radical solidarity were heard from the crowd, even from the rapt Saint John, and after fifteen or so monotonous minutes Rick floated the accusation that Professor Bear was delivering the class lecture that had been scheduled for John's eight-thirty that morning. John tartly disagreed, but none of the other three on the blanket were anxious to take John's side this time. Even the clutch of would-be speakers standing behind Bear seemed to be concerned that he was discouraging the still-growing crowd. Groups of those assembled had started to search out other amusements, so that toward the back, high up the lawn, students were standing in cocktail-party-like clumps from which an increasingly loud buzz of conversation and laughter was coming. At last one of the technicians was convinced to accidentally let forth a blast of the Grateful Dead ("Living in the Past," some thought, although the excruciatingly loud music lasted for only a few seconds under a withering look from Professor Bear). Still, Bear took his cue and wound his speech up to polite and scattered applause. Even Saint John did not rise to his feet at the anticlimactic end.

While Bear had been speaking, the five had restlessly shifted their weight on the blanket, looking for a comfortable spot. At one point Susanna, who was sitting behind Andy, companionably fitted her legs behind his back, supporting part of his one hundred and seventy-five pounds. "Feels good," he said distractedly. "Mais, oui," she replied. He'd only known Susanna part of spring semester, since she'd begun spending more time with John. He wasn't sure what her relationship with John was, but he had his suspicions. They were well matched, both tawny and blond and quietly confident as young southerners often are who know themselves to be of a certain class.

This proximity to female flesh, even flesh presumably dedicated to someone else, made Andy think of Shelley, with whom he hadn't spoken in three months now. They'd broken up, inconveniently enough, on Valentine's Day, and on the phone. He couldn't really remember why, just a vague sense that her distance from him—she had gone to school a state away in Greensboro—somehow pleased her. He'd bummed rides to see her early in the fall, and she had come up for homecoming and a few other weekends, and there had been Thanksgiving and Christmas of course. But since Christmas break it had seemed increasingly inconvenient for each of them to visit the other. January had been shot by semester exams. He had studied hard trying to make up the ground his public school education had placed between him and what Concord evidently expected of the likes of him. *This* Shelley had not quite understood and perhaps not quite believed. In any case, they had been unable to agree on a plan to see each other in the weeks between exams and Valentine's Day, and each had found it harder to reach the other at night when they'd try to call the hall phones in one another's dorms. It was only in the final hour of Valentine's Day itself that Andy had been able to find Shelley, and he was firmly in the grip of jealousy by the time he did. And so the Valentine's Day call had been nasty, brutish, and short—and had been the last communication between them of any kind.

Since then, Andy had had a few dates with girls from the nearby women's schools, and a crush of several weeks' duration on a friend of John's from Richmond now at Hollins, a girl with the most porcelain skin and the chilliest disposition he had ever known. Whenever they had been together, he had felt that he was viewing her from slightly behind—her long, straight, sparklingly brushed hair revealing only an oblique profile of her face, a wonderful face, but one always concentrated on some distant and invisible spot. Her name was Mab, and he could not help but think of her then and now as Queen Mab, from the land of the faeries. Her unapproachability had touched him at first, as had her odd willingness to see him at all. But that latter quality disappeared soon enough, and in the few weeks he had been acquainted with her he had made no progress in coming to know her in any way. It had felt like having a bit part in a fairy tale whose happy ending was destined for somebody else.

Susanna shifted her legs slightly, stirring Andy from his reverie. He turned to give her a smile and watched as she wriggled out of the oversized pea coat, Saint John courteously lending a hand, although his attention was fixed on the speaker who had taken up the microphone after Professor Bear. Susanna looked up and caught Andy watching her. "Quoi?" she said, but her look showed she was pleased to be watched. Despite the reddish blond of her hair—the color of heart pine—her eyes were dark and her skin had a slight olive tint. Beneath her bangs her face narrowed from broad cheekbones to a narrow jaw. A fox in more ways than one. Andy did his best to dazzle her right back.

The red-bearded law professor had followed Bear at the microphone, and although he was a more dynamic speaker by far—and had dressed carefully for the occasion in hunting boots, a red flannel shirt, and faded Oshkosh overalls, over which he wore a threadbare but once-expensive tweed sports coat—he also seemed trapped by his own academic specialty. This specialty, it appeared to Andy, was constitutional law, a fact soon confirmed by Rich, who despite his professed aversion to the law, knew the names and courses taught by each of the dozen professors at Comity's small but undistinguished law school. In this way, too, Andy learned that the speaker's name was McGrew. The professor had begun winningly enough by addressing the students directly, a somewhat more personal and certainly more realistic approach than Bear's imagining a worldwide audience for himself.

"Are you comfy, lads?" he'd started ingratiatingly in a low voice. "Sun not too strong in your faces?" He continued by praising them for putting themselves forward at this early hour—by now it was close to 10 A.M.—and praised the loveliness of the day and of the season. Everything he said was soothing, as comfortable as the way he was dressed. McGrew tugged now and then at his flaming beard and this, too, was comforting to the hundreds of students now sprawled before him. A long silence began, one in which the professor stroked his beard contemplatively, a silence broken as the clock in McCormick Chapel's steeple tolled out ten times. The professor pointed up at the steeple with an impish grin, as though he had timed his speech for just this event. Then, after waiting for the reverberations of the bell to fall away, McGrew straightened himself and without further warning yelled into the microphone the words "WAKE UP!" It was a bellow that needed no amplification to startle his listeners, but the microphone chipped in a teeth-rattling exclamation point in the form of screeching feedback. The effect was of course quite literal—any student who had been half asleep or who had dozed off during the Bear era or anyone whose interest, had, like Andy's, drifted, was now paying what felt like highly caffeinated attention. But McGrew's meaning also turned out to be metaphorical. He urged his listeners to wake up to the misdeeds of the Nixon administration. The deeds he chose to enumerate, the continuance of the war without proper declaration, the widening of it into Cambodia and onto the campus at Kent State, each had for him profound constitutional implications, none of them reassuring. These he began to spell out in a brisk but possibly too detailed way. From professor he seemed to slip slowly into the role of prosecutor, chief prosecutor at Nuremberg, say. Although the audience listened soberly, very few of its members could in the end follow McGrew's arguments. When he wrapped it up half an hour later the applause was certainly more enthusiastic than that for his predecessor, but it could not be said that, beyond the startling wake-up call, he had electrified them, or even told them clearly why they were there.

At this point one of the law students who had begun to take charge—he had introduced Professor McGrew and thanked him afterward—had the wisdom to urge the students to take a five-minute break for stretching and other nonrevolutionary behavior, such as taking a pee. For this purpose many members of the crowd ascended the hill, and it felt like nothing so much as halftime at a football game. Sensing this as he led John and Hubert away, Rick called back, "Can I bring anyone a bag of popcorn?"

Andy and Susanna were left facing each other, Susanna standing slightly uphill, so that she seemed the taller of the two. They covered their shyness at being alone together by elaborate stretching, maneuvers that caused Susanna's breasts to rise and fall exuberantly beneath the thin material of her pale blue work shirt, and just inches from Andy's face. Seeing his dazed expression, she rubbed his head briskly, her fingers penetrating his thick brown waves right to the scalp. "Wake up again, Andy," she said with a smile.

"You speak English," was his reply. "We can communicate after all."

"Mais, oui," she said. "I do believe we can."

THE FIVE-MINUTE BREAK stretched to half an hour, but by the time the law student reclaimed the microphone, as the last strains of Jimi Hendrix—his "Star Spangled Banner" from Woodstock—echoed up the hillside, the sun was warm and nearly every available patch of grass was now occupied by young men and a surprising number of women, who had apparently come from surrounding colleges and the local high school. This time the law student was not at the mic to cede the stage. Instead he began an hour-long address that changed everything for those who listened, changed the listeners, and changed Concordia, since those now assembled made up a large percentage of its students and not a small percentage of its faculty. This law student—his name was Ringwald and he was a moot court star, according to Rick—had a perfect halo of tight dark curls, an Afro such as Andy had never seen before on a white head. He wore blue jeans and a blue-jean jacket, which he would shed to reveal a black T-shirt, and he actually had a red bandanna tied across his forehead. For this cliché Andy forgave him as soon as he recognized the impressive rhythm and control of Ringwald's words. He spoke without notes and in the face of increasingly rowdy eruptions of support, and yet it was a speech that even Andy's English professor said might be printed unedited. This professor, handsome and easygoing, had taken a seat on Andy's blanket on the other side of Saint John from Susanna, who had resumed her role of supporting

Andy with her bent legs. What Ringwald's speech did that the others had failed to do was to give the big picture, to list the range of grievances that these mostly well-to-do young college students ought to realize were their own: The war itself, of course, and the draft; the attack on a college campus; the Nixonian program to turn the antiwar young into the enemy at home. But the subtlety of Ringwald's approach was his appeal to these self-satisfied, basically conservative kids as an elite, as people who owed something to those further down society's ladder. The poor and the Black were losing their lives in this pointless war, not to mention the tens of thousands of peasants in Vietnam itself who merely wanted to return to growing their rice and fishing the sea. He could not speak the words that hovered over this appeal, so satisfying to his audience's sense of social superiority, not in these egalitarian times. The words were *noblesse oblige*.

Ringwald controlled his listeners like the conductor of a big-city symphony, like Herbert von Karajan himself, and the crowd produced a most pleasing noise. It wasn't long before these usually self-conscious kids were yelling without irony the most hackneyed phrases of the youth movement, words so stale that the writers at *Time* and *Newsweek* had begun to appropriate them: not just "Strike" and "Right on" but chants of "Hell no, we won't go" and "One, two, three, four/We won't fight your dirty war"—chants that didn't precisely express the spirit of solidarity that Ringwald's speech was aiming for. But the most lasting impact of that hour was the model this shaggy young man created in the minds of his listeners, a model of earnest and rational critique.

What he was able to show these kids, what many of them now realized for the first time, was not only that the large events reported by Uncle Walter touched their lives in a very immediate way, but that small decisions they made in their everyday lives could profoundly alter the seemingly immutable forces of government and industry. Ringwald was the first person Andy heard to use the metaphor of the butterfly in Brazil whose flapping wings could cause a howling storm in China. And, down the years, the next sixty-seven times Andy heard the same metaphor or close variations of it, he could not help but think that Ringwald had invented it, for nobody else elaborated it so eloquently or to such effect. What Ringwald produced in these sons of southern bankers and doctors (and grandsons of segregationists and double-great grandsons of slaveholders) was a searching sense of social responsibility. Many of those he touched, it's true, were only able to maintain that blessed state of knowledge for the glorious month of May in the otherwise pretty dismal year of 1970. Many of them underwent a thorough course of deprogramming when they returned to their comfortable homes for the summer. Their attempts in early June to, for example, have the servants seated at the dinner table with the rest of the household were not, on the whole, well received. Oddly enough, even the servants themselves were made grouchy by the suggestion. And in a hundred other ways, large and small, these students were eventually encouraged to recover their senses.

But another large chunk of that audience listening in the shadow of Cy McCormick's statue was more or less permanently altered. This included perhaps seventy percent of the five people first seated on John's blanket. Rick was hopeless, of course, a sort of Ayn Rander even before he'd had the questionable benefit of reading her. And John was only half-convinced. Or perhaps it would be fairer to say that half of Saint John's personality had had no need of alteration, for there was in John's sweet disposition a real nobility, a selflessness and sympathy for others the source of which was mysterious to Andy. And, it must be said, there was in the other half of John's makeup the unyieldingness and even severity of his aristocratic family and the others like his that thought of themselves without embarrassment as among the First Families of Virginia.

It's true that Ringwald's appeal was simplistic, a reduction of the world's complexities and subtleties to the most rigid binary system: us and them, good and evil, reactionary and revolutionary, fascist and socialist, and even young and old. Ringwald was far too bright and far too aware of those in his audience to float the pretty silly idea of the untrustworthiness of anyone over thirty. But his rhetoric was sufficiently shaped by the rhetoric of the time to make it clear that the revolution was to be a revolution of the young, a youth movement. Ringwald also knew his audience well enough to understand what limits to place on his critique of the college itself. Much of that criticism was abstract, and when it did focus upon Concordia he made it clear how inappropriate any form of violent protest would be, a fouling of the nest, an unproductive form of self-destruction.

"Remember, friends," he said. "We're the university, those of us sitting right here, not those," pointing up the hill toward Comity Hall, "not those sitting up there." To burn the ROTC building would be pretty stupid, he said, especially since that building on the backside of the campus also housed the departments of physics, chemistry, and biology. Once the free university they were about to create had taught its lessons, "We'll need the sciences to build a better world."

Andy's English professor, Martin Wainwright, repeated the phrase "a better world" in a tone that Andy couldn't quite name. It was neither critical nor approving. Perhaps wistful got closest to it. When he said it he lay back on the blanket and took a meditative drag off the unfiltered French cigarette he was smoking. This prop was always on hand when Professor Wainwright lectured on American poetry, or read the poems in his sonorous southern voice, so slowly that you could almost believe you understood what they meant, even Wallace Stevens—"We live in an old chaos of the sun/ And old dependency of day on night …" Andy guessed that the professor was nearly forty, although there was something youthful and robust about him. For one thing he always had a healthy tan, from summers on Crete and a long winter break in Key West. And although he did not dress like the students, he did dress youthfully, in leather boots and neat Levi's. He wore a tie, as all professors and indeed all students had until this epochal week, but it was a knit tie carelessly knotted, and his shirts were plaids or wool. His hair, too, was somewhere in length between student shaggy and professorially trim. He had a distinctive style, but it was a style that was careful not to alienate any group. His manner also said that he was as comfortable on this blanket full of students as he would be at a faculty meeting. And despite his elaborate casualness, there was something slightly thrilling about him to Andy. He was single and it was said that he had slept with many a colleague's wife. Perhaps it was this sexual danger that Andy sensed.

The end of Ringwald's speech was a call for a free university, open to all the people of the town of Concord. "We don't need to take over Comity Hall," he said, again pointing up the hill. "We'll just move the college right down here." He proposed a series of lectures over the next few days and weeks that would be conducted not just by professors of law and history, economics and political theory, but by potters, yogaists, transcendental meditationists, organic foods proponents, and experts in the arts of peaceful mass demonstration. And, of course, "You'll tell us what you want to learn," Ringwald promised, and "we'll find someone to teach it." Rick muttered something about a course in group masturbation, but for once something he said under his breath was not audible several hundred feet around him. Then for the second time in two days Andy found himself standing in a crowd of people yelling the word "Strike!" at the top of their lungs. The general absence of marijuana on this morning gave a greater sense of reality to the proceedings, and something about it made the hair on Andy's arms go all prickly. This seemed more like disobedience to Andy, who had always been such a good boy. It made him feel just a little bit scared.

3

STORM TROOPERS DID not descend upon Concordia College to beat the protesting students black and blue. Nor did any administrator appear on the scene to interrupt the day's events in any way. By late in the afternoon the college president had acquiesced to demands booming up the hillside from the microphone in front of McCormick Chapel that the college shut down for the last few weeks of the term. This could be seen as a courageous decision by President Prettyman, given how unlikely it was to ingratiate the school with its wealthy and conservative alumni. But many other colleges and universities made similar decisions during those dangerous days—even colleges in such peaceful and out-of-the-way places as Concord. Only a single small incident marred Day One of the Revolution in any way, when a group of groundskeepers on riding mowers attempted to cut the grass on the sweeping hillside below Comity Hall. More than a few of the students assembled—sleepy though they were from having eaten lunch, lounged an hour or so afterward in the sun, and in some cases indulged in one of the many fat joints now passing through the crowd—more than a few were roused to their feet and to verbal protest. Wednesday afternoon turned out to be the scheduled time to cut that particular patch of grass, and the presence of five or six hundred people densely populating the space was not seen by the head groundskeeper as an insurmountable impediment to this routine. Of course some of the students reacted as though a Panzer division had been loosed upon them by the administration. Dean Quirk, the assistant dean of students, who had been discreetly monitoring the day's events from behind the shade of a second-story window of Comity Hall, sensed the possibility of trouble and quickly made his way to the north end of the hillside.

There the flanking maneuver of the Panzer mowers had been stalled by a group of shirtless students hurling not insults, quite, but words the groundskeepers might well have felt were tinged with condescension. The students said things like "Look here, comrades" and referred loudly to the men on mowers as "Our fellow citizens" and even had the nerve to offer the flagrantly offensive "Join us in our protests, proletarian brothers." Before the tensions could rise to a more explosive level, the assistant dean had advised the head groundskeeper that, given how little rain had fallen lately, perhaps the grass could wait another week. With that the blue-shirted workers raised their mower blades and rumbled off in the direction from which they'd come, leaving the shirtless students with not so much as a nod of the head in solidarity. The students were so stunned by this rudeness that they forgot to call out "Peace" or "Right on" at the happily defused situation. The barriers of class would have to fall some other day.

For Andy Watson the twelve hours between noon and midnight of May 5th would be among the most significant hours of his life. That morning even Andy himself would have admitted that he was still little more than a big boy. By midnight he would be … not a man, exactly, but no longer quite a child, either. For one thing, by midnight he would not be returning to his solitary dorm room alone, something that he'd done each night since the Valentine's Day breakup with Shelley and, given how rarely she'd visited, for most of the nights before the breakup. No, by midnight the foxy Susanna Agincourt would be at his side, eager or at least willing to hazard the unchanged sheets of his narrow iron bed. And as they embraced just inside the door, the room dark except for the uncertain light filtering in through the open window, there was little of the trepidation on either side that the moment might have borne for two young—and at least in Andy's case, fairly inexperienced—lovers ready to dive into bed together for the first time. This confidence was undoubtedly in part because Andy and Susanna had already vigorously and more than satisfactorily coupled twice that evening, once in Professor Wainwright's sauna and once on the concrete footbridge that connected the back campus to the athletic fields on the other side of a ravine.

Like the porridge at the Three Bears' house, the first taste of love had been just a little too warm and the second just a little too cool—not that either party really cared. But this time was just right. An appealing thing about Susanna for Andy, who was years away from mastering the art of separating women from their undergarments, was her utter eschewal of any. Earlier in the day he'd noticed at close range the unfettered state of her breasts, and in the sauna, of course, she had been wrapped fairly casually in nothing but a not-large towel. On the footbridge he'd wondered whether she'd left her panties at Professor Wainwright's, but it had not been the moment for even solicitous inquiries. Once Just Right unfolded in the dorm bed and Susanna had whispered several apparently sincere "Mon Dieu," they began to speak of simple things, waiting for their breathing and heartbeats to slow.

"So what's the deal with you and underwear?" Andy ventured.

Susanna ran her hands down the sweaty front of her body. "Don't own any," she said with one of her radiant, foxy smiles.

"None?"

"Pas du tout," she said firmly.

"Far out," was all Andy could think to say.

They lay side by side with the sheets off, listening as the

music from perhaps a dozen stereos reached them through the open window. Simon and Garfunkle. Procol Harem. Three Dog Night. Black Sabbath. Even a little Motown. On an ordinary weeknight stereos would have been silent after 11 P.M., but because all studying had ended with the suspension of classes, so had many of the small number of dorm rules the college had until this day tried to enforce.

After a little while a more serious consideration occurred to Andy, and he blurted it out as soon as he thought it.

"What about, um, birth control?"

Susanna gave his cheek a little pinch. "How gallant of you to think of this now, Andrew Watson, now that you've added what feels like several quarts of oil to my crankcase."

"Oh, I'm sorry. It was just that in the heat of the, uh, moments … But, really …"

"The pill, Andy. Even my mother insisted on it. 'You'll be one of ten coeds with thirteen hundred boys?' she asked. 'I don't much like those odds.'"

"Your mother sounds pretty cool," Andy said.

"My mother is a realistic lapsed Catholic lady from New Orleans, who thinks of herself as mostly French."

"Got it."

One other serious subject came up as their damp bodies cooled in the night air, eventually to the point of chilliness, which caused them to pull the sheets up and hold each other. That was Saint John. John had been the reason they'd gone to Professor Wainwright's, to a dinner that had also included several older students and four young faculty members from the English department. During the afternoon Rick had eventually wandered off in disgust (muttering, as a critique of the rhetoric he was hearing, "Fuzzy-wuzzy was a bear …"), and Hubert had started to come down off the Black Beauty he'd taken the night before. So Hubert (with a parting peroration that Andy thought was a tribute to his native Savannah, but was in fact an elaborate good-bye to Susanna) went back to his room to sleep for what would turn out to be about thirty-six hours.

Professor Wainwright had lingered on the blanket with Andy, John, and Susanna until late in the afternoon. Then he'd asked them to his house outside town for supper, and departed to go to the grocery store and to have a nap before they were to show up at about seven-thirty. Because she was a junior, Susanna was permitted to have a car, and John knew the way. In the hour or so after the others had left and before Professor Wainwright had, the four of them on the blanket had seemed to pair up, and even when the older man departed John did not seem to be reclaiming Susanna. Once the speeches had ended for the day, the three of them climbed back up the hill to their rooms to shower before supper. They met later at Susanna's newish Peugeot and John made for the back seat, acknowledging without saying so that Andy should be up front with her. John gave no hint of a sulk or of having had to relinquish Susanna. During the brief ride he had been his usual friendly and well-mannered self with both of them. He had been in a good mood, and his fine-featured face, reddish from the shower and the day's sun, seemed lit from within. Once they reached their destination, down a twisting dirt driveway, and been introduced to the guests who had arrived before them, John had gravitated toward the kitchen and Hal, as they had been encouraged to call Professor Wainwright, whose middle name was Harold. It was a friendly group of people, and although Andy and Susanna were comfortable in it, they had hung together and been accepted by the others as a couple.

Now, their eyes having adjusted to the indirect light entering through his dorm window, Andy looked at the disheveled Susanna and said, "I'd thought you and John might be a pair, especially when you showed up in his coat this morning."

"No," Susanna said. "We're good friends, but being together would not be possible."

Andy still didn't get it. "Why not? You seem so well matched."

"How to say this, Andy. Our Saint John, for all his many virtues, doesn't, um, like girls." She wore a careful little smile that condemned neither John for his nature nor Andy for his naiveté.

Andy was quiet for a few minutes as bits of information fell into place like tumblers in a lock.

"And Professor, ah, Hal?"

"Prince Hal seems to have an eye for John."

"But what about his reputation as a lady-killer? All those faculty wives?"

"I guess you'll be holding the lady-killer title after today, Andrew. As for Hal, who knows? Is his hetero virility a myth the students hand down year to year so they don't have to acknowledge the truth about him—a guy they, let's face it, find pretty cool and even attractive? Perhaps it's a myth Hal encourages? This is a conservative campus, or was until this week. Not a very safe place to be too obviously pink."

Andy did not have any more questions for the time being. He was spent in every way it was possible to be—physically, emotionally, mentally, and certainly sexually. He held Susanna tight, so tightly that the line where their bodies touched grew slick again. Soon Andy could tell from her breathing that she was asleep. By all rights he should be too. The stereos had shut off one by one and it was quiet on his hall and outside his window. But Andy's mind still raced.

THE DAY HAD filled Andy with revolutionary zeal, or at least the sweet Virginia version of it, and he had found without knowing he'd been searching for it a new way to look at what he experienced day by day. In effect he'd learned for the first time to think about his life—what it meant, how it measured up—and to think about the lives of those with whom he came into contact. Either of these two revelations would have been more than enough to mark this day in his memory, but there had been more. Not least, Susanna, the first girl or woman he'd known who had frankly wanted him and hadn't waited long to claim what she wanted, a woman (at least in this sense) whose experience matched his ardor. As they had been playing out their desire for each other in the last hours of the day, it had seemed that each took on an aspect of the other's defining quality, so that he became more confident as she became even more unguarded. ("It's not my habit to do it in public," she told Andy as they'd hoisted themselves up from the cold cement of the footbridge.) And then there was what Susanna had told him about Andy's professor and Saint John. Andy was not so much shocked at them as shocked at his own unawareness. If he had not seen this, then what else out there was he missing? Was Rick a narc, Hubert a dealer? Was Susanna's interest in him something impersonal, something that the day's exertions had satisfied and so concluded?

And yet he'd learned one more thing that day.

The party at Professor Wainwright's, so successful in Andy's estimation because of where he and Susanna ended up, had worked yet another change in how he saw the world. Concordia was a college that prided itself in the easy relationships between its faculty and students. Concord's small population and lack of diversions had as much to do with this as anything the college might try to sell (in alumni magazine photos) as the Socratic model at work in the co-op or on the handball court or, most improbably, under a picturesque tree. Many members of the tenured faculty did invite students into their homes. The event might be a small seminar that meets one afternoon during the semester at the professor's handsome Federal-style house, where his bright but stir-crazy wife, who gave up on her PhD to raise the children who were now gone, had busied herself in preparing a high English tea. Or it might be a garden party in the late spring at the chairman's towering Victorian honoring all the graduating majors of his department. But there were also a handful of faculty members, often single, who like Hal Wainwright had grown tired of most of their colleagues and had chosen to associate with students, often asking them alone or in small groups to their houses for dinner. Andy had got wind of such events but never been invited to one. Not many freshmen were, perhaps not any besides the likes of John, who had caught the eye of a professor and known himself well enough to offer a frank gaze right back.

Although the end of classes had certainly been the reason for the gathering that evening at Hal Wainwright's, all of the guests tried to remember the larger political situation, which made anything like a celebration inappropriate. This was the evening's tone, at least, until the first bottle of jug wine had begun to have its effect. When John had confidently introduced Susanna and Andy to the two young members of the English faculty who'd already arrived, a horse-faced but appealing blond woman and a robustly athletic man, the instructors had tried to look sober without being in any way aloof. Three older male students, all English majors, took their cues from their teachers, and also were understated but friendly. It had seemed to Andy that Susanna's arrival had charged the room, that all the young men and perhaps even the horse-faced woman had felt a burst of adrenaline at her presence. It was hard to tell for sure, though, because they'd all been on the lawn that day, and their complexions, like John's, showed the effect of the early-May sun. It was as if they were now meeting for drinks after having spent a day at the beach together. And all of them had to feel the excitement of a day unlike any that Concord had yet seen.

"Who knows this Ringwald fellow?" the athletic young instructor, named Jeff Charger, asked. He was dressed in unpressed khaki pants, a blue work shirt, and an ancient, greenish corduroy coat that was a little tight across the chest. He rocked back and forth in his well-oiled hunting boots, his long face, which made him seem taller than he was, looming up with each forward rock. "He certainly has a quicksilver tongue. I believe he could have made us all enlist if he'd wanted to."

Andy noticed that Charger was talking directly to Susanna, but she had nothing to say on the matter and the three English majors had quite a lot to say.

"He's from Chicago," was the explanation of one.

"I've seen him in the weight room," said another.

"How's a white guy maintain such a perfect Afro in a place like Concord?" asked the third.

These three also addressed themselves to Susanna, and when they were through, an expectant silence fell. Susanna held their gazes confidently, and looked splendid in a tunic of some unbleached white material, a sort of rough cotton just thick enough so that the dark areolas of her nipples were faint shadows beneath it. The light color of her blouse made her tan look deeper and brought out the red in her auburn hair.

"Something about him," Susanna finally said, "made me think 'outside agitator.' He looked like a union organizer, a gun for hire, someone who had given this sort of speech before."

"Perhaps that's just his legal training," said the young woman professor, whose name was Francine Poutier. Her peasant blouse and blue jeans should have given her the look of a student, but her face said she was twenty-five going on forty. "He's learning to speak with conviction what he does not believe. How much more persuasive might belief make him?"

"Still," Susanna replied. "There was something just a bit too theatrical about him. He was effective, it's true, but his conviction seemed—what?—forced, a conviction trying too hard to be convincing."

Her words hung for a second in the air, and Andy saw in the faces of those encircling her that she'd planted small seeds of doubt. Had there been a false note in this day that all of them seemed so satisfied with?

Just then Hal Wainwright walked into the room from the kitchen. "What's this? Wordplay from a student?" The look on his face assured them that this was not a surprise at all, but something to be expected, at least among the students of his acquaintance. He urged them all to sit near the far end of the long room in sofas and chairs arranged near a stone fireplace. John then began to set the table at the end of the room where they'd been standing. Hal offered wine to Susanna and Andy, and they accepted. It was not yet dark out the picture window across from where Andy had taken a seat, and the view was a long one of valley and distant mountains on which the last rays of the sun were playing.

As he was looking at the view he lost track of the conversation for a moment, but was drawn back into it when he heard a question aimed at him. "What about you, Andy," Charger was saying. "Where are you from?"

"Me?" he said. "Oh, I'm from just up the valley in Strasburg. A smaller town even than Concord."

"Our one true blue Virginian, then," said Poutier, a little condescendingly, it seemed to Andy. He wondered if he should point out that Saint John was also a Virginian, but perhaps the word blue disqualified him in some way. "How in this valley of Scots-Irish did a name like Strasburg pop up?" Poutier asked in a tone that was playful without quite making Andy feel included in the play. "A lonely Alsatian wanderer, perhaps?"

Andy was thoroughly lost, wondering what a dog might have to do with his hometown. He blushed and looked at Susanna helplessly. "I don't really know," he finally muttered, feeling miserable. Susanna, who was sitting beside him, slipped her hand to the inside of his leg, just above the knee. She gave a friendly little squeeze and left her hand there until it had the desired effect of ridding him of any embarrassment. He was amazed by the self-possession of Susanna's small gesture, and by how much power she so simply and generously exerted over him and all of those seated there, who seemed mesmerized by the position of her hand.

Then the last two guests arrived, both men who, Andy would learn later in the evening, were holding temporary jobs in the English department while trying to finish their PhDs in Charlottesville. One had black hair in a bowl cut, a bushy black mustache and very red round cheeks that made him look either flustered or deeply embarrassed. The other was tall and thin and wore his long straight hair pulled back in a ponytail. He was dressed in blue jeans and a vivid Hawaiian shirt. In his arms was a paper bag from which he drew two half-gallon bottles of a California red wine.

"Hearty Burgundy," said Hal, heartily. "My favorite."

"Don't anyone report us to Cesar Chavez," said the ponytailed man, who introduced himself simply as Jim to Andy and Susanna, the only people there he didn't know. "And this sturdy fellow," Jim said, turning to the dark-haired man, "this is George, but we call him Gustav because he loves Mahler so much."

"George will be sufficient," he said, shaking hands earnestly with Susanna and then Andy. "We mustn't inflict our little jokes on others."

There were now more people than seats, so Andy and Susanna followed Hal into the kitchen to see if they could help. Hal handed Andy a cheese grater and a wedge of Parmesan and asked him to grate it all onto a plate. He gave Susanna a cutting board and knife and a large bunch of parsley.

"This needs to be washed, spun dry, and minced," Hal said. "Can you handle that, Miss Susanna?"

"Mais oui. D'accord," she said with a smile. "In New Orleans we are very good at mincing. It is taught at an early age."

On the stove an enormous pot of water was heating, and Hal was tending an iron skillet in which bacon softly sizzled. Andy saw a carton of eggs and one of cream on the table where he was grating the cheese.

"May I ask what you're cooking?" Andy said.

"Yes, spaghetti carbonara. It's the only way to feed a crowd this big. That and a salad and enough bread and butter and of course wine and you can even fill up young male undergraduates."

He said this with a confidential wink for Andy, as though Andy both was and wasn't a member of the group he was speaking about.

"And when you finish your chores feel free to wander around the rest of the house. Check out the study. It was here when I bought the place so I can say in all modesty what a great room it is."

When the cheese and parsley were ready, Andy and Susanna did what Hal had suggested. The room was two steps lower than the rest of the house. It had a stone floor and the walls were all windows and bookshelves. The books made the room a study, but there was no desk. Instead there were facing couches with an Oriental rug between them. In piles at the ends of each couch were stacks of books and the shelves were spilling over with them. The effect was not sloppiness but a warm, lived-in feeling. Andy had never seen a room quite like it, certainly not in his own house, a conventionally furnished postwar colonial in Strasburg's nicest subdivision.

"Great room, isn't it," John said to them from the doorway. He stepped down into the room and approached them. "Hal lets me study here sometimes. I flop right on that couch and study while he reads and smokes on the other one. The views from these windows are amazing when it's light out."

"How does he happen to have so many books?" Susanna asked. Andy had wondered, too.

"He edits a literary magazine, you know, the *Concord Review*. Publishers send him books for review. And he's been reading for a contest he's judging. Boxes of novels come in every week. Those are the books stacked on the floor."

"But this isn't even the best room in the house," John said, a mischievous little smile playing on his face.

"What is?" Andy asked.

"The basement. That's where Hal's sauna is."

"Oooh, a sauna," Susanna said, chucking Andy on the arm. "We'll definitely have to check that out."

Before Andy could respond, Hal poked his head into the room. "Supper's almost ready. Fill your glasses and John, would you round up some chairs?"

Dinner unfolded slowly. The large pot of carbonara was placed on the table, along with several loaves of crunchy French bread, from which the guests tore chunks onto which they knifed pats of sweet butter. Each serving of the pasta was small, but Hal encouraged seconds and thirds, and indulged in them himself. With the wine, the conversation grew from one general exchange, polite and witty, to four or five more boisterous ones among smaller groups. It was a long time before Hal rose to dress the salad, but nobody seemed to mind. Once the salad went around, served right on top of the scraps of congealed carbonara, there was another long pause before dessert. For a while the fumes of vinegar rose from the plates now empty of salad, but then Jim, the pony-tailed PhD candidate, passed a small brass pipe of marijuana, and the rich smell of burning leaves fought the vinegar fumes and won. Hal put on a record of highlights from *The Magic Flute* at a volume that discouraged conversation, and they all listened contentedly as Mozart's music and the vibrant voices washed over them. Eventually Hal and John produced a dessert of ice cream and Pepperidge Farm cookies. Just as the wine and dope and sweets and music began to make the table drowse, Hal brought out a large espresso pot of the blackest coffee Andy had ever seen. Taken with sugar, the espresso jolted the table back into fervent conversation, and Hal would bring out several more pots of coffee and another half-gallon of burgundy. Andy felt a bit as though he were in a dinghy in large swells, as his energy level rose and fell.

Eventually part of the group moved near the fire, as Hal and John and Susanna and Andy worked on the dishes. Once Susanna and Andy had cleared the table, John said, "Four of us can't work in this small kitchen. Hal turned the sauna on several hours ago, and it ought to be good and hot. Why don't you two check it out?"

"There are towels on a chair down there," Hal added encouragingly, "and a stall shower in the corner."

Susanna bounded down the stairs ahead of Andy, who was taking in the dimly lit basement. By the time Andy had turned a corner toward the source of light, a red bulb in a floor lamp near the sauna, she had already shucked her clothes and wrapped a small blue bath towel around her.

"Don't tarry, mon ami," she said as she popped open the sauna door and entered.

"Right behind you," Andy said. The wine and pasta and dope on the one hand and the espresso and sugar and music on the other had made Andy feel just a bit dazed. As if things were somehow moving both very quickly and very slowly. The red light and the redwood smell of the heated sauna and of course the presence of Susanna in just a towel on the other side of that door added to Andy's sense of disorientation as he fumbled out of his clothes. But then he had at last gotten everything off and into a pile on the floor and found another blue towel to wrap around himself, and opened the door. The heat hit him like a hard slap. Inside the sauna was a yellow bulb and under its light Susanna, her skin already rosy from the heat, was piling her hair up on top of her head, her arms raised like a slender Renoir nude, the towel just covering her breasts and her crotch. Suddenly Andy felt as alive as he ever could remember feeling. He moved forward to take a seat beside her with the confidence of, if not a young god, at least a young English instructor whose prospects for tenure were looking very, very strong.

4

THE LAST FEW weeks of what would have been the spring semester at Concordia College passed as the sort of idyll that even Andy, flushed in as many ways as he could imagine—with intellectual excitement, with sexual pleasure, with the effects of spending so much of his time outdoors without very much, if anything, on—even he knew it was an idyll that could not last. Susanna was right there in his iron cot the next morning when he woke up, as lean and tawny as the fox-like creature she was, as full of expostulations, in French yet, as any new lover could hope for, and she would be there or he would be in her bed every day for the rest of that most merry month of May. Yes, there was a strike on, and yes, the world had been revealed as a dangerous and heartless place, as different a place, in its essence, as anyone in Concord could imagine from the piece of earth that they inhabited. If the administration of the college and its puppet government in the town were deeply distressed by the daily gathering in front of old Cy, they were wise enough not to exacerbate the situation by making demands of any sort—or even by making themselves visible. The crowd would never again be as large as it was on the first day, and since the facilities of the college remained open even if classes were not being held, it was a crowd that continued to be well fed in the dining hall or the co-op or the faculty club. It was a crowd with access to squash and handball courts, to an indoor pool for swimming laps, to emerald athletic fields and a cross-country course cut from what seemed like virgin woods. It was a crowd not even in need of port-a-johns, given the marbled bathrooms of the classroom buildings and the dorms, nor of an unusual amount of maintenance, since the leaders of the strike urged the strikers to keep a tidy lawn, to police up after themselves so that the fascist cops working undercover as the maintenance crew would have no excuse to invade their space bearing sticks with little nails on the end, ostensibly, of course, for spiking trash.

A world away, as they were often reminded from the podium, young men such as themselves were dying in a foolish and hopeless, not to mention imperialistic, cause, as were the peasant inhabitants of that distant and, frankly, impossible-to-imagine nation, peasants who were as dignified and innocent as peasants are everywhere, including, of course, those noble native Concordians who made the strike so painless for all of them, cooking their food and cleaning their bathrooms, and who would not be caught dead within sight of the uplifted arm of old Cy. And the young college men who turned out each day at the crack of midmorning, if not the cream of southern manhood then at least its whole milk, knew that they were obliged to feel guilt at their good fortune, a guilt that burned in them all the way until lunchtime, after which they would slink off for a joint and a good nap. But not Andy and Susanna. Because she had a car and was familiar with the glorious countryside within a short drive of Concord, a knowledge borne of the two years she had spent dating Concordia men even before she had come here for a sort of junior year abroad from Hollins, the two would set off each afternoon in search of waterfalls or mountain whirlpools or remote ponds or granitic outcroppings that offered both spectacular distant views and utter privacy. It turned out that it was not just underwear that Susanna eschewed; she preferred to be without clothing of any kind whenever possible, except for sandals where going barefoot could be painful.

On Day Two of the revolution there would have been ample

time for wakeup lovemaking, but the exertions of the night before had made them both even hungrier for nourishment than they were for a continuation of the happy coupling that had left Andy, at least, still a little dazed. After he showered and then guarded the door to the hall shower room for Susanna—not that modesty was a high priority with her—he naturally assumed that they would head first to the dining hall. But wouldn't you know that as if by magic Concord's first funky, hippie, mostly organic bakery was now in business up on Lee Street, and so Susanna steered him past the home fries and over-easies he was expecting to wash down with institutional coffee at the dining hall, and into a darkish storefront establishment offering an assortment of muffins and teas. Who knew, in that benighted era, that teas even came in varieties more exotic than Earl Grey, and that muffins could be made of a brownish substance known as bran? Fortunately there were also less colon-friendly varieties of baked goods for sale: Andy pointed to a perky looking blue-berry muffin in the display case, while Susanna took some sort of walnut thing. Once they had settled into the frumpy stuffed chairs near the window and the girl from behind the counter, whose granny dress seemed to be made of the same dingy and not-quite-clean material that covered the chairs, had plopped two mugs of tea down on the table between them, they picked at their respective breakfasts and gazed, for the first time, perhaps, into one another's eyes. Hers, it turned out, were a rich shade of gray, unlikely given the rest of her coloring, which might have implied brown or gold. She gave him a confident smile, tinged with irony.

"Alors, what a student of amour you are," she said. "I admire your dogged application to your work."

"Merci beaucoup. I try always to be prepared for a pop quiz," Andy replied, his verbal confidence somehow deepened by her own, and by her inexplicable but apparently growing affection for him. "Let's plan to do a lot of cramming for the final exam."

"Ooof, cramming. Not a good word, mon ami, especially on this morning after, when I'm feeling a little, um, rubbed."

She was such a wonderful color, Andy thought, and perhaps the word *rubbed* put him in mind of a coppery genie's lantern, her skin color offset by an embroidered turquoise peasant's blouse she had fetched from her room as he showered, along with a snug pair of cutoff jeans. Her hair was pulled back into a loose braid that hung well down her spine. She sat up very straight on the edge of her chair, so she could lean her elbows on the table and grasp with her long slender fingers the little spiked wooden mallet from which she drizzled honey into her tea. He thought he could sit and look at her all morning.

And yet dawdling was not really in his nature. One of the older members of his fraternity, who could always be found occupying a certain leather chair in the KA house, offered as his trademark expression the thought that "Time wasted is time well spent." Andy admired the flair and even brilliance of the maxim, but he himself often grew restless without something specific to do.

"I wonder what's on the agenda for the free university this morning," Andy asked, as he watched sleepy looking students pass down Lee Street in the general direction of Cy.

"Je ne sais pas," Susanna replied. "Banjo strumming? Marxist economics? Norman O. Brown? Here's my proposal, and I hope this doesn't shock you too much, Andy. Let's cut class and head into the mountains. This perfect weather can't last. Let's make hay while, well, you know."

The strength of Andy's revolutionary zeal was here tested for the first time, but given the plump nipples straining at the thin material of Susanna's blouse, it was hardly a fair test. Was he not flesh and blood, and was not a pint or so of blood now rushing to a certain untimely protuberance of flesh?

"Let's just sit here for another moment or two," Andy countered, while trying hard to conjure up the sound of nails on blackboards or the feeling of a hammer blow to the thumb or of a naked plunge into an ice-cold mountain pool, this last thought proving to be both prophetic and effective. He smoothed the front of his fatigue pants and headed to the counter to pay the modest bill. He realized then that he might have conjured up the greasy hair of the counter girl as another effective de-stimulant, or the passivity unto narcosis of her manner. Still, when he turned back to Susanna he felt so strong a sense of gratitude that he left the hippie chick a tip sufficient to pay for her next tab of whatever it was that she was on.

WHO NEEDED PSYCHEDELICS, given the view through the sunroof of Susanna's Peugeot? The new green foliage of the trees (oaks, maples, beech?—Andy made no claims as a botanist) winked stroboscopically against the deep blue sky as Susanna darted through the switchback curves of a mountain in the Blue Ridge. She had driven briskly and without any doubt about where she was going from Concord to the foothill town of Belle Vue, and from there gone what seemed to Andy to be straight up. Once the road reached the crest and crossed the Blue Ridge Parkway, she drove just as confidently downhill, slowing only once she'd turned onto a gravel road that soon dwindled to dirt. She parked in a wide place along a curve and rolled the sunroof shut.

"Dust," she explained, not that there seemed to be much traffic on this road. "Nobody else around," she added, "a good thing about a weekday morning."

Andy smiled then, but he hoped not lasciviously, and fumbled with the door release.

"This would be a good time to change into those shorts you brought along, mon petit soldier boy. Those fatigues are going to get hot. We've got a pretty steep walk for about twenty minutes."

Andy did as he was told and was soon following her up a well-worn path. After a few minutes the path flattened and crossed a creek. There were steppingstones, undoubtedly placed by some early pathfinder, but Susanna strode right into the water, which was only ankle high but surprisingly cold when Andy followed her across. The path then twisted upward and followed the creek from about ten or fifteen feet above it. The sunlight was dappled on the water but along the path there were long open stretches of sunshine and Susanna was right, it was getting hot, especially because Andy was carrying a brown bag containing a six-pack of warming beer and the best sandwich-making ingredients they could find at a 7-Eleven just before Belle Vue.

"Not getting winded, are you, André?" Susanna said with a smile that was more sweet than taunting. "We could rest for a moment, but it really isn't far now."

"No, I'm okay," Andy said, "but that muffin didn't make much of an impression. I'm starved."

The woods were alive with sounds, of course, the calls of birds, the soughing of the trees, their squeaking sandals on the hard path, the creek below. Still, it sounded like quiet. But in a few more minutes Susanna stopped and held out her hand to stop Andy.

"Listen," she said. "Can you hear it?"

And he could, the sound of falling water. It was not thunderous, or even the hiss of a hard rain, but something in between, a steady thrumming that had a deeper pitch than rainfall.

"Just up this one last rise … here you go."

As Andy stepped up beside Susanna he saw that the ravine they had been following upward now widened dramatically, and in the opening were a series of pools and waterfalls—three of each, it looked like from here. The fall farthest up the slope was the tallest—perhaps twenty feet in height—and the pool closest to them was about thirty feet wide.

Great boulders surrounded the pools and the bleached gray bones of large trees lay at the periphery of the clearing, with smaller piles of debris near the falls. But the water was clear and dark.

"The middle pool is the best," Susanna said, leading him up to it. "It's deeper and gets more sunlight."

As if to offer proof, Susanna walked up to a flat boulder on the sunny side of the clearing and in a twinkling had shucked her clothes and climbed up.

"We should get nice and toasty before we try the water," she said, brushing the smooth surface of the rock with her hand to make a comfortable place to stretch out. "I promise you you'll never forget the moment when you plunge in."

The thought rose up into his consciousness that everything about this moment would be pretty unforgettable, but before he was able to complete the thought, much less savor it, a sort of buzzing in his brain pushed it aside, and the buzzing grew until he was wholly inarticulate and barely able to send commands to his extremities. Still, he was able to pull off the already aromatic red polo shirt that was now on its third day, struggle out of his khaki shorts and the ignominious jockey shorts beneath, and claw his way up on the rock beside her. He remained stupid with lust, able to muster only one thought of any kind, that he might literally be drooling, and to register at some sub-verbal level an observation that he would be able to call up later: that his body looked white and cold—like Carrara marble—against the warm rusty gold of her skin. He swept his hand and arm along a wide swath of her ventral side, not even registering breasts, belly, pubis, thighs, but feeling only the heat that she had already absorbed from the bright sunshine.

She turned to him and gave him a searching look, and suddenly he realized that she too had gone dumb with desire. But then her lips were moving and they were forming words but not sounds—the words were each only one syllable and his eagerness but inability to understand them at first put him in mind of gentle Hubert of Savannah. But then apparently herself realizing that no sound had emerged the first time around, she made a bolder effort and out came the words one by one: "Not … Just … Yet … Jack." She fell back away from him with the effort and then in what seemed one motion rolled up off her back and jackknifed into the cold dark center of the pool. Even the bottoms of her feet looked golden, Andy noticed before they disappeared with barely a splash.

Susanna remained beneath the black surface of the pool long enough—was it actually only a second, or three, or five?—for Andy to wonder if she'd conked her head on a big rock or wedged the V of her gracefully pointed hands into whatever the bottom of the pool offered. But no, her head emerged at the shady far side, her braid roughly intact, and then she turned to show him teeth made whiter even than usual by the surrounding dimness. She began a lazy breaststroke into the sunny part of the pool and to the side where he still lay.

"Cold?" Andy asked, knowing there could only be one answer.

"Cold enough that you should get that beer out of the sun and into a shallow spot."

"Oh, great. Ice-chest cold," Andy said, already off the rock and moving toward the paper bag.

"It's brisk," she admitted. "I'll be the same blue as you if I stay in here long. Come join me."

He found a shady place for the bag of lunch stuff and put the beer—Schlitz in cans—in a little eddy near the spot where the water fell down to the next pool.

"I'm not going to dive," he said, feeling more self-conscious about his paleness than his nakedness as she smiled up at him. "My mother taught me don't ever, ever dive into a strange body of water."

"It's plenty deep, but do what you like—just get in here."

With that he obediently leaped, jumping straight over her and as far out toward the center of the pool as he could manage, making sure to cup his genitals with his hands as he entered the water. This precaution streamlined him, so he shot downward beneath the surface for what seemed like twenty feet, never touching the bottom, before he began clawing up for air, the water around him so cold that he felt as though his lungs had contracted and his heart might at any moment stop.

"You call this brisk," he said when he could get enough breath to produce speech. "You, a New Orleans girl?"

"We used to go to Maine in the summer," she explained.

Andy did a quick crawl across the pool and back, hoping to get the blood moving in his veins. He wiped the water from his eyes in time to see the perfect heart shape of her behind as she pulled herself out of the pool and walked quickly to the warm flat rock where she had first lain.

"I couldn't stand another second," she admitted. "Mmm, this rock feels great. My goose bumps should be gone in only a matter of weeks."

Without even realizing he was doing it, Andy hauled himself out of the pond and was up on the rock beside her, both of them warming their stomachs, their hands pillowing their faces as they quietly looked at each other and laughed with anticipation. She did indeed have goose bumps on her arms, whereas he had the slightly bluish tint that she had predicted, wrongly, for herself. They lay there side by side, not touching, waiting for the sun to warm and dry them. At first they were too shivery to talk much, and then as they warmed up, Andy's tongue once again grew thick with lust. Soon he was engorged elsewhere, too, so that he needed to roll on his side for comfort's sake. Susanna rolled on her side, too, facing him. She reached carefully for the thing that was now bridging the space between them.

"Mon Dieu," she said softly, with only the gentlest sort of irony.

AN HOUR OR more passed before they found their way down the path again. After their lovemaking and a quick washing off—Andy thought of Narcissus as he watched Susanna leaning over the pond's edge to dab herself clean—Andy hauled the now-coolish beer out of the water and Susanna did her best with a loaf of white bread and sliced salami and Swiss cheese. With a small jar of yellow mustard and a plastic fork she was able to moisten the bread enough so that they could swallow, although as hungry as they were they could have choked it down even mustardless, with a beer chaser. They each carried two sandwiches to the flat rock, where Andy had already set down the beer, and they sat facing each other, cross-legged in the sun, and ate earnestly, without any sort of mugging and only monosyllabic conversation. Andy wondered if he had ever tasted a better sandwich, or if a Schlitz had ever been more refreshing, and vowed to himself that although this was the first meal he had ever eaten in the nude, it would not be his last. Would not be their last. They finished the sandwiches and a beer each and then shared a second one before they lay back down and drowsed a bit in the sun until Susanna sat up with a start.

"You're getting pretty pink, Andy," she had said, reaching out to touch his arm, which indeed already showed the effects of the sun. "And it's not your arms I'm most worried about getting a good scorching sunburn. At least they're used to the sunlight. We should get you back into your clothes."

The little nap had reinvigorated them and they had chatted animatedly as they went along the path. Now they were walking carefully down the steep place that led to the spot where the path flattened out to cross the creek. They could hear voices below, and as they peered from the bright sunlight into the deep green shade of the creek they could see three young men picking their way carefully across the steppingstones.

The two parties reached the side of the creek at the same time.

"Susanna!" one of the men said. "What are you …" and then he stopped and had a look at Andy, who was still toting the now soggy-looking paper bag. Under the appraising look of this fellow, whom Andy recognized as an upperclassman at Concordia, he felt, though clothed, more naked than at any time he had been naked with Susanna. Andy could sense the heat coming off his face and wondered if it was sunburn or embarrassment.

"Hello, Jeff," Susanna said with utter self-possession. "I see that you boys are up to your usual games." The two burly guys with this Jeff, who was himself a jockish-looking sort, carried a huge metal cooler between then. All three were wearing athletic shorts of various descriptions, and tennis shoes with long white socks, and one of the three wore a T-shirt that read *Property of Concordia College Lacrosse*.

"The same could be said of you," Jeff said, but without any particular rancor, and his buddies, when Andy looked at them, offered not a snigger, but had studiously blank looks on their faces. Although it could have been Andy's natural charity that attributed their blankness to studied effect.

Without another word, Susanna was threading her way across the creek. Andy gave a nod and followed. The two blank-faced fellows nodded back and headed up the path behind Jeff, the backs of their shirts already damp from their exertions with the cooler.

Susanna was mostly silent as they made their way down the last short stretch to her car. But she did not seem, when they stopped, to be glum or moody or embarrassed or in any of the frames of mind Andy might have expected. Nor was there a car parked in the wide part of the road, as they might also have expected.

"I wonder where …" Susanna said, almost to herself as she started the car. She executed a deft three-point turn in the curve in the road and after they had driven for a minute or two they came upon a shiny black Pontiac GTO parked slantwise, partially blocking the narrow dirt road. If a truck or a school bus were to try to pass by, there would be trouble.

"Idiot," she said as she nosed carefully around the jutting tail of the car. "Not only does he not know how to park, he doesn't know where."

And that was the last that either of them ever said about Jeff.

When they got back to the campus and were walking to Susanna's dorm, the first person they saw, returning from the commons, was Saint John, still the most neatly dressed revolutionary in all of Concord, wearing good leather sandals, pressed navy-blue shorts, and a white button-down shirt, the sleeves rolled up with a careful haphazardness.

"Just look at you two," John said. "You're beaming happiness. A quick trip to Disney World?"

"Something like that," Susanna said, squeezing John's arm.

"What's been going on around here," Andy asked. "Things look pretty quiet."

"We've been advised to break up into small study groups for the afternoon," John said. "But Prof. Bear was not in evidence this morning"—with this he gave a charming and self-deprecating smile, all perfect teeth and boyish, regular features—"so I'm going to have a private tutorial out at Hal Wainwright's. In fact, here he is now, come to give me a lift."

Professor Wainwright ambled up to their group, books and mail under one arm. "My goodness, Andy, you've gotten some color since last night," he said. "Are you taking care of this boy, Susanna? He's looking healthier already."

Andy felt tongue-tied, but attempted a smile of Saint John-like intensity.

"Happier, too," the professor added.

"You seem to be the only person on campus doing any work," Susanna said, nodding at Hal's mail.

"Well, revolution or no revolution, those books and manuscripts just keep coming in."

They said goodbye and as Andy and Susanna turned toward her dorm, Hal called out to them.

"Do you have plans for dinner? Why don't you come back out to my place tonight, say about six-thirty? We're going by the store now and we'll get enough for four of whatever it turns out to be."

"We'll bring some wine," Susanna said.

Andy looked at John and Hal sheepishly. "She just turned twenty-one a month ago," he said. "Very useful, these older women."

The upper-class dorm was arranged in suites, four private rooms sharing a central living area and a bathroom, and two suites at one end of the top floor hall had been given over to the exchange students from nearby girls' schools. Three of the eight girls in the suites had already been called home by parents unimpressed by the revolutionary ferment of the moment and concerned that their daughters might be exposed to Commies or even liberals. And the very idea of their living in the midst of the unkempt had made the decision non-negotiable. Not that these three had put up much of a fight, Susanna reported, their main concern having been that they really didn't have anything appropriate to wear and didn't much want to acquire the sort of clothing that would be appropriate. Two of the remaining five—these two were from the most intellectual of the nearby all-women's colleges, Randolph-Macon—had dropped acid the night of the Kunstler rally and not been heard from again. This was not a matter of huge concern because the two had been together when last seen and there was evidence that one or both of them had stopped by for fresh clothes and a shower.

Andy was impressed by how neat and even decorated Susanna's suite looked. The posters on the walls were framed and hung, not thumbtacked into the sheetrock, and the couch in the common room was not threadbare or beer-stained, and featured pillows in coordinated colors and a throw quilt. The worn oriental rug on the floor looked as if it had been vacuumed at least twice that semester, and there were no athletic socks or candy wrappers or moldering half-filled paper cups of coffee anywhere on its surface. One of Susanna's remaining roommates was having a snooze in an easy chair, wearing only panties and a T-shirt, and sprawled in a position that nobody would have described as ladylike. Susanna and Andy crept past her and into Susanna's room, closing the door behind them. Susanna's bed was unmade and there were a few articles of clothing on the floor—not including panties or bras, of course. The clothing there—a khaki skirt, a blue cotton blouse, a lightweight yellow sweater that had the appearance of cashmere—all looked pre-revolutionary and put Andy in mind of a skin that had been shed, left where it fell as a reminder of a former self. Susanna made no effort to pick it up or to straighten up the bedclothes, but went to her desk and shuffled through a few pieces of fresh mail that her roommate had apparently fetched for her, not opening any of it.

"I have an idea," she said. "Let's go to the bibliothèque. After all, we've eaten, we've napped, we've stretched our legs and gotten some fresh air and sunshine—a bit too much sunshine in the case of one of us—and we've done the dirty deed four times in sixteen hours. What's left but intellectual stimulation?"

"Do you really think it's dirty?" Andy asked. "You Catholics …"

"Only an expression, André. Don't be so sensitive. I mean it's only dirty in the best possible sense."

She walked over to him and held his sunburned face with both hands, her gray eyes burning holes in his bluish ones.

"Have I seemed to you in any way, um, unhappy?" Her smile showed how ridiculous a question she had posed.

Not waiting for an answer, she kissed him quickly on the lips and then clapped her hands.

"Allons-y. Enough of this moping about. I'd like to see a newspaper or two to learn how the revolution is playing out. With any luck, Tricky Dick has already been guillotined on the steps of the Lincoln Memorial."

"Vive la révolution!" Andy cried, but softly so as not to wake the napper.

The library was as empty as Andy had ever seen it. Even when he had been grinding away at his studies late at night at a carrel deep in the stacks, he could wander down to the periodicals room on the first floor and find a few warm bodies. But today the periodicals room had the look of abandonment. There were a few library workers in occasional evidence, but their practiced invisibility did nothing to enliven the scene.

"No need to whisper," Susanna said. "You check out the news-papers, Andy, and I'll just catch up with the art magazines." She was an art history major, and although she'd spent what she called "lifetimes" in the Louvre and the Prado and the Uffizi, she was most excited about the art of what she called without irony the avant-garde. Somehow when she used the term it seemed only descriptive, and did not raise in Andy's mind the images of black capes and berets, or of artists who were trying too hard to be noticed. Still, she was not without irony about herself. "Like every rich girl of an artistic bent," Susanna had explained to Andy, "I hope my daddy will buy me a gallery in Greenwich Village. Or at least in the Quarter."

Thus the trendy art magazines of the day, or at least the members of that set stolid enough to find their way into the college library, had for Susanna the wonderful appeal of being both work and play. She couldn't wait to read the latest news of this small world and feel the satisfaction of both sating her curiosity and doing something responsibly preparatory.

Andy pulled first *The New York Times* and then *The Washington Post* from the racks. He hated reading the papers pinched into the long wooden hangers for the racks. When he sat to read, the bottom of the hanger always wanted to be between his legs, up high, and there seemed to him something masturbatory about having the post sticking up from your crotch. Of course today there was really nobody but Susanna to notice, and she was rifling a shelf of magazines several rows away. He nonetheless called out tidbits to her as he found them on how things were going with the Cambodia invasion, the latest body count in Vietnam, the unlikely campuses that were now on strike—were there any unlikelier than his own?—the inadequate explanations of the Ohio National Guard about the Kent State shootings, the elaborate way in which Tricky Dick was ignoring the exploding campuses.

A voice came from what Andy had assumed was an empty leather chair facing one of the library's tall windows.

"All very interesting, camouflage boy, but some of us can read the papers on our own."

Up popped the shaggy black head of Rick the ultra-rationalist, who had been slumped in the chair and out of sight, either snoozing or eavesdropping.

"Oh, Rick. I'm really sorry. I thought the place was empty."

"Some of us have our futures to think about," Rick said, turning to face him. "Are you reading that paper or jacking it off?"

And then he said, "Jeeze, Andy, nothing to be embarrassed about."

"Sunburn," Andy explained.

"Yeah, no kidding."

Susanna stood up, her head showing above the magazine shelves.

"Bonjour, Monsieur Randolph. Enjoying your solitude?"

Even the sarcastic Rick responded like every other male Andy had observed in Susanna's presence, softening the fierce expression on his face and addressing her almost shyly.

"Not that much, really. Even the librarians won't talk to me."

"Perhaps you only frighten them," Susanna said. "They might think you are looking up instructions for making bombs."

"No, just trying to keep up with the reading assignments for my philosophy class," he explained. "Nietzsche."

"Oh, how very counter-revolutionary," Susanna said playfully.

Rick actually smiled.

"So what are you kids up to?" he asked. "All done throwing pots and eating macrobiotically?" It occurred to Andy that Rick was lonely.

"We're playing hooky," Andy explained.

"Yes, well, aren't we all?"

"You apparently aren't. But we're even playing hooky from the free university."

"My god, is nothing sacred to you people?"

Rick turned back to his book, Andy to his newspapers, and Susanna to her magazines. Things were quiet for another twenty minutes or so, and then Susanna stood up again and said, "Let's all go get a Coke at the co-op." So she had noticed Rick's loneliness, too.

As they approached the co-op they could see several groups of professors seated at the picnic tables on the open porch of the building. What sounded at first like the usual sort of bickering and posturing among the younger faculty members who didn't mind hanging out in public, exposing themselves to students outside of office hours and class, turned out to have an ugly edge to it as the three students passed by. And as they swept their eyes over the scene while trying not to stare they noticed several older faculty members, distinguished not only by their gray heads but because they dressed their age in ancient Harris Tweed jackets and nubbly knit ties. They could only conclude that the generational warfare had enlisted even the mostly undistinguished members of Concordia's faculty.

They made a beeline through the co-op to the bookstore one floor down, and approached the manager, Sally Wilkins, who always knew exactly what was going on anywhere on the campus and didn't mind offering a strong opinion about it.

"It seems," she told them, her graying hair pulled back in a sleek ponytail, "that in their wisdom Provost Marshall and Dean DeBenedetto asked some department chairmen to 'talk some sense' into the younger faculty who are active in the strike. My understanding is that this is not going well."

Their curiosity satisfied, Susanna, Andy, and Rick thanked Mrs. Wilkins and ascended the steps to the co-op, where Rick ordered a BLT on white toast and French fries to go with his Coke. The three took their drinks to a booth while Rick's food cooked.

"Late lunch?" Susanna asked him. "Early dinner?"

"Both," Rick confessed. "The dining hall gives me the creeps lately."

Beyond the window next to their booth was one of the picnic tables filled with intemperate faculty members. It had grown warm enough this late in the afternoon so that the air conditioning was running in the co-op, and the window was closed. Only muffled sounds accompanied the histrionic gestures a few feet from them. It was hard not to smile at the overheated faces and jabbing fingers or pounding fists, and the three did not try very diligently to conceal their mirth, certainly not from each other.

"The slave revolt spreads to Arcadia," Rick said, shaking his shaggy dark head. "The old ways are under attack even here."

Andy had no idea what he was talking about, but Susanna seemed to want to encourage him, either because she was actually interested in what he was saying or because she wanted to make him feel less solitary.

"Surely you are not opposing yourself to the will of the masses, are you, cher?"

"The masses will always have their way, Susanna," he explained patiently. "Even in a dictatorship, where they have the will to be dictated to."

Rick was pulling at his beard as he said this, and Andy thought he seemed as crazy as an Old Testament prophet, although the look in his eyes might just have been hunger. The smell of the browning fries had wafted to their booth from the fry rack behind the counter.

"It is the stupidity of the masses that we can regret," he continued, "not a lack of power."

"Have you read any history at all," Andy asked grumpily. "Or are you confining yourself entirely to the philosophical and theoretical?"

Just then the friendly Black woman who cooked the short orders hoisted Rick's sandwich and fries onto the counter.

"Saved by the BLT," Susanna murmured. And indeed, as Rick tucked into his meal she was able to steer the conversation into safer waters.

Supper at Hal Wainwright's followed much the same pattern as the night before, even though it was a more intimate group. Hal had fixed a simple risotto, which Saint John had stirred unceasingly as Hal added broth and made the other preparations, and Susanna and Andy had been given small tasks like setting the table, putting the butter out to soften, grating cheese. The volubility of the evening had risen steadily along with many glasses of bad wine and good food and bread and salad, a couple of cups of espresso, followed by more wine. And then silence had descended as Saint John produced a couple of joints and Hal turned up the recording of *Der Rosenkavalier* in the background. After what was approaching several hours at the table, Saint John began to clear, urging another sauna on the two lovers as he and Hal tidied up. With only minor protests about helping, Susanna and Andy acceded, and even Andy's sunburn on the hot redwood bench did not diminish his ardor.

In this way the days and nights of that most impassioned May acquired a rhythm. Susanna and Andy did partake of the offerings of the free university, eschewing crafts but attending lectures on politics or literature or art, roaming the countryside in the afternoons either alone or with others, allowing themselves to be drawn into intense discussions about the issues of the day at the commons or the co-op, but finding Hal Wainwright's, where they often ended up having supper, to be a mostly politics-free zone. They were together all the time, in his dorm room or hers, at the library, at meals, or naked to the intensifying sunshine, for which Andy was developing a growing tolerance. He looked almost tan, as the increasingly bronze Susanna would point out. The whole month felt like a single continuous moment in time, and Andy tried not to think about when or whether it would end, even as the campus grew emptier as what would have been the last day of the semester arrived. The dorms and commons would stay open until what would have been the end of the exam period, and then the campus would close down entirely except for a couple of days for graduation. The seniors would get their degrees even if they came up short on hours or hadn't taken departmental comprehensive exams.

Then one afternoon in the middle of the non-exam period, the idyll ended without warning.

Susanna and Andy were walking from the library to her dorm room when Susanna touched his arm to stop him and said, "Andy, I'm going home to New Orleans. It's been lovely, it's been more than lovely, but I think we both need to wake up from this dream and pick up our real lives."

"What can be more real than this?" Andy managed to ask, but he could see by her expression that the decision had been made and there would be no talking her out of it.

"When?" he asked quietly.

"Tomorrow," she said. And by the middle of the next morning she was gone.

PART II

KEY WEST, 1975

5

T HE MONSTER HAD been Hal Wainwright's idea. It was the biggest and best-known gay bar in Key West that winter of 1975, and probably the safest one for a straight couple like Andy and Shelley Watson. Safest for their hetero sensibilities, that is. It would be pretty hard to find a gay bar in that time and place where you would be in danger of getting stomped— unless, of course, that was what you were looking for. Hal knew about that sort of bar, too, but his young companion John Brockenbrough did not approve. "When Hal has to scratch that particular itch," Saint John had said somewhat primly, "he's on his own." But the Monster was pretty straightforwardly a pickup place. A few drinks, some dancing, and then the proposition. Unless you were a complete horror show, Hal reported, chances were that the answer would be yes. "And after all," Hal said, "how many queer horror shows are there?" But even if the club was all about sex, no sex was permitted on the premises, which made it tame in its category.

As the four of them wound their way to a table just off the dance floor, Hal seemed to enjoy the quizzical stares he was getting from the young men lining the walls of the club. There were men at many of the other tables, but standing with beer or drink in hand must have been a better way to get checked out. Once the waiter approached—"How're you girls doin' tonight?" he'd greeted them—and had taken their orders, Hal hustled the still-beautiful John off to dance, knowing that those wallflow-ers' looks would quickly turn from questioning to envious.

"Did you happen to notice that I'm the only female in this place?" Shelley whispered loudly to Andy. "Whatever the waiter might think."

"Pretty hard not to," Andy said directly into her ear, because the DJ had just gotten another record spinning. "It was like the Zulus seeing their first white woman."

By then the dance floor was jammed with young men, all of them seemingly bronzed, thin, and wearing shorts a good bit shorter than Andy's Bermudas. They were dancing wildly and screaming out something that sounded like French.

"What are they saying?" Andy now had to yell to Shelley.

"It's 'voulez-vous coucher avec moi?'" she said. "And then when they really scream it out, they're saying, 'ce soir.' That's the LaBelles. Lady Marmalade."

"So you aren't the only lady in the house," Andy said, and took a long draw from the bottle of Budweiser that had just arrived, delivered with a flirtatious flourish by the waiter. The smattering of French put Andy fleetingly in mind of the elegant and often lamented Susanna Agincourt and the distant dream of their brief love affair.

When the song ended, Hal and John returned to the table, Hal soaked in sweat but John looking characteristically crisp and cool. "Aren't you two going to dance?" Hal asked.

"What, with each other?" Andy asked with a smile.

"Well, if you aren't going to claim her, I will," Hal said. He took a long swig of his beer and then grabbed Shelley's hand and led her through the parting crowd.

Seeing Shelley and Hal on the dance floor reminded Andy of how the two of them had danced together at Andy and John's graduation.

"Are you thinking what I'm thinking?" Andy asked John.

"How could I not be," John responded with a little shake of his golden head.

The night before graduation, at a dance well attended by seniors and their dates and families, and by other members of the Concordia College faculty and administration, Hal had led Shelley in a waltz so sweeping that the other dancers had all stopped to watch and to inch backward to give them more room to maneuver. They made a handsome couple, Hal still youthful and light on his feet, Shelley lithe and dark and beautiful, a bright smile flashing as she turned, and clinging to Hal as though her feet were hovering just above the well-waxed linoleum of the dining hall. Shelley had not known Hal that well then—Andy and Shelley had only begun dating again toward the middle of their senior year, after a long separation in a relationship that stretched back to their early teens—but she had found both Hal and the moment curiously captivating. "His intensity was amazing," she told Andy later. "I really felt as if the prince had chosen me to dance at the ball." Hal loved to dance, and was good at it, and his philosophy had always been to flaunt whatever charms you've got. But in a college environment where Hal was at the very least circumspect about his sexual nature, the public display with Shelley would tamp down the rumors, among those who still might care about such things, about Hal's apparent inseparability from Saint John. That relationship was another sort of flaunting, not a welcome one, in the eyes of some of the older members of the faculty who were still cautious about revealing their own orientation.

But if Hal had had an ulterior motive back then, he could not be accused of having one here at the Monster. Even as good as Shelley looked—after only a few days in Key West as bronzed as the wallflowers and as thin and skimpily dressed as they—she could not be earning Hal any points with the many probing eyes. Although it must be said that there no longer seemed to be the astonishment that first showed in the looks of all those gay young men, but something more like a mildly patronizing bemusement, as though Hal had brought his cute new puppy into the bar, and was spinning with her on the dance floor.

"They do look good together, don't they?" John shouted to Andy, nodding at the two sweating dancers as they kept up with the relentless demands of the rhythm. "And it's so clear they just adore each other. As who could not adore the adorable Shelley?" And the two young men watched the respective loves of their life utterly absorbed in the moment and each other, dancing energetically, striking poses when they were not mimicking or humorously mocking some new move that the other dancer had introduced. Every now and then Hal would clasp Shelley to him in a slightly avuncular way, saying by the awkwardness of the gesture that no, he was not some elderly pervert who had found his way into the wrong club, but was instead the sort of elderly pervert who very much belonged here. Elderly being a relative term, of course, and one that Hal only applied to himself with heavy sarcasm.

When the song ended and Hal and Shelley showed no sign of returning to the table, Saint John took a careful sip of his beer and, as the first few notes of the next song promised a reprieve from the disco they'd been hearing, a familiar song from the previous decade—was it the Supremes?—he said to Andy, "Well, pal, since I know you're not going to dance with me we'd better get out there and pry the two of them apart."

Andy was often self-conscious on the dance floor, but he knew that on this night he was invisible to those around him, who lost their interest in Shelley when she allowed herself to be pulled away from Hal by the straight guy in the golf shirt and baggy shorts. And Shelley was still so involved with the situation and the music that Andy was drawn in, too. They gyrated as Diana Ross sang about baby love and then danced clingingly as the Temptations were wishing for rain. After the '60s reprieve they were back to disco, and Andy gamely trotted through a few more numbers before dragging Shelley back to the table. By this time Hal's sleeveless T-shirt was utterly soaked and Saint John was visibly urging him to take a break, too.

"Save your strength, old man," Saint John said when they returned to the table. He said it with a kindly smile, and without any of the overt lasciviousness of, say, their waiter, who overheard John's remark as he was sashaying up to the table. "Ooooh," he said with a visible shiver. "Count me in."

John gave the waiter an indulgent look and Hal just beamed, like a proud father or the owner of a shiny new toy that all the other kids wanted to play with.

Andy agreed to the proposal of another round of beers, just so he wouldn't seem to have been offended by the waiter's aggressive overtness. But the disco beat was beginning to irritate him, and the air in the club was thickening, and not only with cigarette smoke—with clouds of testosterone, perhaps? The four of them watched in amusement the growing frenzy of the dancers, but after the beers arrived and he and Shelley had had a sip or two, Andy grasped Shelley's hand and said loudly to Hal, "Well, this has been so, um, so special. But I'm ready to shove off." Shelley nodded her assent. "What about you guys?"

"Let's stay for another dance or two," Hal said to John, and seeing no objection, said, "Well, you kids have a key. Stay off the little side streets and you should be quite safe getting home."

John waved Andy off when he reached for his wallet, saying, "You're our guests. We can't have you receiving a credit-card statement from the Monster. What if you run for office someday?"

"There is a thing called cash, John," said Hal, ever careful with a penny.

"We'll take care of this," John said firmly. "Go."

Shelley and Andy walked through the club without drawing

so much as a glance, and out into the night air. It was heavy and warm but still a lot fresher than the air inside.

Andy turned them not toward home but down Duval Street in the direction of Mallory Square. It wasn't late, really, and there would be a bit of life still at the square beside the water. This was the famous sunset spot, where visitors like themselves and assorted local freaks would gather for the nightly ritual of applauding the sun as it made its way into the watery horizon. By now, just after midnight, the freaks were gone—the fiddlers and guitarists, the druggy panhandlers of both sexes with their dusty tans and skimpy unclean bathing suits, the man with skin as leathery as the large iguana he displayed on his shoulder, the jugglers and trinket hawkers, and the narcs in their Hawaiian shirts and wife-beater T-shirts who made Mallory Square at sunset a very bad place to buy marijuana, whatever the bed-and-breakfast lady told you. Now the crowd at the square, considerably smaller than that at sunset, consisted mostly of couples like the Watsons, vacationers with a few drinks in them and an unwillingness to go quite yet back to their narrow rooms.

"To think it's actually cold up in Virginia," Shelley said as they joined the slow perambulation—there were not many places to sit down or even lean up against, so it was necessary to keep moving.

"It's so balmy," Andy said. "I love the feeling of tropical air at night. Like a warm bath."

They had known each other since they were in school together in Strasburg, and had dated off and on since junior high, but they'd been wed just six months—this trip was a celebration of that fact—and it still seemed strange to think of themselves as being married. Especially since they were the first of their real friends to take the plunge. Some of their friends from high school had already been married for years, but these couples now seemed more like their parents' friends than their own.

They were living the sort of life Andy associated with his parents—raising small kids, hustling them to lessons or practices, socializing mostly at home rather than in bars or restaurants, even going to church on Sundays. Lots of grocery shopping and homework and television. It was a life that made Shelley and Andy leery, a life that his other distant dream, of, well, revolution, was supposed to have made impossible. The word *revolution* felt a little grandiose and a little silly by now, and perhaps had felt that way even five years earlier, but the beliefs it represented, if you were young and American and, now that the war in Vietnam had reached its ignominious but inevitable end, lacked any significant form of oppression to rebel against in a world filled with the real thing, those beliefs, whatever they were, still mattered to people like Andy. If Shelley had been less swept up than he by the events of May 1970—was she more naïve or more mature than Andy and his friends?—still she saw the significance of those times when everything could and should be questioned, and felt especially their significance for Andy, and sympathized. So much so that she had shared with him his hesitation about marrying as young as they had, shared his fear that they, too, would take up the same routine as their parents and their high-school friends, that the two of them would be old before they hit the age of twenty-five. One thing they both agreed upon was that they could not go back to Strasburg to live, not ever, ever. It would be too easy there to fall into the same traps their friends had, to be beaten down into the same dull Strasburgian conformity.

The trap that many of those high-school friends had first encountered was a surprise pregnancy before which marriage had not been contemplated and after which nothing else, short of suicide, could be. Some of those surprises were now in the first or second grade. Pregnancy had not yet been a factor, happy or otherwise, in Shelley and Andy's long relationship.

And they intended to wait a few more years before going for it. But it wasn't as if they were making a radical break with their upbringings. They had never discussed, for example, decamping to an ashram in India or a commune in Vermont or even a group house in Adams Morgan, for goodness sake. Yes, they had thought how nice it would be if they and their friends could buy a big house together in the country someday, a house that would become the main lodge for the small cottages each of them would build on the periphery of the property. Yes, they would all take their meals together and hang out together and watch from the front porch as all of their children played—a band of little wild Native Americans. And they would have fruit trees and a communal vegetable patch and perhaps a small stand of marijuana somewhere inconspicuous—all organic, of course. And a little pond where they would all swim ... but this was where the dream veered off in directions that Andy really didn't want to sketch out for Shelley. Still, the whole earthly paradise thing really was only a dream, a pipe dream of the most literal sort. At best it would be a weekend sort of place, and to make it come true would take wealth they had no prospect of having anytime soon. Andy was working as a newspaper reporter in Charlottesville, where Shelley was teaching at a private school near the foot of Monticello Mountain. He wanted to go back to graduate school in English, something they could ill-afford to do even without a child or children. Their other friends, the ones with whom they might someday embark on this part-time communal journey, were scattered about in law schools or film schools or jobs as ill-paying as Andy and Shelley's. None of them had prospects of any kind, not even for marriage or a stable relationship. The Watsons were the one exception to that.

They walked past the palm trees to the dock and sat at the edge, their feet dangling above the water. Andy scrunched his toes so he wouldn't lose one of the flip-flops he had bought the day before.

"So, do you think this marriage can be saved?" he asked Shelley.

She smiled at him, her teeth flashing white in the semi-darkness. She put a hand on his leg.

"It's calmer here, isn't it?" she said. "No pressures. We'd be fine if only we could spend all of our time on vacation."

"Maybe we should move here," he said. "I could check with the local paper about a job. I saw the office today—we walked right past it. You could tutor and eventually get a teaching job. How much can it cost to live here in these shabby little houses? We'll eat at the Cuban restaurants or catch our suppers off the dock here."

"Whoa, pardner," Shelley said. "You're just kidding, right?"

"I don't know—am I? What's to keep us in Charlottesville? Not the jobs we have. Not the weather."

"What about our friends? And our families? Do we really want to move so far away from everyone we love? And what about graduate school? I don't see a lot of opportunities for graduate study around here. Mixology, maybe. Scuba diving."

"It wouldn't have to be forever. Maybe just a few years. But, you're right. It probably would get lonely down here. Even Hal and John go back north in a couple of months. And how hot must it get in the summer. Still …"

"Well, don't make me be the one to say no. Go by the *Citizen*'s office and see what you find out."

"So you did notice!"

"Notice what?"

"The *Citizen* office when we walked by it."

"You're crazy, Andy. It's on the side of every paper box in town. Key West *Citizen*. I'm not blind, you know."

"So you're saying if I get a job we can stay?"

"Of course I'm not. I'm saying until you get a job we might as well not even talk about it. I'm not working as a cocktail waitress just so we can afford to live somewhere warm."

"Hey, with boobs like those you could make us very, very rich." He reached into the top of her blouse—a blue work shirt, actually—where, with no bra to in any way diminish his delight, he copped a feel.

"Yeah, so could you if you work on your tan and buy some short shorts. If you know what I mean."

They sat for a while happily watching the water and letting the warm air wash over them. It was getting quieter and emptier on the square at their backs.

"Maybe we should mosey on up Whitehead," Andy said.

"I bet we'll still beat Hal and John home," Shelley said as they got to their feet. "I got the feeling that Hal was just getting started."

ALL FOUR OF them slept in, but when Andy arose at about eight-thirty he found Hal sitting in the small garden beside his kitchen, smoking a Gitanes in a contemplative way, a small cup of dark coffee at his elbow and a large espresso pot on the table.

"Grab a cup and have some of this café cubano," he said after greeting Andy.

Andy did not smoke, and found the smell of American cigarettes acrid and unpleasant, but the Gitanes Hal smoked left a sweet, rich cloud that Andy didn't mind at all.

Once Andy was settled beside him, Hal said, "You should have seen this place a year ago. Just bare earth under deep, deep shade."

Now it looked like an Henri Rousseau painting, almost impossibly lush with plants that had oversized, often jagged leaves. But not out of control. A certain order contained its wildness. Hal had bought this little one-story cinder block duplex on the far end of Whitehead late in the winter before last. He rented out one side year-round to an older gay man named Frank who was constantly pushing for expensive improvements, but who had the touch as a landscaper. Hal had paid for the plants and the soil and the necessary tools, but Frank had made it into a garden, tending and watering it through its first months and bullying it into shape.

"Of course now Frank gets to enjoy it all the time and I only get to during the winter."

"Poor you," Andy said, "wintering in Key West and missing it the other nine months. But, I wonder, could you live down here full time? What would you do?"

"I'd move down here in a flash. College life just bores me to death, especially now that I have John. All those years of teaching were just a protracted search for John, I believe." He said this softly, and without any sense of irony. His southern accent—he came from Savannah—seemed stronger when he was speaking sincerely.

"But what about the magazine? Could you give that up?"

"I most certainly could. It's been fifteen years and the unsolicited manuscript stack never gets any shorter, no matter how much I read. If I make a big push to get to the bottom, writers somehow just sense it, and the manuscripts come in even faster till the stack rebuilds. But I could pretty easily do this job from here with three or four brief trips north each year."

"What would you do the rest of the time? What would John do?"

"Well, we would just live, of course. You don't need to hear my big gay liberation speech yet again, but this is a place where I can live as myself, where I can live among my own kind, and, not least, where I can make up for some of those repressed years—with a vengeance!

"I'd be ready to do anything necessary, really. Frank works in the library. He was once a New York publisher. Of course that was when he was straight and the father of four. I'd even sell real estate if I had to."

"But Hal, you'd be the worst salesman in history. You don't have a dishonest bone in your body."

"Hmmm, well I have one that makes me a bit untrustworthy. At least that's what young John would say.

"And what would John do if we lived here full time? Who knows? Our John is still finding himself. But there is one thing about that aristocratic Richmond upbringing of his. He *knows* who he is. Nothing as trivial as an occupation is ever going to change that astonishing confidence of his."

"Yet he seems so lacking in ego," Andy said.

"Exactly! It isn't really about him. It's about his family, the social order. Even as this incredible black sheep, this beautiful gay boy, he feels confident about his place in the world. It honestly never occurs to him that anyone else could be better than he is, or that he might be better than anyone else. It's a complete equanimity."

At just this moment John pushed open the screen door from the kitchen. His golden hair was still wet and his tanned face was pinkish from his shower and perhaps a vigorous toweling off.

"I love it when you talk dirty, Hal," he said with a smile, and gave the older man a squeeze of the shoulder. "How'd you sleep, Andy? Was that you two or a couple of alley cats I heard last night?"

"Not guilty," said Andy. "Besides, the walls are cinder block, so I know you're only fishing."

John held the espresso pot to his nose and said, "I think I'll make some fresh."

When he was gone, the proud papa look of the night before had returned to Hal's face, and even Andy could appreciate John's freshness and the grace with which he moved.

"I guess I can see the two of you making a life here," Andy said.

Through the door John said, "Oh, Hal, you're not singing that refrain again, are you? Poor Andy doesn't want to hear about how you intend to escape from a life that anyone else would kill to have."

"You might be a saint, John, but you'll never be a pope till you master infallibility. Andy brought up the subject, I'll have you know."

"It's true, John. I've even been fantasizing about moving here myself."

"Terrific," John said. "You and Hal stay here and I'll return to civilization with Shelley. Like me, she wouldn't be caught dead living on this ratty key. Not when there's a Virginia to return to."

With that, Shelley must have appeared in the kitchen, because John said, "Here's my angel now."

Shelley came through the door, wearing the T-shirt of Andy's she had slept in and a pair of blue jeans. She still had bed hair and her face showed signs of sleep, but that bright smile dazzled them all, straight or gay.

"Show them your T-shirt," Andy said. She'd had her arms crossed over her chest out of modesty, but she did what she was told.

Andy had just bought the shirt the day before. Its message was, "Your proctologist called. They found your head."

"Very nice," Hal said. "I'm glad you only wear that to bed. Otherwise, Andy might have to fight a Conch or two who took offense."

"Oh come on, Hal," John said. "No Conch knows what a proctologist is. It would take a visit to the library for him to get the joke."

Shelley crossed her arms again and announced, "I'm ravenous. All that dancing, I guess."

"Let's go for a big breakfast at the Fourth of July," John said. "It's our favorite Cuban place. There's nothing like plantains with your huevos."

The others agreed and Shelley asked for five minutes for a shower while the men had another round of Cuban coffee. She was as good as her word and soon reappeared with the same pinkish look that John had had, and pulled a chair into a patch of sunlight while she combed out her shoulder-length, dark-brown hair, which looked almost black when wet.

The men hadn't stirred, so Shelley, who really must have been hungry—and there was not even a crust of bread in Hal's kitchen—said, "I'll be ready when you fellows are."

They walked in the bright sunshine the few blocks to the Fourth of July. It was still early enough that the sea air felt almost brisk, in spite of the humidity. The restaurant was plain inside, with white paper tablecloths, but it wasn't small and because it was in a freestanding building, it was bright with light from the windows on three sides. The kitchen at the back of the room was open beyond a counter. An American flag hung from the ceiling above the register. Unlike every other restaurant in Key West, it seemed, this one was staffed with women. Even the cooks at their griddles were female.

"Buenos días," the waitress said. "Welcome to the Fourth of July." She had reddish hair and a not-especially olive complexion, but what struck Andy most about her was the complete absence of sexual innuendo in her greeting, something that he and Shelley had noticed not only from waiters in gay bars but from virtually everyone with whom they came in contact. The naturalness and even shyness of the waitress charmed him and he could tell that Shelley had noticed this quality in her, too.

They ordered four cafés con leche and various juices and when the waitress went off to fetch them John took over the ordering, going beyond plantains and eggs with jalapeños to sausages and ham and breads and fruit, with side dishes of black beans and rice, a breakfast that quickly evolved into a brunch.

"So Andy told you he wants us to pull up stakes and move to Key West?" Shelley asked.

"He masked it at first by feigning interest in whether I, or we, could live here," Hal said. "But he soon confessed his real motive for asking."

"Unfair," Andy said between bites. "If you were here it would certainly make a big difference. Then we'd know at least one other old married couple like us."

"Hmmm," John said. "I don't recall the proposal, much less the wedding. And I'm not holding my breath, since doesn't marriage tend to include pledges of fidelity?"

"Right," Hal said with a snort. "Because all straight marriages are so pure and free of extracurricular activities."

"I said *pledge,* Hal. And when did you become the expert on heterosexual marriage?"

"Are you kidding?" Hal said, with what felt like real incredulity, not just rhetorical flourish. "This is the ocean we swim in—our novels, our newspapers and magazines and television, our own families, our friends. It's the water that we are fish out of. Surely we're all experts on heterosexual marriage."

"Funny you should say so," Shelley said quietly. "One reason we're here now is that, after six months of marriage following many years of knowing each other, we're puzzled about this thing we've gotten into; we're even flustered."

Andy was surprised that Shelley was saying this. One ongoing point of dispute between them was how private their life together needed to be. She was always getting annoyed at him for saying something to his mother or to their friends that she thought was out of bounds. "Can't we just keep our business our business?" she would say. Andy felt that she had an unrealistic belief in how happy any two people could be together, and that the stresses they felt were not unnatural or embarrassing, but simply the way things were. Why should they hide it from others, especially others who knew them well and might have some advice to offer? And here she was telling Hal, of all people, that they were having troubles. Hal who loved any evidence of heterosexual love gone wrong. And John, who would never show the bad manners of offering any sort of advice to others, why tell him?

"But that's impossible," Hal was saying. "You two are perfect together, you're the exception to the rule. When I look at you two I can almost understand heterosexuality. And marriage seems like a quite credible institution. If there's any sort of problem, it must be Andy's fault. John, take him out back and beat the shit out of him. Then everything will be fine."

They all burst out laughing, but none of them were laughing, Andy thought, because they felt John *couldn't* have throttled him, just that he never would. Although Andy probably outweighed him by twenty-five pounds, John was taller and would have the longer reach, plus his catlike grace suggested a coiled athleticism. Andy had been an average athlete at best, shining only slightly in college when he joined the Concordia rugby club and participated in the barely controlled chaos of Saturday matches. Still, the idea of John using his fists on anyone, especially Andy, was of course absurd.

When they stopped laughing, the table grew quiet, and John reached for Shelley's hand. "We love you both, you sweet thing, and if there's anything we can do ..."

"Isn't it obvious?" Hal asked. "Clearly you two have been fine since you've been in Key West. We've been with you almost every minute. You need to move here pronto and what we can do, John, is move here ourselves. That will solve everything."

They all laughed again, not only at the simplicity of Hal's

solution, but at how transparently he was pleading on his own behalf, not Andy and Shelley's.

Still, Andy thought, as they staggered out of the restaurant, filled beyond full and carried on legs that had not moved in ninety minutes or more, sometimes the simplest solution really is the best.

6

THE DAY BEFORE, at Hal's urging, Shelley and Andy had booked spaces on a snorkeling trip for early this very afternoon.

"Good lord," Andy said. "We'll go straight to the bottom with all this food in us."

"That's okay," John said, "the bottom is where the fish are. Down in the reef."

"And we still have a couple of hours to digest our food," Shelley said. "You'll be hungry again by the time we get on the boat."

"The water isn't that deep," Hal added. "And it's crystal clear. One of those lovely deck hands will dive in to save you if you need it. Makes me almost want to go myself."

"You're still invited," Andy said. "Whatever your motive for coming along."

"No, we'll let you two lovebirds have some time to yourselves," Hal said.

When it got close to one o'clock, Shelley and Andy jumped on their rental bikes and pedaled over to the marina on William Street. The boat had been out when they signed up for the cruise, and now they saw an aged charter fishing vessel, with a wide back deck behind an enclosed cabin, below an enclosed captain's bridge. Andy imagined that the boat had had a varied career, ranging from deep sea fishing when it was new, to smuggling dope and Cubans at midlife, to its banal geriatric present task of hauling tourists the few miles across calm, shallow waters to the reef.

The weathered sign on the dock by the slip where the boat was backed had the age-appropriate name Sunset Tours. Across the stern of the boat, in blocky black letters, were the words MISS MELISSA and KEY WEST.

"Must be a story there," Andy said. "Especially if *miss* is being used as a verb."

"That doesn't sound likely, Andy. I think of a sexy girlish heartthrob who today is gray-haired and missing a few teeth."

A bearded and shirtless young deckhand was hosing down the deck of the boat. His skin seemed impossibly brown, and he had lean, ropy muscles above his faded denim cutoffs. His curly hair and beard were bleached by the sun.

"You here for the one o'clock trip?" he asked with a shy smile. "Come aboard if you like, but don't slip."

He offered Shelley a hand as she scrambled onto the stern and hopped down to the wet deck, and waited to offer help if necessary as Andy did the same.

"We're getting your clean deck all dirty," Shelley said of their footprints.

"No matter. Nothing else on this old wreck's that clean anyway. I'm Rick. Up there in the air conditioning is Captain Dave."

He pointed to the bridge, where the tinted-glass doors were indeed shut to keep out the warm, humid day. They could only take Rick's word for it that there was someone up there.

"How many people do you take on these cruises?" Andy asked.

"Ten if we can get 'em," Rick said. "We're full this afternoon, I hear."

Just then a clatter of bikes pulled up to the dock, each of them commanded by a healthy-looking young woman. What struck Andy first about them was how unmiscellaneous they were. Each of them seemed to have reddish tans and long, straight hair ranging in color from blond to darker blond. They weren't muscle-bound or dikey looking, but they all had athletic builds and carried themselves like athletes. Only one of them was what you would think of as short.

And they were calling Rick, the mate, "mate."

"Is this the tub that's taking us out to your tiny American reef, mate?" one of them asked with a confident laugh.

Rick seemed as astonished as Andy and Shelley were, and by the time he could welcome them aboard they'd gathered their packs from their bikes and scrambled onto the deck. There was never any question of Rick offering them assistance, as he stood there with his mouth open and his hose in his hand.

"Where you gals from?" he managed to sputter.

"We're from Borneo, mate. Can't you tell by the bones through our noses? A lost tribe of cannibals, that's us." This, too, from the confident one.

But the shortest of them, who had the darkest hair and seemed to have the biggest boobs, gave him a kind look and said patiently, "Don't believe a word she says, mate. We're from Australia. We're ruggers from Canberra."

"Ruggers?" Rick clearly could not imagine what this word meant.

"You play rugby, too?" Andy said. "I played in college."

"Not in the scrum, clearly," a broad-shouldered, very blond girl said. "You're far too scrawny for that."

"Fullback, actually," Andy said with a smile.

"Ah, a golden foot," said the big girl. "I'm Kate."

She offered a hand with a firm but not quite aggressive grip. Her teeth were perfectly white when she smiled.

"This the missus?"

"Yes, this is Shelley and I'm Andy. Pleased to meet you."

There were handshakes and introductions all around, and as the girls stripped off their T-shirts and put them in their packs, the door to the captain's deck opened. The view from the bridge of the assembled bikini or low-cut one-piece tops must have been splendid, Andy thought.

Captain Dave wore a soiled white baseball cap that said "Capt. Dave" on it in blue letters. He looked to be a man in his forties, and an expanse of Hawaiian print, mostly orangey shirt somewhat contained his girth. He doffed his cap and said to them all, "Welcome to the *Miss Melissa*. Rick will help you with the equipment and if you want a cold soda there's some in the ice chest." The captain recited this brief speech as though he had memorized it once long ago, and then he returned to his small cabin. His outline was faintly visible behind the dark glass as he stood there, apparently continuing to check out the girls.

It was clear that Rick would not be handing out many soft drinks to this crowd. Each of them had at least part of a six-pack of beer in her bag, and they soon had the large built-in ice box, bigger than a coffin and designed for holding fish, and now half-filled with crushed ice and a smattering of soft drinks, well stocked with beers of various sizes and makes, ranging from one-pint cans of Fosters to the ubiquitous Buds.

"Have a beer?" another of the girls said to Shelley and Andy, holding open the top to the chest.

"Yes, great," Andy said and reached in to pull two out. "We've got some nice fat joints we'll share once we get off shore just a bit."

"Groovy," she said. She wore a lime-green knitted bikini top and looking at her made it just a bit difficult for Andy to swallow. "We've been here for two days and haven't yet procured any. Those blokes at Mallory Square didn't feel quite right to us."

"Wise decision not to buy from them. We have friends here, though, so we'll get you some good information from them for you. Meanwhile, this is home-grown from Virginia."

"Ah, Vir-gin-i-a," she said, enunciating each syllable. "It must be beautiful there."

"It is. You should come visit us," he said perhaps a bit too eagerly, because Shelley shot him a look. "We live in Charlottesville," he added. But his voice was trailing off at this point and the girl in the lime green, whose name turned out to be Lydia, seemed to sense not to pursue it.

Soon Captain Dave had the big diesel engines of the old boat thrumming, and Rick scrambled around the deck to untie the lines. The *Miss Melissa* chugged so slowly across the little harbor that it felt almost as if they were adrift, and then they took a wide left turn into the channel that separates the key from some small nearby islands.

The ten of them stood around on the deck, the Aussies chatting amiably with Shelley and Andy, seemingly starved for company other than one another. They had left Canberra a week before on what would be a month-long team excursion in the United States, a bonding experience that would not actually involve playing any rugby. Only about half the team had been able to afford the trip, which had begun in Miami and would end in San Francisco. All of them were in their early to middle twenties, roughly their own age.

Once they cleared Sunset Island and headed out to sea on a trip that Rick had said would take about thirty minutes, Captain Dave opened up the engines a bit, creating a wind sufficient to make joint smoking, or at least joint lighting, a problem. So Andy fished a couple of those fat joints and a pack of matches out of his backpack and urged Shelley and the girls closest to the door to the cabin to join him inside. This included Lydia, who had offered them the beer, and the short, stacked girl who turned out to be the team's scrum half. Her name was Susan. She was wearing a maroon one-piece tank suit and a pair of multi-pocketed shorts in fatigue green. The sides of the cabin were lined with short cabinets on which seat cushions had been fitted. The four of them sat in a row and Andy lit a joint and passed it.

Susan inhaled deeply, stretching the maroon material over her breasts to a pinkish color. "Blimey," she said, after a long, leisurely exhalation. "That's some good ganja."

The joint went down the line quickly, ending with Shelley, and when Andy went to fetch it he noted with satisfaction that not one of them was a drooler. Nothing worse than a soggy joint, especially when it was the first one in circulation, permitting no excuse for any failure to control bodily functions such as saliva production. He could be forgiving after four or five joints of sufficiently good marijuana, but a spittled joint at any time was still gross.

Soon Susan and Lydia were reporting in detail about snorkeling in Australia, the Great Barrier Reef and so forth, and after the third pass of the joint Andy went to get them all a fresh beer. Determined as he was to complete this mission as quickly as possible, he could not help noticing that out on deck several of the ruggers had removed their bikini tops and were offering their already sunkissed breasts to the midday sun. A couple of the girls who remained mostly clad intercepted Andy as he carried the beers back to the cabin, asking what was up, mate. A little innocent dope smoking, he reported soberly, and he urged them to see for themselves.

The three of them entered the growing haze of the cabin just as Lydia popped the little butt end of the now-extinguished joint into her mouth, and swallowed.

"So it's going to be like that," Andy thought, without quite knowing what he meant. After distributing the beers he pulled the other joint out of his pocket and scrambled around till he found the matches where he had been sitting. He handed the joint once lit to the taller of the newcomers, a girl with big teeth and a pert nose. Andy was trying his hardest to be calm, as if smoking dope with a roomful of lovely, no, beautiful young Australian women was an everyday sort of thing for him. He shot Shelley a look, and her stoned smile suggested that he had not—not yet, anyway—done anything to arouse her ire.

He mentioned very casually to Shelley that some disrobing had occurred outside, something that Shelley could plainly see for herself through the tinted cabin windows, which made looking in difficult but looking out pretty unhindered.

"You stay safe in here, then," Shelley said, "and I think you'll be okay."

"Well, I might have to get another joint out of the back-pack …" Andy began.

"Let me know and I'll fetch it for you." She still seemed to be speaking more in jest than not.

But the room had become so smoky that Shelley and Lydia soon pushed outside for some fresh air, and a couple more of the Aussies slipped in for a toke. Andy tried not to notice that one of them was quite bare-breasted. Still, she and the other girls seemed utterly unfazed by this, although the air conditioning was already having its effects on the nipples of the topless one.

Soon Susan was pulling a Lydia by consuming the end of the second joint and Andy, not wishing to be a faithless sort by fetching a third joint over Shelley's expressed if possibly insincere preference that he not, asked Susan if she would ask Shelley to dig out another cigarette. He did not wish to explain that because there were more bare-breasted women outside than inside he was obliged to stay here, so he simply hoped that Susan would assume he was just too stoned to make the journey himself. Whatever other cultural differences might have been at work on board the *Miss Melissa,* Susan did make this assumption, or at least showed no hesitation in heading out the door.

Andy busied himself in conversation with Kate, the big girl who had pronounced him scrawny. He was afraid he might not be able to keep his eyes off the erect nipples only a few feet from him, so he stared at Kate intently.

"You in the scrum yourself?" Andy asked, innocently, he believed.

"Oh, yes, I like to mix it up with the other mathildas, not that I'm like that. Nothing sexual about a good scrum, unless scratching and sweating and the occasional fart is your sort of fun."

"Well, one out of three, actually," Andy said amiably.

"You look like a fellow with fairly conventional tastes, not to suggest there's anything plain about Shelley. She's glorious. But I don't see you getting turned on by being scratched or smelling farts. And don't we all enjoy a good sweat?"

"Yes, indubitably."

Andy feared that this conversation had nowhere else to go, but then Susan returned, joint in hand, accompanied by another nudish goddess. Susan bore him the joint like a host and he ceremoniously lit it and sent it on its way. He realized that if he hoped to actually snorkel once they arrived at the reef, he had had enough reefer for now. He thought about sharing this witticism generally, but the second set of nipples were setting up, and he felt that he should make himself as inconspicuous as possible. In fact, now that there were likely as many bare breasts inside the cabin as out, he thought it might be his moral obligation to join Shelley on the deck.

When he did he found a flaw in his math, but it was not really his fault, because Lydia had now dropped her top, too, the lime-green knit one that he knew would be a part of his fantasy life for years to come. And yet here was what that green knit had sheltered. Should he approach or not? Would Shelley want him at her side or would she suspect that he was cozying up only to get a close gander at Lydia? This was becoming a very difficult day to navigate, and the THC coursing through his bloodstream did not offer much promise of a successful outcome.

Andy decided to pull himself together by standing near the ladder to the bridge, along the starboard rail, staring out at the turquoise water. Soon Rick was scampering down from the bridge, where he had evidently been driving the boat so that Captain Dave could get a continuing eyeful of the deck scene from behind the tinted windows of the bridge.

"I highly approve of the dress code on this vessel," Andy told Rick as he stepped to the deck.

"Nothing surprises me anymore," Rick said. "You see a bit of everything out here. I'm just glad it's ladies and not the homos. They come out here with their baby-oiled hairless bodies and skimpy tank suits and giggle like a bunch of damned girls."

Andy gave Rick a noncommittal look and said, "We getting close?"

"Yeah, I gotta start hauling out the flippers and masks and snorkels from the cabin. Looks a little smoky in there."

"Feel free to partake," Andy said.

"Maybe on the way in. I'm the lifeguard for the next hour and a half. Even in Key West it would be trouble if a girl drowned and the crew failed a drug test. Besides, what I'm seeing makes me want to hang on to my senses."

"Yes, stimulation enough for any man," Andy agreed, hoping that his own memories of this day would be as specific as possible.

Rick began carrying armloads of equipment out to the deck and dumping them on top of the ice chest. The girls drifted out of the cabin with him and soon they were picking through the flippers and adjusting the straps on the goggles. Rick encouraged them to put a little suntan oil on their feet so the flippers would slip on easily and to spit into the inside of their masks to keep them from fogging up. There followed a scene reminiscent of a Renaissance painting of Purgatory, with half-nude bodies writhing on the deck to try on their flippers. Andy and Shelley slipped off their own T-shirts and shorts, revealing their bathing suits—Shelley's a pink two-piece with white polka dots that looked good if a little demure on her in this company, Andy's a baggy nondescript navy-blue thing. They also began rubbing their feet with lotion and fiddling with the masks and snorkels and then they heard Captain Dave cut the engines and it grew very quiet. There were some other boats within sight strung along the reef, but none within a thousand yards of so of the *Miss Melissa*. Rick scrambled along the port side of the cabin up to the bow, where he opened a hatch and began to feed the anchor and its chain carefully down into the water.

When he returned he gave a quick lesson on breathing with the snorkel and how to clear it with an explosion of breath, garnering the same sort of bored looks that stewardesses get when explaining the operation of a seatbelt. Then he went back into the cabin and returned with a ladder that hooked to the side of the boat. "Please stay on the surface nearby till you get used to the snorkel. You get in any trouble, just holler."

With that, several of the girls jumped overboard, their equipment nestled in their arms against their breasts. Once they surfaced they each, as if by plan, slipped off their bikini bottoms and flung them up to a teammate in the boat, inspiring raucous laughter. They soon had their flippers and masks on and were slowly propelling themselves away from the boat, staring down at the reef below, their creamy white bottoms protruding from the calm surface of the gulf. The girls in one-piece suits, including Susan, shed right on deck, offering mild apologies for their immodesty, and were soon also paddling around, joining the flotilla of bouncing buttocks.

Even Rick stood gaping, and Captain Dave had emerged

from the air conditioning for a frank look. Andy and Shelley stood on deck, not quite knowing what to do.

"I'm feeling a bit Victorian right now," Andy said.

"Oh, don't be such a liar," Shelley replied. "You know you like to strip at any excuse."

"Should we, then?" Andy asked.

"Not this girl. I don't want fish nibbling at my privates. You'll have to keep your own counsel on that. I'm not going to be the one to say no."

They both jumped in with suits on and soon Shelley had wriggled into her equipment and was flippering away on a heading at a slight oblique to the one the Aussies had taken. Perhaps it was the good Virginia marijuana or the two or three beers or the bright sunlight or even the jalapeños in the eggs at the Fourth of July, or the unholy combination of them all, but Andy made a fateful decision. He shucked his own suit and flung it onto the deck, heading off in Shelley's direction, but at an angle that kept the ruggers in sight.

The reef was as Hal had promised, easy to see from the surface through the clear water, and only eight or ten feet below them. The fish were plentiful, darting in small schools in their various sizes and colors, seemingly oblivious to each other and to the humans moving slowly on the surface above them. Shelley stayed on the surface, following the edge of the reef, but Andy dove several times down to swim among the fishes, often looking through the clear water toward the Aussies, who were also now diving to explore the reef at arm's length. As they returned to the surface he could see the black triangles of their pubic hair or the white flash of their muscled buttocks. Naturally, he would like to have had a closer look, but he was careful not to stray too far from Shelley or to be too obvious about his voyeurism. But was that really the right word, given the girls' apparent obliviousness to his glances? They were so unselfconscious that he imagined he could have swum with them without engendering a second thought from anyone but Shelley.

A problem with his mask, though, was somewhat obscuring the views he did get. It was not only steaming up on the inside, but had a leak he couldn't stop. When he kicked up to the surface and pulled off the mask to reline the inside glass with fresh spit, he noticed a pitted place along the rubber edge of the mask that was making it impossible to get a tight seal. He swam over to Shelley and patted her on the shoulder.

"I'm going back to the boat for a different mask. This one isn't right. Come back closer to the boat or get nearer the other girls in case you have a problem. Be back in a minute."

Shelley nodded, her snorkel bouncing up and down dramatically, and he swam back to the boat. He asked Rick to toss his suit to him so as not to subject Rick and Captain Dave to his genitals, especially given that he was in a state of semi-arousal. He let his flippers float on the surface as he struggled into his suit and then was up the ladder and on the deck.

"See any grouper down there?" Rick asked as Andy was inspecting the masks remaining atop the ice chest. When Andy asked what they looked like, he described their unmistakable ugliness and girth.

"Yes, I think I did," Andy said.

"Want to try something fun?" Rick asked as he headed back toward the cabin. He came out holding a small spear gun and spear. The shaft of the spear was perhaps two feet long and the tip had a small barb on it.

"This ain't recommended for this kind of trip, so be careful and stay away from the others. You don't want to spear anything but a fish, and a big fat grouper would be the easiest fish to hit and good eating, too."

He showed Andy how to engage the safety before loading the

spear, but demonstrated the loading process without actually doing it. "You don't ever want to load this except under water and when it's loaded keep it in the water even when the safety's on. You got it?"

Andy jumped back in with his flippers and new mask in his arms and then thought what the hell and shucked his suit again. This way, he'd be able to regale his friends with tales of nude spear fishing among the Australian mermaid mathildas. Once he had his goggles and flippers on again he swam over to the ladder and Rick handed him the spear gun. When he pushed off he found himself surrounded by several of the girls. Susan gave him a smile.

"Having fun?" Her breasts were bobbing on the surface of the clear water. "Hey, be careful where you point that thing."

She gestured in the general direction of his penis, which was now approaching an embarrassing state of erection. But he realized quickly that she meant the spear gun.

"Will do," he said weakly. He treaded water with them for a few more moments, hoping the girls were planning to scramble up the ladder in the altogether, but instead they asked Rick to fetch them some beers.

Shelley had indeed joined the other girls. He needed to tell her about the spear gun and to urge her to keep an eye on him from a distance, so he kicked off in their direction, giving his dick a good rough squeeze to encourage some semblance of flaccidity before he got too close to Shelley.

When he explained his plan, she asked, "Is this really wise? How stoned are you, anyway?"

He assured her it would be okay, the water and exercise (and although he didn't mention it, the blood rushing into his groin and perhaps pulling some THC away from his brain), having sobered him up considerably.

"I'll be careful. And this thing has a nine-foot cord on it, so as long as I keep my distance I won't be able to shoot anybody but myself, and I promise not to do that."

Off he went. Once he had separated himself from the girls and stopped to load the spear, he was surprised at how easy it was. When Rick had explained the process Andy had had a little trouble concentrating. It was like asking directions when he got lost driving. Something always made his mind go blank about halfway through the explanation.

Now, the gun pointed straight down, he slowly flippered along the surface, following the ridge of the reef and watching for an unsightly and unfortunate grouper to happen into the moving cone of his vision. The mask was working fine, now that he wasn't looking at the girls. Rick had told him not to shoot down from the surface for fear of hitting a rock and catching the ricochet of the spear. And of course the target was much bigger if you could shoot at the fish from the side instead of from above. Soon the magnified sound of his rhythmic breathing and the beautiful but, frankly, somewhat boring view unfolding beneath had begun to lull him. His thoughts drifted away from the business at hand to Susan's ample breasts and to the firm roundness and reddish-brown areolas and nipples of Lydia's, once so imperfectly hidden by the lime green top. He was becoming aroused again when, blimey, as Susan would say, two pudgy groupers swam into his sight.

Andy took a deep breath and dove stealthily, he believed, down to their level. He trailed them at just beyond the range of the spear until his breath began to give out. Before his lungs really burned he gave a couple of hard kicks to get within range and, like ducks in a shooting gallery the fish turned to the side, offering a choice of broad targets that just needed to be led by a foot or two. He tugged the safety off and pulled the trigger. The spear seemed to burst off its spring, but the fish had disappeared before the spear was halfway to them.

It traveled harmlessly to the end of its cord, bounced back a foot or two, and drifted to the bottom. All of this happened faster than Andy could actually register it; he would remember this sequence after he had reached the surface, cleared his snorkel, and taken a few deep breaths. Already the smaller fish beneath him were swimming around as though nothing had happened.

He spent another fifteen minutes or so watching for grouper and taking two more shots with a similar result. He had loaded the spear a fourth time when he heard Rick calling them back to the boat, now several hundred yards from him. Because the girls, including Shelley, were between him and the boat, he didn't dawdle, hoping to get one last view for his memory bank. The Aussies were not really paying much attention to Rick's announcement, and Andy soon found himself among them. He was careful to keep the spear gun pointed at the bottom, but his fleshy spear was less easy to control. It pointed enthusiastically in the direction he was swimming. Shelley was at the far side of the group, edging toward the boat while keeping an eye in Andy's direction. Much as he would like to have frolicked with all those robustly naked bodies he kept on a steady heading toward Shelley. The water around him seemed to be sizzling with erotic energy, his own if nobody else's. The girl's did not engage him as he swam, but neither did they scatter or show any signs of modesty. As he broke out of the group and approached Shelley, he was still in a highly aroused state, something that was pretty easy to spot in the clear gulf water.

"Good god, Andy. Can't you show a little self-control?" Shelley at last seemed deeply annoyed, evident even with her mask still on.

"Well, it's, um, it's sort of involuntary. I don't really get to tell it what to do in circumstances like these. Not that I've ever really been in anything like this sort of situation before."

He knew there was a pleading tone to his voice, but Shelley turned without comment or any sign of understanding and led him toward the boat. When he had to ask Rick for his suit while Shelley was pulling off her flippers, she just got that much more furious. He handed her the spear gun, thinking he would unload the spear once he'd gotten into his suit. When she let go of her flippers to grab the gun, they started to drift away. Once she'd corralled them and turned back toward the boat the gun discharged and the spear shot out in the general direction of Andy's groin. He had been getting his own flippers off and had not yet slipped into his suit.

The spear struck him with what felt like a hammer blow at the top of his thigh. He registered the force even before the pain exploded into his brain. By the time he could understand what had happened, Rick was in the water supporting him and the water was pinkish, whether from blood or simply from the pain, Andy would have to sort out later. He looked up to see Captain Dave's burly form reaching down and felt Rick pushing him upward and soon he was lying on top of the ice box with Shelley pressing a towel hard on the spot from which the spear end was sticking. Captain Dave had cut the cord but because of the barb could not pull the spear out.

Rick was hustling the girls up the ladder. He would tell Shelley later that he was terrified that the bloody water would bring a shark within a matter of moments, so there was no time for modestly pulling on their suits first. Andy was soon surrounded by solicitous-looking nude women. He himself was still nude, although the towel covered his now flaccid privates, and Captain Dave was bringing armloads of towels and a blanket to keep Andy warm to prevent him from going into shock. When Andy looked up at the dripping women hovering above him, nearly blocking out the blue, blue sky with its puffy white clouds, the thought occurred that he had just won the Miss Nude America contest and all his fellow contestants, so deserving of the honor themselves, were leaning over to congratulate him. And then he blacked out.

He came to briefly when the medics were moving him from the ice chest onto a stretcher and over the stern onto the dock, where an ambulance and a fairly sizable crowd was waiting. But Shelley would tell him later that they had given him a shot before moving him, and he soon passed out again, not waking until he was in the recovery room in the hospital, the spear having been removed and his thigh bandaged. A nurse was saying "Mr. Watson, Mr. Watson," and he thought of his father. She was hovering over him as the Aussie girls had, and was quite thoroughly dressed in blue hospital garb. He did not feel any pain in his leg but did feel nauseated.

"We're going to prop you up just a bit so your wife can have a look at you," the nurse was saying. "Can I bring you some juice and crackers?"

"Sick to my stomach," Andy managed to say.

"Okay, we'll start you with some ice chips, then. Sitting up should make you feel better."

Another nurse in blue was leading Shelley down the open ward in his direction. Her expression showed that however angry she had been with him, she was now far more chagrined than annoyed.

"Oh, Andy, how are you?" Shelley said as she kissed him on the forehead. "I'm so sorry. I have no idea how it happened."

"Groggy. Don't know how I am. Doctor say anything to you?"

"Yes, he said you were incredibly fortunate—given, of course, that being shot in the first place isn't too lucky. It missed a big artery in your thigh by only a few inches. If it had severed the artery you probably would have bled to death before they could get you back to the dock. Although one of the Australian girls turned out to be a nurse, so perhaps she could have done something. As it was, she put a lot of pressure on the wound and you really didn't lose that much blood. The doctor said it would heal fine and he isn't too worried about infection given all the salt water."

The nurse came back with ice chips in a Styrofoam cup.

"They anesthetized him to get the thing out of his leg," the nurse explained. "It's given him some nausea. See how he does with these and then we'll get him to eat some crackers."

Shelley began feeding the chips to him slowly with a plastic spoon.

Sitting up did make Andy feel a little better and his head was beginning to clear.

"They want to keep you in overnight just to be sure you don't develop a fever," Shelley said. "I called John and Hal and they're going to come visit as soon as you're in a room.

"And all your new girlfriends want to pay you a visit, of course. Susan and Lydia actually pedaled up to the hospital and sat with me while they were working on you. They're really very nice girls."

"I'll never forget them," Andy mumbled with ice chips in his mouth.

Shelley smiled indulgently so he knew she wasn't really that mad, at least not now, but he decided not to say anything more about the girls.

"Wasn't that thing supposed to have a safety on it?" Shelley asked.

"Must not have pushed it in right," Andy said. "All my fault."

"I have a feeling Captain Dave would like to hear you taking the blame for this. He's probably sitting in a bar somewhere, waiting for a call from your lawyer. He was incredibly solicitous. He let Rick drive the boat part way in so he could tend to you, after calling ahead so the ambulance was waiting at the dock. If you really want to live in Key West, you could probably own his boat if you wanted to."

Andy shook his head. "Don't think so. Not much interested in being on the *Miss Melissa* again soon. I'm ready to go home."

"You're going to get that wish, but who knows when. Let's wait to see how much that baby hurts once the drugs wear off." Shelley's face was pinkish on top of her tan from being in the sun. She was still wearing the denim cutoffs and sleeveless gray sweatshirt that she'd worn over her bathing suit when they'd set out from the dock, what, six hours ago? She must have been exhausted from the stress of the afternoon, but, to Andy, she'd never looked better.

TWO DAYS LATER, Andy was sitting in Hal's garden with Frank, the older man from the other side of the duplex, the one who had transformed Hal's yard into the beautiful space surrounding them. Andy had his leg propped up on a chair to keep the throbbing down. He was still taking Percodan for the pain, and he had managed to sleep fairly well the night before, his first night back from the hospital. Shelley and John had gone on a bike ride and Hal had walked to the grocery store to get some stuff for lunch.

"By the way, Frank, my new Aussie friends were looking to score an ounce of dope. Do you have any ideas for them?"

"I'll buy a baggie from a friend on the way to work. One of the girls can come by the library this afternoon and pick it up. Tell them to give you the twenty-five bucks. Even I'm not comfortable taking cash at the public library."

"You do like to live on the edge, though, don't you Frank? Was it always this way, or has Key West done it to you?"

Frank took these as rhetorical questions and just nodded his head companionably, staring into the foliage.

"Thanks for doing this for the girls," Andy added. "My motive is I get aroused every time I talk to one of them, but I take it your motive is something else."

Frank was tall and slender, with cowboy good looks, although the deep freckled tan of his head beneath his thinning hair suggested he'd never worn a hat of any number of gallons. Today he was dressed for work in seersucker shorts, black high-top Keds and a blue knit shirt.

"I liked women once, you'll remember. I liked them quite a lot. And they liked me right back. A lot. So I get your motivation. Mine's just a chamber of commerce sort of thing. I want everyone who comes here to love it as much as I do."

"Yes, you're very chamber of commerce. What could be a better business practice than procuring marijuana for the needy?"

"Saves jail space if people aren't buying from the narcs on the square. Fewer prisoners, lower taxes. Good for tourism, too."

Frank was not much of a kidder; in fact, he didn't really have a sense of humor. Nor did he tend to try hard to ingratiate himself to others. But perhaps it was his chamber of commerce persona that motivated him this morning to be a bit charming and confiding with Andy. Just because he was going home with a serious leg wound didn't mean he had to be dissatisfied with his Key West vacation.

"But, truly, Frank, I'm curious. You've lived two very different sorts of life—and I don't only mean straight and gay. It's more straight and outlaw, within the bounds of social expectations and beyond them. I guess, since this is the life you're leading now I know which one makes more sense to you. But do you miss your former life?"

"Well, okay, if you're looking for wisdom, I'll give it my best shot." He ran his hands along the sides of his head, smoothing back the longish hair there.

"My seventy years have taught me you just can't plan your life out. I never thought about whether I would get married, whether or not I would have children—much less four sons— run a publishing company, ride the train in from Connecticut every day. I just did it. One thing led to another. And as I say, I was never very good at being married. There were lots of women but never much in the way of love or affection, even with my wife as time went on. I never thought about whether I was straight or gay, but I went to prep school, you know, so the gay side of things was always familiar to me, didn't shock me. I was a dabbler but it never meant any more or less to me than the women."

"So you weren't like Hal, who knew from his early teens that he was utterly and enthusiastically gay?"

"No, and perhaps it's only a libido thing. Sex just never inter-ested me that much. I had more than my fair share, but it never defined me, never transported me in the way that just the idea of it transports Hal or the way those firm Aussie lasses must have transported you on that wild outing of yours.

"And as for the job, the responsibility, I could live that life but it never seemed like anything more than a play to me, a play in which I was cast in a certain role. I accepted the role, and acted it without much difficulty or much sense of reward. I just did it.

"But here's an important thought, perhaps, amid all this seeming indifference. If I hadn't played that role I'm not sure the life I lead now would seem so authentic to me. I inhabit my life now in a way I did not before. At my age, it isn't about picking up boys or feeling alienated from the heterosexual world. But I do feel more like myself. In fact, I don't feel like an outlaw now—that other life was my outlaw life, the life beyond the boundaries of my true nature. I love my sons and don't feel in any way estranged from them or the life that produced them. And I needed to live that life, perhaps, before I could become comfortable living this one. But I never lived it in order to live this one, never planned in any way for this one, never longed for it. But one day after my kids were grown up I looked at my wife and decided to leave her, and when I left her I realized I wanted to leave everything else, the job, Connecticut, everything but being a father to my sons. And I've never looked back."

"Wow," Andy said. "That's quite a speech." His elevated leg was going numb so he used both arms to lower it to the ground. It almost immediately began to throb.

Just then Hal walked through the garden gate with two bags of groceries in his arms.

"What'd I miss?" he asked, his face almost boyish with real expectation. Hal was the fellow who never wanted to miss anything.

"I was just explaining to Andy," Frank said, stretching his long arms high above his head, his face unsmiling, "I was telling him how I became a faggot."

"Ah," Hal said. "With the week Andy's had, I can see how he'd be interested."

PART III

CHARLOTTESVILLE. 1976

7

WHEN ANDY AND Shelley had both been working full-time jobs, they had lived in what was little better than graduate-student housing, a small rented cottage on a large estate well south of Charlottesville. The rooms had been tiny, the heating and insulation inadequate, the air conditioning nonexistent, and although the rent was low the utilities were high. The best thing about it was the wide-open spaces for their golden retriever, Jim, who had been free to roam the acres of the estate far from any highway. Even when Andy and Shelley were gone for the day, Jim could be trusted to hang around outdoors, amusing himself in the woods or fields or ponds while keeping an eye on the driveway so he could be there to welcome them home. But now that Andy was in graduate school and only working part time, he and Shelley were living like they were rich. A good friend from the paper had joined the Peace Corps and offered them an apartment downtown he had inherited from his parents. The rent was only a little more than they had paid in the country, and the utilities were included. The hitch was it was theirs only until Andy's friend returned in two years. "Yeah, just try to get us out," Andy and Shelley would say to each other as they grew used to their upscale new surroundings. The apartment was one of two penthouses in an eight-story building on a small hill just north of the downtown, on a street called Altamont Circle. From its wrap-around balcony you could see Monticello Mountain to the southeast, the Rotunda to the southwest, and the Blue Ridge to the west, and look almost straight down at the downtown, its streets bricked in and closed to traffic as part of a pre-Bicentennial facelift. Even Jim loved the view and thus, in their estimation, had given up his rural kingdom happily for long walks on the leash and an occasional run in the country.

Andy had trouble explaining, especially to himself, why he had quit his job to go to graduate school, and to study English no less. He admitted that he had no desire to be an academic even if his academic work had been so stellar as to make such a career possible. But that was hardly the case. He knew he didn't want to keep reporting for the *Daily Progress*. It was an intermittently interesting and even, given Watergate, a somewhat glamorous job, but Andy noticed that there were not many older people doing it, and those who were had become burnt-out cases, alcoholics, or worse. And the pay was rotten, so bad that his current job, working as a waiter at a fancy new restaurant on the downtown mall, did not represent much of a loss of income, even though Andy worked only three nights a week. He supposed he might want to become some sort of editor, not that he was at all sure what editors do. Certainly the editors at the *Daily Progress* did as little as possible. But perhaps not a newspaper editor, perhaps instead an editor of books or magazines. He also had a secret fantasy of becoming a film critic, but this was more than anything in homage to Pauline Kael and Penelope Gilliatt, whose reviews in the *New Yorker* he read obsessively, and talked about excessively, or at least Shelley hinted as much. But the truth was that many of the films those two tough women wrote about never made it to Charlottesville, and he couldn't imagine having as much to say on his own as they did about even those films he did see. What kind of pressure would that be?

So he toiled away at papers about Milton or Whitman or the eighteenth-century English novel without thinking too much about what these tasks were preparing him for. Shelley liked her job teaching Virginia history to eighth graders at the private school, so she didn't begrudge Andy this interlude. His being in graduate school gave both sets of parents in Strasburg the vague hope that he was going somewhere, and also gave them something to say to their friends about what Andy was doing. They only shook their heads with sheepish smiles when one of those friends would be so rude as to ask what Andy would *do* with a graduate degree. But such was the prestige of the university in the state that just knowing he was enrolled there was accomplishment enough to soothe the social anxieties of their parents. "Andy's in school in Charlottesville" was all the explanation required with most of the people with whom they came into contact. If the university was a place that few of their children or they themselves had aspired to, still they were all too aware of how little success such aspirations would have met. The one-sentence version of Andy's present situation was enough to induce a satisfying silence in the other Strasburg parents, or to get them to change the subject with a pleasing eagerness.

A moment of real hope was taking hold in the country, the first such moment Andy could remember in the years since he had begun paying attention to anything so large and vague as the notion of a country. Vietnam was finally over, Nixon disgraced, the likable if hapless Ford defeated, and the lusting little peanut farmer was finally installed, a man so innocuous that he could walk right down the middle of Pennsylvania Avenue after his inauguration without fear of anyone's bothering to knock him off. Still, in a country not yet recovered from the monstrous Nixon, innocuousness was welcome. And with the national Bicentennial only a few months away, it was possible to see beyond the vigorous commercial exploitation of the event to the ideals of the hedonistic Jefferson, the roguish Franklin, the dour Adams, and the dimwitted Washington. Ours was a country founded on principles, however hypocritical were the

Founders who articulated and installed them, and even the most grudging and querulous members of Andy's generation could hardly argue with liberty and the pursuit of happiness as guiding ideals. In fact, those were the principles that pretty much defined the ambitions of everyone he knew. Where that might lead was a question that Shelley had a better sense of than Andy did. But for the time being it was enough to consider that the world was once again focusing on our more idealistic qualities, and that for Andy there was the birth of an utterly unfamiliar feeling about his country. Was it simply the absence of anger and shame or was it an actual presence, the first gentle waves of what might be called patriotism? Whatever that growing impulse was, the Fourth of July fireworks promised to be outstanding, especially those on the big mall, the one in Washington, where Andy and Shelley were planning to park themselves on the auspicious day.

HAL AND JOHN had returned to Concord after another winter in Key West, and Shelley had planned a dinner party to celebrate their return. The four of them had not been together since before Christmas, and now it was late March. Hal loved the new apartment in Charlottesville, which he had driven over the mountains to see a couple of times after Shelley and Andy had taken possession of it last fall.

"I'll just move into the extra bedroom and you'll hardly notice me," he'd said more than once. "You know I'm low maintenance." This was a joke that all of them got immediately.

Shelley had invited a third couple to the dinner. She had become friends with a woman at work, a Spanish teacher who was just a year or two older and was married to an assistant professor of anthropology at the university. Jan and her husband had met as undergraduates at Berkeley—both were from northern California. She and Shelley had started at Belmont School at the same time, and Shelley had immediately been drawn to Jan's high spirits and rebellious nature. The two even looked a bit alike, although Jan, who was four or five inches taller and had a long neck, seemed like a stretched version of Shelley, especially because her dark hair was short, like a mushroom cap on the top of her head, and Shelley's hung down straight past her shoulders. But Jan had the same bright smile as Shelley and in spite of her height had the same loose-limbed comfort with her body. The way she dressed, both in school and out, left little to the imagination about the contours of her lean, girlish figure. Her husband was named Carlos, but with her dark complexion and almost black hair and eyes, she seemed to have more Latin influence in her blood than he did, with his sandy brown hair and light-brown eyes.

Hal and John arrived first, and as they were wriggling out of their coats the always-enthusiastic Jim made his usual frontal assault on Hal, nosing his crotch and licking his hands obsessively, giving little yips of pleasure. Hal gave little yips himself, yips of protest more than pleasure—"Get … this … beast … away … oh, the slobber … not cute"—but was as always pleased to be the center of attention. John crouched down to Jim's level and distracted him by calmly scratching his ears, cooing "Good boy" and "That's my Jim" as Jim stared contentedly into his eyes. Hal escaped and made a beeline to the kitchen to see what was cooking, Shelley trailing him as Andy hung up the coats. Andy marveled, not for the first time, at John's ability to mesmerize Jim, but then John had an animal magnetism that impressed itself upon every creature he came in contact with.

"You look great, John," Andy told him. "Both of you look so tanned and rested. Maybe we really should have made the big move to Key West ourselves."

"I'm not surprised you didn't," John said, "given what must

be your main association with the place. Is everything healed down there?"

"I still have a knot of scar tissue and will probably always have a scar of some sort, they tell me," Andy said. "Not exactly a place that requires plastic surgery, however."

"No, I shouldn't think so. Be hard to explain to Shelley, I imagine, if you got too concerned about the cosmetic appeal of your groin area. As long as it doesn't repel her or anything."

"She seems to have mixed feelings about it," Andy said with a chuckle. "Guilt, of course, although it was my fault that the safety wasn't on. But I think it gives her some satisfaction to see the scar as a spousal warning or perhaps as a primitive connubial scarring ritual. We'll have to ask Jan's husband, Carlos, for his interpretation. He's an anthropologist."

With that there was a knock at the door and in they came, Jan bearing a molded cake draped with plastic wrap and Carlos carrying a bottle of wine in each hand. As Andy and John greeted them and unburdened them of their presents, Jim made another crotch attack, this time on Jan.

"Oh, Jim," Jan exclaimed. "You know what I like. But let's just save it for later."

Hal and Shelley returned from the kitchen, and in the general chaos at the front door, as Shelley and Jan were hugging, Andy noticed Carlos giving John the same attentive look that John inspired wherever he went. Carlos was an inch or two shorter than Jan, but in his lined denim jacket with the collar flipped up, and his bushy brown mustache, he looked substantial and confident. He had the bulk and bearing of a weightlifter. Hal was clearly impressed, and poured on the charm as they were introduced, an attentiveness that both John and Carlos seemed to notice and to take in stride. Meanwhile, Jan was giving Andy a full-bodied hug and a resplendent kiss on the lips.

The party broke in two as Andy, now holding the cake,

followed the two women into the kitchen and John led Carlos and Hal to the bar set up on a table in the living room. Andy put down the cake and watched for a moment as the two women talked animatedly, both clearly excited to be together away from the school. Andy interrupted Shelley's description of what was in the oven—a beef burgundy she had fixed that morning that was now becoming aromatic as it heated—to ask what they would drink. They both wanted a glass of the white wine Carlos had brought, so Andy went out in search of it. The three men had gotten their drinks and were standing out on the balcony, gazing toward the last streaks of salmon-colored light in the western sky. Hal seemed to be pointing out features in the view for Carlos, who was nodding appreciatively. Andy slid open the door and, as he was starting the corkscrew into the bottle of white, asked if they had what they wanted. They all toasted him with what looked like stiff, straight drinks from the bottle of blended scotch that Andy had sprung for that day. Fortunately he had decided to go for quantity over quality—so far there was only a small dent in the large bottle of Cutty Sark. After serving the women and pouring a scotch for himself, Andy joined the men on the balcony.

"A little brisk out here," Andy said, but Carlos still had his jacket on and the other two were in sweaters.

"This scotch is keeping us warm," Carlos said. "I don't drink that much hard stuff and I'd forgotten that lovely burn as it goes down straight."

"No pleasure without pain," Hal said with a devilish smile.

"Stop showing off, Hal," John said amiably. "He doesn't really mean that. Well, sometimes he does."

"Carlos was agreeing with me," Hal said to Andy, "that even if the landscapes closest to our hearts are elsewhere, there's something about the Blue Ridge that is hard not to love."

"What place do you long for?" Andy asked Carlos. "I think

John and I agree the Blue Ridge is our first love." He patted John on the back and John nodded in assent.

"Mountains appeal to me, too," Carlos said. "These beautiful worn old Blue Ridge are great. But I suppose my favorite landscape is the northern Sierras, their jagged bulk. But it's all a matter of what you've grown up looking at, probably."

"Must be why you love Key West so much, Hal," Andy said. "Growing up close to the ocean in Savannah."

"Yes," John said. "That and the fact that there are ravenous gay boys on every corner."

They all laughed, and Carlos said, "You must come visit San Francisco."

"Oh, don't worry," John said. "He has, he has. He can tell you all about his favorite bath houses."

"What about yours?" Carlos asked John with an even look.

"Call me old-fashioned," John said. "But I'm content to bathe alone. Or if absolutely necessary, with Hal."

"Ah, this is why we call him Saint John," Andy told Carlos. "He's had the nickname since freshman year in college."

Then they were silent for a moment, gazing out at the dark forms of the Blue Ridge. Andy preferred to think that the other two were not focused on the image of John in his bath, but were wondering like he was at how John managed to combine such dignity with such good humor. He was not a prig, but neither was he flirty like Hal.

Just then the door slid open and the women joined them at the railing.

"Don't jump, guys," Jan said, tousling Andy's hair, since he was closest. "The cavalry is here to save you from your gloom."

"Not gloomy at all," Hal said. "You caught us in a rare moment of reflection."

"Well, don't make a habit of it," Jan said. "Thinking will get you nowhere." She was wearing a long-sleeved black leotard and tight-fitting black denims. "Warm me up, baby," she said to Carlos and slipped between him and the railing. He opened his jacket and enveloped her in it and his arms.

Shelley's cheeks were red, a sign of her excitement and perhaps of the warm kitchen, the glass of wine, the laughter she had undoubtedly been sharing with Jan. She watched Jan eagerly, like the little sister she resembled. A few stars were beginning to appear in the darkening sky. Jim was scratching at the glass door to join them.

The appreciative silence lasted a few more beats and then Shelley broke it, saying, "Too chilly out here for me. Let's go back inside and get some music on." The warm light from the living room drew them in. "Who needs another drink?" she asked.

THE BEEF BURGUNDY had been a success. Even without any marijuana—Shelley had asked Andy not to produce any joints, since they really didn't know Jan and Carlos that well—the six of them had eaten heartily, several of them wiping their plates with the good day-old French bread Andy had brought home from the restaurant. After drinking Carlos's Napa cabernet they had polished off a Beaune red that John had brought, and then gotten into the jug wine. By the time they had eaten generous helpings of Jan's carrot cake with ice cream and drunk a cup or two of strong coffee, the men were back to drinking the Cutty Sark neat. Once the women emerged from some preliminary straightening in the kitchen, Andy was pushing the coffee table up to the couch to make room for dancing. The music was all rock and roll—CCR, Led Zeppelin, the Who, the Band—and everybody was dancing with everybody, screaming out lyrics, jumping up and down, no inhibitions. Jan roved, facing off with Shelley, then John, then Hal, and finally with Andy. Someone had put on Randy Newman's song "Sail Away," and Jan threw her arms over Andy's shoulders and buried her face in his neck. He felt as if every inch of her body was touching every inch of his, and as he pulled her closer their dancing slowed and was more rhythmical. Meanwhile, Hal had commandeered Shelley for a perkier sort of waltz, and John and Carlos had been left to chat confidingly, swaying but not quite dancing together.

Soon Jan was chewing gently on Andy's ear and when the song ended she whispered to him, "Let's get some air." She led him by the hand through the sliding door and around the corner of the balcony where they were out of sight from the living room. Andy was not so loaded as to be unaware of the potential unwiseness of the situation, and said to Jan, "This could be a mistake."

But she pointed through a crack in the curtains at the other four and said, "Look, they haven't even noticed we're gone." That did indeed seem to be the case, and with this observation, however skewed by lust, Andy abandoned any pretense of caution.

In a second their tongues were in each other's mouths and their hands were taking the complete inventory. Jan's nipples were as hard as pebbles through the thin material of her leotard, and as she rubbed his bulging groin with the palm or her hand her fingers brushed the lump of scar tissue that she could feel even through his jeans.

"Jesus, what's that?" she whispered.

"You don't want to know," he said, and he licked the sweat running down her neck off her face. He was sweating from the dancing, too, even in the cold night air.

"Really, it's like you've got an incipient dick right here, a dick transplant, a baby brother." She gave the lump of feelingless flesh a good tug.

With that, his brain kicked back in and he pulled away.

"It's where Shelley shot me with a spear gun when we were snorkeling in Key West last winter."

"Christ, really? A spear gun? She must really have been pissed to shoot you there," Jan said.

"No, an accident. Not that I didn't somewhat deserve it."

"She isn't armed now, is she?"

"Not that I know of."

They both began to laugh and, without any further conversation but a few minor clothing adjustments, returned to the living room. John and Carlos were still locked in conversation, but Hal and Shelley were out of sight. Jim came padding in from the kitchen and quickly turned and padded back, as if to say, "Follow me."

When they did, they found Hal and Shelley vigorously applying themselves to the dishes.

"Can we help?" Jan said perkily.

"You bet," Shelley said, turning from the sink. Andy thought that she made a point of not looking at him.

He and Jan began ferrying dirty dishes in from the dining room. They gave each other a wide berth and did not talk, except when Andy said, "Let's leave the wine glasses here. Shelley read somewhere that you should never try to wash them until you've sobered up the next day."

Jan put the glasses she was holding back on the table.

"Sobriety," Jan said without a smile. "Highly overrated."

AFTER JAN AND Carlos left, Andy took Jim for a walk as a way to get back on Shelley's good side. Hal and John were spending the night, and Hal offered to accompany him so he could have a smoke. They had crossed the mall, quiet now except for small knots of teenagers with their fake IDs screwing up the courage to go into the few establishments still open and serving alcohol. As a university town, Charlottesville had never expected its drinking establishments to be too exacting about the authenticity of ID cards, although flagrant disregard could result in the occasional bust and fine, especially if city council elections were approaching. They walked down by the old C&O train station and turned left on East Water St. They had been chatting about the dinner party, with Hal asking more questions about Carlos than Andy had answers to.

They turned right on Market Street. Then Andy said, "Did it seem like Jan and I were out on the balcony a long time?"

"No, not really. Any longer might have been a problem, though. Shelley definitely noticed."

"Did she say anything?"

"No, but she took the first opportunity to head for the kitchen and then she was pretty quiet cleaning up.

"Jan was just a little bit out of control, wasn't she?" Hal asked. "I wonder if it's because Carlos doesn't seem quite straight."

"You think so?"

"I got the vibe immediately, and then he was all over John. Not literally, of course, like Jan was all over you."

"So it was more noticeable than I thought. And you're suggesting that it wasn't just because Jan found me irresistible?" Andy said with a laugh.

"I've never gotten what women see in you," Hal said, with what Andy hoped was a bit of sarcasm. "You're just far too wholesome."

There were a few cars on Ninth Street. As they waited for them to pass, Jim took the opportunity to hit yet another streetlamp.

"Where do they get all the piss to water so many lamp posts?" Hal marveled. "Do you suppose the sight of a post or a tree triggers some sort of reaction that extracts all the extra fluids from their system?"

"They seem to have good on/off valves. He knows how to spread it out, just a good sprinkle here and a good sprinkle there. Never a puddle."

"If only you could learn to hold back, too, Andy, you'd make fewer messes."

"This coming from you?" Andy said, a mock defensiveness rising in his voice. "From the Bath House King, Mr. Fuck Every Male Who Moves?"

"Guilty as charged, and proud of it. But, unlike you, Andy, I'm single. Not pledged to be faithful. Besides, John doesn't really care, and clearly Shelley does."

They were walking down East Market Street, and it was getting darker and the houses more modest the farther they went. Andy was never concerned at night in Charlottesville, even when he was alone, because of Jim, who could let out a vicious-sounding stream of barking when necessary.

"Hmm, I wonder about John," Andy said at last. "He seems pretty faithful."

"Yes, he is perplexingly so. But he grew up gay in a different era," Hal said. "He's never had to repress anything, and certainly not for the years that I had to. I'm making up for lost time."

"Maybe his libido just isn't as overwhelming as yours is. I sometimes wonder about that with Shelley and me."

"Well, how do you measure that sort of thing, anyway? But his libido seems fine to me, happily. Forgive me for being serious just for a moment, but I think it's something deeper than that. It has to do with that rock-solid sense of who he is. For me, being gay is the end-all and be-all of my existence. But for John it's just one more thing to put alongside his social standing, his being from Richmond, the extraordinary physical specimen he is, so beautiful, so perfectly formed. He's like a Greek sculpture with eyeballs."

"It's true. John seems so utterly self-contained. So oblivious to the yearnings that the culture imprints on the rest of us. He's lucky not to need money, of course, but he doesn't need the prestige that the rest of us are so worried about, doesn't need to keep score. So why *would* he be affected by all the messages about sex the culture sends us? Those messages in the movies or on the news that say if you're not naked at Woodstock or wife-swapping back home then you're missing out on something everyone else is having. It's just another form of acquisitiveness—don't let the neighbors get something you don't get."

"Speak for yourself. There aren't a lot of messages on the networks or in the movie theatre urging gay sex upon the general population."

"Yes, I guess I was talking about me. But the message is easily translated: 'If it feels good, do it.' Carpe diem. The pursuit of happiness. We've all got to have our share, whatever it is that makes us happy—drugs, sex, a fancy German car."

"Golly, Andy. And I just thought you had trouble keeping your dick in your pants."

"Yeah, well, name me someone who doesn't. Someone other than Saint John."

"So true."

"Besides, I kept my dick in my pants tonight, at least literally. And the only time I've really had my dick out of my pants since Shelley and I were married was that day in Key West, and look where that got me."

"Yes, you came so very, very close to never having to face that problem again."

"Still, there must be something between actual castration and a self-imposed figurative version."

"What about connubial bliss, my boy? You have a splendid wife who loves you, and I know you love her. Even if neither of you is exactly my particular sexual delectation, I can certainly see why you'd revel in each other."

"Yes, we do revel." Andy tugged Jim's leash to indicate he was ready for them to start back up East Market toward home.

"She's perfect; she's thrilling; I can't get enough of her, sexually and every other way. But when Jan sticks her juicy tongue in my mouth, I find it very, very hard to count my blessings."

"Well, Andy," Hal said, casting a friendly arm over his shoulder, "that sort of math just isn't our strong suit, I suppose."

THE NEXT DAY Shelley and Andy put Jim in the back of their little Fiat and drove him up Rt. 29 to Chris Greene Lake on the airport road. Jim was used to the car and generally just watched the scenery quietly, but whenever they turned onto the airport road he knew he was in for a swim and a good run and began to slobber and trill. Shelley and Andy always tried to calm him down but nothing ever worked, and he was always the first out of the car when they got to the lake. Perhaps because it was a reservoir for the county, the trees and foliage had all been cleared away and there were acres of grassy land around the part of the lake you could see. Everything about it looked as if it had not been open as a park for very long, but the contours of the lake suggested that it was not man-made. Jim always sprinted directly to the water's edge and leaped in, no matter how cold the weather, and would be contentedly paddling around, his nose straight up in the air, by the time they caught up. At least it was sunny on this day, and there were hints in the air of warmer weather to come. They always kept a tennis ball in the car so Jim could show off his retriever genes, and he loved retrieving in water as much as on land. He'd repeatedly crash into the lake, swim the two or three dozen yards to the ball and bring it back to them, only stopping just this side of exhaustion. Then he would wander off along the shore, happily searching for something to lift his leg on.

"I'm sorry about last night," Andy said. "Nothing really happened."

"It's okay, I guess," Shelley said, watching Jim as he became smaller in the distance. "At least we know you're not gay. But don't make a habit of it. It makes me look and feel a little foolish."

"You're right. It was stupid. I don't know what got into me. No dope to blame, and I didn't even drink that much. But Jan is just so, um, what's the word?"

"Sexy?"

"Well, she is that, but I meant something more like vibrant. It's one of the things I love about you. She's just so present. Not that I love it about her, of course. It's just something I must be a little vulnerable to."

"You seem to be a little vulnerable to anything with breasts, Andy. Just try to be more careful." Andy tossed the slobbery ball up by the car and they both ambled off along the lake after Jim. They were wearing jackets but it was breezy by the water and not terribly warm.

"But don't be mad at Jan," Andy said. "I didn't get the sense that it was anything personal, that she was coming after your man or anything like that."

"Look, I like Jan. But she needs to be more careful, too. It might not have been personal for you, but it was for me. It wasn't a very friendly thing to do." Jim had finally found a sign a couple of hundred yards from them, and was giving it a good long dousing, presumably having factored in the dearth of other such opportunities.

"Hal thinks Carlos is gay, and that might be why Jan is a little over the top."

"You talked with Hal about this? Oh, that's just great."

"He brought it up, Shelley. If you noticed Jan and me, why wouldn't he notice? I couldn't say I'm really not allowed to talk about this."

"But he isn't, you know. He isn't gay or at least he isn't only gay. Jan has told me she's worried about him with his students. His female students."

"Maybe," Andy said, "she only thinks it's the females."

"No," Shelley said, stopping to look at him for the first time, it seemed, since the night before. "There have been incidents. Girls coming to the house. Parents phoning the dean. That sort of thing."

"Oh, god. That's terrible."

"And Jan herself has been pregnant at least twice," Shelley said. "She doesn't want to have a child until she knows if she and Carlos are really going to make it. She doesn't want to become the typical faculty first wife, abandoned with a couple of kids for a younger model."

"Poor Jan," Andy said. "And that's even assuming that Hal has got it wrong." They were quiet for a few minutes as they walked along the lake.

"And what's the lesson of this story, Andy?"

Andy gave her a blank look, assuming that she really didn't expect an answer.

"The lesson is that we don't want to be that couple, do we?"

"No," Andy said. "Of course we don't. We'll never, ever be like that, Shelley, because I'm not like that. When we got married, I meant it. The vows. The 'till death' part. I might be a little warm-blooded, and in spite of your best efforts with the spear gun, I'm not a eunuch. But you're the one for me, and I'll never do anything to mess that up."

"You'd better not," Shelley said, and he was surprised to see that there were tears in her eyes.

He pulled her to him and he could feel the tension draining out of her body. He loved the way she fit him, the way her very feminine curves pressed into him, her softness, her smell. Not just the smell of her shampoo, which was there in her hair this morning, or the faint fragrance of the perfume she had dabbed on before the dinner party, but her actual musk, the essential odor of herself. It was almost as familiar to him as his own musk, and a lot sweeter, but he never failed to notice it when he snuggled his face into her skin, as he was doing now.

Soon Jim noticed them clinging to each other. He always seemed to think they were dancing whenever they were holding each other in any way. Now he was sprinting at them, and would soon be barking and jumping up and down beside them.

"Here comes Jumping Jack Flash," Shelley warned. "Unless you want to get wet you'd better let go. He might just knock us over like bowling pins."

"Let him try," Andy said, still hanging on and turning his back to the golden streak heading their way, bracing himself for the attack. "I'm not letting go."

8

T HE FIVE AND DIME restaurant was in a nineteenth-century building on the bricked-in, auto-free part of Main Street, about two-thirds of the way up what was now called the Downtown Mall. It was said to have been a general merchandise store before becoming a Five and Dime in the 1930s. Now the downstairs was a bar in the front of the building and a gleaming new kitchen in the back. The upstairs, almost entirely given over to the long main dining room, had utilitarian wide-plank flooring and bead-board walls and ceiling. The floor had been sanded, stained dark, and heavily varnished, and the walls and ceiling painted a high-gloss silvery gray that reflected, day and night, the light from the tall windows on the street. On its fifteen tables were white cloths and napkins and heavy silver-plate utensils. Each table had a glass vase with a single bright flower, a yellow rose or tulip, or sometimes a red carnation, which would offer the only note of color in the room. The restaurant's sterling aesthetics—in its first months people came as much to admire the room as to enjoy the food, although the food was well above the Charlottesville standard—belied the intentions of the owner, who had lavished so much of his own time and care, and of course money, on the project. These intentions were primarily carnal.

Randall McRogers had moved to Charlottesville from Scotland in the 1960s, and his brogue had proven sufficiently charming to the people of Albemarle County to afford him a good living as an agent for the large estates that were often changing hands there. He had made a killing a couple of years before by selling an estate of several thousand acres near Barboursville to an Italian conglomerate that intended to realize Jefferson's dream of making central Virginia a home for world-class vineyards and winemaking. Randy's imposing height and reddish goatee, which gave him the look of a Confederate general, had not seemed to charm the unexpectedly dour Italian representing the vintner. Sig. Novelli had been all business but had made the fatal mistake of focusing too narrowly on the Barboursville estate, displaying only a cursory interest in the other properties Randy showed him. When he detected this weakness, Randy cut a deal with the owner of the estate to split any profits above the asking price. Then through a combination of bravado and brogue—Randy always wondered just how much the mumbling Italian actually understood of what he said—he had played and finally reeled in the conglomerate at a number that gave Randy vast amounts of disposable income. Because Randy's dowdy Scottish wife wanted little more than the small farm he had bought her in Greene County in a spot that reminded her of home, and because they were childless except for her Old MacDonald's farmyard of animals, Randy felt little compunction to save the money, securing their old age, when he could dump the windfall into anything he desired.

What he desired was women and lots of them. He had made a steady diet of the wives of rich men who'd parked them in far-off Virginia so that they themselves could have their own mistresses in New York or Boston or wherever they were making their millions. But since the university had gone co-educational in the early 1970s the city was crawling with young women, and it had to be said that the rich men's wives, although often beautiful and fit, were rarely young and even more rarely happy. Randy had come to America in the first place because its optimism matched his own, and he had lost as little of that optimism at forty as he had lost of his sexual vigor. What better way to refresh and extend these qualities than by steadily meeting the bright young women that the town offered so plentifully? Since none of these women were buying or selling property in the county, he needed to find a second line of work that would increase his availability to them, and vice versa. Clearly the best way of all to prey on these fawns was to be a university professor, but there was just as clearly not much chance of that, given his own lack of a university education. What did young women need, anyway? Clothes? Their use for upscale clothing had dipped dramatically in recent years, as had the related necessity of dry cleaning. And in any case, running a dress shop would have been a little too prissy for Randy and a dry-cleaning establishment far too proletarian. He had a brief fantasy about starting his own call-girl business, with *belle-de-jour* graduate-student wives servicing the diplomatic community in Washington. But that seemed a little complicated and although as a real-estate agent he had long since made peace with his own ethical deficiencies, even he did not really want to think of himself as a pimp. He resorted to asking advice of some of the rich women he knew. Before long one of them offered up the perfect solution. What did young women want? Why, young men, of course, and the alcohol necessary to lubricate the ways of meeting them. What better opportunity to satisfy this need than to open a bar? Yes, Randy thought, a good local pub like those at home, one that would be classy enough to be comfortable for young women and sufficiently uncomfortable for the drink-buying young men to create a disparity—an excess of tipsy girls at closing time.

One small drawback to this plan was that the Commonwealth of Virginia, in all its southern Baptist wisdom, made it illegal for anyone selling alcohol to derive more than half of the revenues from those sales. Thus, owning a bar per se was not possible, he believed. Legally, the only thing that you could logically sell with alcohol was food, and that is how Randy McRogers got into the restaurant business.

This was the story that Andy had been able to piece together from the other waiters in the upstairs dining room. Since the restaurant had only been open for a few months and Randy was far from circumspect, figuring that his thick accent and the unlikelihood that his wife would ever set foot into the Five and Dime made circumspection unnecessary, Andy tended to believe it was true. Certainly the regularity with which Randy showed up at the downstairs bar an hour before closing and the regularity with which he left the bar soon thereafter with a young woman on his arm gave credulity to the main thrust, so to speak, of the story.

If all of the servers upstairs were men, downstairs they were all women. Why this was the case, Randy had never revealed to anyone, and nobody had ever asked him directly. But the feeling was that male waiters made the upstairs restaurant more Continental in Randy's mind, whereas having waitresses downstairs made the bar more welcoming to single women. Randy was always scrupulous about not hitting on the bargirls, as he called them with so amusing a number of r's that the waitresses let him get away with calling them that. The inviolability of this policy, even as applied to the occasional off-duty waitress who might come in and have a few too many, suggested that Randy knew how destructive it would be to the atmosphere he was trying to create. So he never, ever, as Joe the dishwasher succinctly put it, "humped the help." If this hands-off policy had the effect of implicating the waitresses in his scheme, it did so passively, something all but one or two of the sluttier ones were deeply relieved about.

"Where does he take them?" Andy had asked a fellow waiter named Sam. Andy had by then been at the Five and Dime a week or two and had not only heard the stories but witnessed firsthand some of Randy's accompanied departures.

"Have you ever seen what he drives?" Sam replied.

"Doesn't he drive a Mercedes like every other real-estate agent in town?" Andy thought he had once seen Randy in one while he was while he was walking Jim.

"Well, yes, but that's during the daytime. When he comes here at night he drives his Ford pickup, which has a camper on the back. He's got a mattress in there. And, according to Joe, who has a problem with authority, 'an extra-large box of extra-small rubbers.'"

"What's Randy's charm?" Andy asked. "How does he do it?" There was his stature, of course, and the fact that he owned the place. But he wasn't especially handsome—his face was unnaturally red, as though badly sunburned, and there was some pitting along the jaw line that suggested the goatee might be hiding worse horrors.

"Gotta be the accent," Sam said. He was pulling small white ramekins of butter out of the big refrigerator so they could warm to room temperature before the first diners arrived.

"Really? The brogue sounds kind of stagey to me," Andy said.

"You'd think he might have lost a bit of it in the decade or so he's been away from home. But I think he understands its strategic advantages. For instance, any pickup line, no matter how banal, sounds interesting if only it has an r in it. 'Come here often?' or 'Are you enjoying yourself?' and 'You look very familiar'—twice the fun—have a whiff of romance about them, especially when he heaps on the word 'lass' at the end of the sentence."

"Smart university girls fall for 'lass'? That's disappointing," Andy said. He was filling cut-glass shakers with salt and pepper.

"And never underestimate the power of being hard to understand. The girls are always a step behind as they try to suss out what he's just said. That puts him in control."

Unintelligibility made Andy think of his marble-mouthed friend from college, Hubert, who had returned to Savannah, given up his various drug habits and gone to law school, not necessarily in that order, and after his imminent graduation would go to work for the city prosecutor's office. How many juries would he befuddle into convictions?

"So do you and the other guys get any spillover?" Andy asked? "Not asking for myself, of course. Just idle curiosity, given that I'm married and everything."

"Yes, of course. Officially it's frowned upon. Presumably Randy feels that a flower unplucked tonight will still be fresh tomorrow or the day after. But once he's gone, he's gone. He either gives them a ride home afterward or brings them back for their cars and leaves his engine running. Never drops in. There are always a few girls still hanging around even after closing. And of course there are a few of the waitresses. Just because Randy isn't bonking them doesn't mean they're going unbonked. They have needs, just like everyone else."

"Awfully good of you to think of their needs."

"Hey, somebody has to."

"Well, more power to Randy," Andy said as he finished the last of the shakers. "To use a phrase of my granddaddy's that may or may not be racially offensive, at least these girls are free, white, and twenty-one."

Sam looked up from his neat rows of ramekins and smiled at Andy. "Two out of three, I'd say, generally speaking."

SHELLEY AND JIM sometimes accompanied Andy on the short walk to work at the Five and Dime in the late afternoon, and very occasionally, if it was not a school night, Shelley would walk over for a nightcap with Andy at the bar at quitting time. Randy steered well clear of Shelley if he found her sitting at the bar alone waiting for Andy to come downstairs, offering her a warm greeting and a limp handshake before moving on to likelier prospects or returning his attention to quarry already in his sights. It was in truth a comfortable place to be alone as a woman, Shelley reported, although that might be because both the waitresses and the bartender—an oddly taciturn sort, given his line of work—treated her as one of the family. But neither Shelley nor Andy had ever had a meal upstairs, so on Shelley's twenty-fifth birthday, April 13th, a date she shared, as she liked to point out, with Thomas Jefferson, Eudora Welty, and Seamus Heaney, they went. Andy had reserved the best table, the table for two in the middle by the windows at the front of the dining room. They went to the early seating, since Shelley would have to teach the next morning. As it happened, Sam waited on them. He did not give them the usual menus—handwritten each day by one of the daytime bar waitresses who had studied calligraphy. Instead he brought two champagne glasses and a bottle of Cordon Rouge.

"Happy birthday from all of us, Shelley," he said. "Do you have anything in particular you fancy, or would you like to put yourselves completely in Jacques' capable hands?"

The chef, Jack Lampert, was a former PhD candidate in philosophy who upon dropping out of the program had gone to Strasbourg, the real one in France, to take cooking lessons. The waiters liked to call him Jacques as their little joke.

"The champagne's delicious, Sam," Shelley said. "What a sweet thing for you all to do. And I'd be more than happy to eat whatever Jack serves up."

"Me, too," Andy said. "I'm up for anything that isn't an internal organ."

"Gotcha," Sam said. "Jacques only makes kidney pie or lamb

hearts under direct orders from the owner. And he's threatened to quit over the very idea of haggis."

When Sam went away, Andy said to Shelley, "I've heard Jack say more than once, 'It's Alsatian food, Randy. Not Alsatian-Scottish. If you're homesick, get your wife to slaughter one of her goats.'"

"Why do you think he decided to start such an elegant restaurant," Shelley asked, "if it really was all about picking up girls in the bar? In fact, he could have had a pub, with lots of good pub food."

She was wearing a blue jersey dress that was tight at the top and showed some cleavage. Her face was so beautiful and had enough natural color that she rarely wore much makeup, but she'd fixed herself up tonight and the result left Andy a little stunned. How had he ended up sitting across the table from this creature, much less being married to her?

"Oh, I don't know. I suppose that, deep down, he suspects that he's a sleazeball, or at the very least his minimal education in such a well-educated town has put a chip on his shoulder. Nobody screws as many women as he does without having to prove something to himself. And the fact that all the women are either society types or college girls has to be meaningful. So he started a classy restaurant to prove to himself that he's a classy guy. And the truth is, it is a classy restaurant, so maybe he is."

"Classy, eh?" Sam said as he approached with a plate in each hand. "Okay, I have classy for you right here." He held out the two appetizer plates for their inspection. "In my right hand I have cold lobster in a celery remoulade with ginger. And in my left I have fillets of trout rolled in bacon and served on sauerkraut. Which would you prefer, birthday girl?"

"Oh, we'll have to share, of course," Shelley said. "But let me have the lobster first, in case someone 'forgets' and gobbles it down without sharing."

"She knows me too well, Sam. I have been guilty of this and even greater crimes."

"And yet she stays with you, Andy," Sam said as he pulled the bottle of Mumm's from the bucket and poured more champagne. "Puzzling."

"Service with a smile—and an insult," Andy said. "That's the little extra we provide at the Five and Dime. But this looks fantastic. Please tell Jacques-Jack thank you."

As Sam slid away toward another table, Andy held up his glass and said, "To you, Shelley. May we be together on your fiftieth, and your seventy-fifth, and ...'"

"Don't be gruesome, Andy. Why don't we hold out for my thirtieth? But this is perfect. Just keep doing what you're doing."

They took their time with the appetizers, but once they had finished and Sam had cleared the plates, there was still a lot of champagne to get through. Sam slowed things down, and even brought them each an amuse bouche—a bite of a smoky cheese melted in pastry—but it was clear they would never finish the Cordon Rouge before the main course. Sam discreetly spirited the bottle away. When he returned, he was accompanied by Jack and two of the other waiters, each holding a glass of champagne.

"How is it so far?" Jack asked, and after they both assured him that it was great he held up his glass. "My goodness, Shelley, we ought to pay you to sit here. Our restaurant looks so much better with you in it. Anyway, we just wanted to take a moment to say happy birthday. We really do love having you here." And then the four drained their glasses and were gone.

"Man," Andy said to Shelley. "You really ought to wear that dress more often. I thought Jacques was going to pounce on you."

After a few minutes Sam returned and told them that Jack didn't want to take responsibility for picking their entrees, so Sam talked to Shelley about several options he thought looked good. She chose trout en papillote and Andy chose the restaurant's signature dish, a classic Alsatian stew that Jack deconstructed—the waiters, who like Sam were grad students in English, used this term, even if Jack didn't—on the plate to make it more appealing to the eye. Andy knew that his wine choice would be reported and second-guessed by his fellow employees upstairs and down, so he took the coward's way out and asked Sam to fetch the wine steward. Allen, who was mainly the restaurant manager, spent most of his time with the books downstairs at a table in the back of the bar near the kitchen. After much discussion they settled on a white burgundy that Allen thought could stand up to the stew without overwhelming the trout. He told Andy not to worry about the price, he'd only charge Andy cost, which was still a good bit more than Andy usually spent for a bottle of wine, even in a restaurant.

Before Sam brought the burgundy, Andy and Shelley admitted to each other that they had already had a sufficient amount to eat and drink, but they supposed if they took their time they could keep going. Once the wine was opened and poured, and Shelley offered the opinion that she liked the taste of expensive on the palate, Andy could not resist a subject they often turned to when their sense of well-being was as high as it was at the moment.

"So tell me again why we don't go ahead and have a kid," Andy began.

Shelley smiled indulgently. "Because, Andy, we both agree that you're not ready for one."

"Really? Remind me why we think that."

"Oh, you know, because you're in graduate school, because our income is pretty paltry, because you don't know what you want to do with your life, because you might not be wholly convinced you want to be married."

"What? That's not fair." He swirled the wine around in his glass. "I admit I don't 'want to be married' in some abstract way, but I do want to be married to you. You make an institution that otherwise makes no sense, uh, make sense."

"That's a sweet thing to say, I guess, and I wish I found it utterly reassuring. But look, you brought this up, not me. I'm not registering a complaint, only answering your question."

"That's fair enough. Maybe what I meant to ask is why don't we get in some practice in making a baby, starting tonight?"

"Okay, I can drink to that." She clinked her glass against his. "We haven't been practicing as much as we might have of late. But I just guessed you thought we'd achieved perfection."

"No, improvement is always a goal worth pursuing. Some of the guys at school mentioned a thing or two I wouldn't mind boning up on, so to speak."

"Oh, lord. Please don't tell me you're getting sex tips from graduate students. In English, yet."

"What would you prefer? Engineering students? Phys ed majors? Residents in gynecology?"

"I don't know. Just anyone who doesn't have to offer up commentary during the act. Anyone who could shut up for, say, ten minutes."

"But I thought you liked it when I talk dirty."

"Is that what you're doing? I don't consider reciting Chaucer, even the good bits, to be talking dirty."

"And I thought we were so compatible."

Shelley took a long sip of her wine. "Okay, enough kidding. I couldn't be happier. You'll see in about an hour. Sooner if we skip dessert."

"I think Sam will understand if I tell him we're having dessert at home tonight."

"Yeah, judging by the way he's been ogling this dress, too, I'd say he will."

"Not the dress, my dear, but what's in it. Or what's not quite in it."

THEY STAGGERED BACK to Altamont Circle, both of them so full, even without dessert, that they were on the verge of nausea. Shelley had not, finally, held up her end on the bottle of burgundy, and given its expense Andy could not bear to leave any behind, although he did send once glass back to Joe the dishwasher. Still, he was feeling fairly drunk, and welcomed the necessity of taking Jim on his nightly walk. The more he and Jim walked in the clean spring air the better he felt, and they went almost up to the mill on the river before Andy turned them toward home. He would have gone farther, but it was just too dark and spooky as you got close to the mill. When they returned to the apartment Andy felt much soberer and not nearly so full. He turned out the lights in the living room and the kitchen and when he went into the bedroom the lights were on but Shelley was out, dozing soundly under the covers. "Ah, well," Andy thought to himself. "No such luck tonight." But when he went around to Shelley's side of the bed he noticed all her clothes in a pile on the floor. She normally slept in a nightgown and put her clothes away as she was changing into it. The fact that everything was here in a pile, even her panties, could only mean one thing. After killing the lights, he went to his side of the bed, shucked all of his own clothes and slid under the covers. She was naked except for her socks, which she always kept on even during lovemaking, so he knew she wanted him to wake her. He warmed his hands between his thighs and then ran one of them along the curves of her side and hips and upper leg. She was warm and her breathing grew shallower and she turned onto her back. He touched her breasts, which pooled out almost flat, rubbed her stomach, and nuzzled her neck. He could feel her rising to the surface of consciousness and he would not have known exactly when she had awakened had she not said, softly, "Boo." He kissed her and the taste of the burgundy was still there in her mouth, along with the familiar taste of her. He reached between her legs and she was wet there. After he'd touched her for a little while she swung up onto him. She liked being on top, which he knew he was supposed to see as fraught with meaning. But her straight-forward explanation seemed more logical to him than any figurative one. He weighed almost twice as much as she did. When he was on top she felt crushed, suffocated. And he loved the pressure of her on top of him, loved it when she balanced every inch of her body on his, right down to her toes. Then when she swung up into the saddle, her breasts rising and falling and her hair streaming down onto his chest as they went from a slow trot to a canter, he loved that most of all.

A FEW DAYS LATER, Andy was sitting on the steps of Old Cabell Hall, killing time between his late-morning Milton class and his afternoon seminar in the nineteenth-century English novel. Spring had really arrived, and as he tried to knock off a chapter or two of *Our Mutual Friend* he kept being distracted by the bright green new leaves on the trees or the undergraduates frolicking on the Lawn with dogs or Frisbees or both, and the people passing by, unburdened of their winter coats.

"André? C'est toi?"

Could it be? The mane of reddish-blond hair and the fox-like face could belong only to the girl who played the starring role in his fantasy life, none other than Susanna Agincourt.

"My god. Susanna? Can this really be you? What on earth are you doing here?"

She dangled her backpack in front of him. It was clearly filled with books. "I'm studying, of course. Getting a PhD in French. And what about you, Andy? You've filled out, mon ami. I love the manly you." She gave his hair a rub as she had that spring day, what, six years before in Concord on the lawn in front of McCormick Chapel. "Still thick as a bear up there, eh?"

"But I'm a grad student, too. In English. Is it possible we've both been here on campus all year and not run into each other till today?"

"Seems odd, doesn't it? But I live in the country and only come in for class. I'm not really on campus that much."

"Still, French and English are side by side. Aren't your classes in New Cabell, too?"

"Oui. But maybe a different floor. In any case, let me have a look at you. Let me have a hug."

Andy stood only then. He'd been so shocked to see her that he'd remained frozen on the steps. She put down her pack and he held his thumb in the thick Dickens paperback as he wrapped her in his arms. She felt familiar there.

"Susanna, you haven't changed a bit." Her breasts pressed against him and she still seemed lean and taut. "You even smell the same."

"Ah, well, you know these feminists. We never bathe or use deodorant."

"No, it's a lovely smell. Eau d'Agincourt. A bit peppery. Unforgettable."

But there was one thing changed about her. "Where are the wire rims?"

"Contacts."

"Did you ever start a gallery? What have you been up to? And thanks for staying in touch, by the way."

"Yes, the gallery. I went to New York on mon père's advice, and went to work for a gallery in the Village. He thought I ought to get some practical experience, and see if I even liked it, before he shelled out for a gallery of my own in the Quarter. But my luck being what it is, the gallery owner was the one straight man in that line of work, and married as well. He gave me a lot of shall we call it personal attention and one thing led to another, with the predictably horrible outcome. Which put me off New York, off galleries, and off married men."

"Hmmm. Sorry to hear that last part."

They were still standing on the steps facing each other. The midday sun had pushed the shadows up the steps and the direct light was picking up the red in Susanna's hair.

"When?" she said. "Who?"

"Shelley, from home. We got married about a year and a half ago. She teaches here at the Belmont School. History."

Susanna made a slight punching motion toward Andy's solar plexus. "In the right circumstance, I could make an exception to the married men ban."

Andy looked so pleased with himself that she added, "I'm not saying you're the right circumstance. Wipe that grin off your face and buy me a cup of café."

"You're skipping class? For me?"

"Non. We're skipping class. We have a lot of catching up to do."

They walked past the amphitheater and over to Newcomb Hall. Lunch was still in full swing at the cafeteria, so they went downstairs to the pub, where they were able to find a table and order beer and some sandwiches. It turned out that neither of them had eaten lunch.

They made a bit more small talk and after their beers arrived, Andy returned to a subject that he'd thought about often since the June day in 1970 when she drove away.

"So why did you hustle off that way, Susanna? And how come we didn't stay in touch? I tried, you know."

"But of course you did, Andy. It was all I could do to resist writing you back. And then the glimpses I got of you on campus the next year—it was hard to turn away. I loved our time together. There's never been another time like it."

"Why, then?"

"Isn't it obvious, mon petit choux? You're a smart boy. You tell me."

"Honestly, I've thought about this for years now. All I can could come up with is that you had somebody back home in the same way I did."

"Mais non. Wrong answer. I did not have anyone at home. Nobody. Look, I'd had many male friends. Many dates. Men adore me, you know."

"I know this one did. Does."

"But I had never swooned for anyone before. Men swooned for me, or boys did. I broke many strong hearts. It was never pretty, and I never wanted to be in that position myself."

"But I swooned for you, too. Breaking your heart was the furthest thing from my mind."

The waitress had appeared suddenly with the sandwiches, and had overheard Andy's last line. She smiled sympathetically, thinking she was witnessing a breakup. Andy was embarrassed but Susanna seemed not to care.

"But you were so young, Andy. Three years younger than I was. You were just starting college, really, and I was getting ready to finish. You had no business getting involved with a dame ancienne like me."

"So was it for you or for me that you ran off?"

"Who knows, Andy? It just felt wrong. Perhaps because I felt out of control I convinced myself that it was for you."

And then an unexpected thing happened. It was something that Andy had not seen once in the few weeks that they had been together more or less around the clock. Susanna began to cry. She didn't hide it, did not cover her face. She did not even wipe her tears at first. She cried for what seemed to Andy to be minutes, but never sobbed, never broke down.

Andy held her hand and at first said soothing things. But then he just sat and watched and wondered that their time together could have meant as much to her as it had to him. And that this news could come out of the blue, at a time when he had finally put the question well back in his mind, at a time when he was completely happy with, um, with Shelley of course.

After a while, Susanna stopped. She pulled a blue bandanna out of her bag and wiped her eyes and face and then blew her nose loudly.

"Bien," she said. "I believe I've answered that question completely. And thanks for crying along with me."

Andy laughed. "I think I was too stunned. I'm still stunned. But I share the sentiment. Truly."

"Vraiment," Susanna said. "Exactement."

They talked till the pub closed for the afternoon and walked over to the Lawn and sat in the sun on the steps of the Rotunda. It felt like no time at all had passed. They talked easily and confidingly and without holding anything back. She told Andy about her life in New Orleans after she returned from New York. She had gone to work at an art supplies house that specialized in conservation, which she had begun to learn. Her parents had introduced her to the son of a neighbor in the District, a resident in surgery at Tulane. He had taken her to the famous restaurants, to black-tie fundraisers, even on a vacation to Kauai, where they had become engaged. She had begun to know her younger siblings again. But one day it had struck her that this was not the life she wanted to lead, that she actually missed Virginia, and so she secretly took the GRE in French and did well enough to be accepted by the university. She had broken off her engagement almost exactly a year ago, and had moved the previous summer to a cottage overlooking the James River near Scottsville, where she lived alone and worked hard at her studies.

"Not even a cat?" Andy had asked.

"Non. Pas du chat."

"Aren't you lonely?"

"I will be now."

She laughed at her own boldness and Andy literally blushed. He did not know what to say.

"Don't worry, cher. I said I was off married men. You're quite safe with me."

"Somehow I sort of doubt that," Andy said. "Let me walk you to your car. I really ought to be getting home. We've talked right through my seminar."

"I had a meeting with my thesis adviser, but I suspect he'll forgive me." She stood and stretched like the cat she did not have. He noticed for the first time that she was dressing better. A white blouse, black trousers that might even have been silk. No adviser would stand a chance with her. Would any male? That was the question on his mind as he kissed her good-bye in the parking lot, saying he would leave a note in her department mailbox the following week, proposing another meeting.

ANDY WAS SO discombobulated by Susanna's sudden appearance that he decided to walk home, leaving his bike chained outside Wilson Hall. It would give him time to clear his head. Somehow it had not occurred to him that he would ever see her again, except, of course, in his imagination, where she maintained a sturdy presence. The pain of losing her had taken more than a year to subside, with disturbing flare-ups each time he spotted her in Concord with someone else. But by his junior year, after she had presumably graduated from Hollins and moved on to he knew not where, he had begun to date again. One girl in particular, a birdlike sophomore from Mary Borden named, appropriately, Robin, had become a steady companion, especially during rugby season, when she had come to all the matches, even the ones involving long car trips to distant colleges, and had endured energetic and often obscene parties following the games. Robin had been a sweet and fun-loving girl, and had always kept her dignity at the rugby parties even when those around her were losing theirs. She had no problem sharing a bed with Andy, either in his apartment or on the road, but there was never any question of her disrobing or engaging in anything more serious than some heavy making out. Andy was fond of her and she of him, but it was clearly more of a friendship than a romance.

Still, to have had any sort of relationship with a girl was probably a necessary transition for Andy after Susanna, and when he next ran into Shelley, his hometown sweetheart, he was emotionally ready for that earlier romance to reignite. Andy had gone back to Strasburg after his junior year in college, but he had not looked for a summer job because he didn't believe he could endure an entire summer there, living at home and wondering what in the devil he would do with his evenings. He'd had a vague sense he might find a job in northern Virginia and live with one of his friends from school, whose parents had a big house in Great Falls. But he was just getting into the ambition-sapping routine of home—with his mother cooking meals, doing laundry, tolerating but just barely his late mornings in bed—when some terrible news came. One of his friends from high school, a high-spirited if not terribly clever boy named Bobby Austin, whose parents lived outside town on a rocky farm, had been killed in the war. Andy's mother had seen the news in the Winchester paper and brought it into his bedroom, waking him to read it. He knew that Bobby had joined the Marines, but he had lost touch with him and didn't even know he'd gone to Vietnam. Now he was on his way home in a box. His unit had been helicoptered in to a firebase that was being overrun in the Central Highlands, near the Laotian border. No sooner had Bobby jumped from the Huey than he had been shot and killed. So the paper reported. His funeral would be on Saturday, five days from now.

Andy spent that time in a daze, poring through his high-school annual to look at Bobby's class photo, his team photo for football, and casual pictures of him. He talked to two or three of their mutual friends, even meeting one at a diner downtown for a cup of coffee. Then the night before the funeral he had gone to the viewing at the funeral home, where the casket was mercifully closed, although it bore a framed color photo of Bobby in his Marine uniform, one in which his eyes twinkled in merriment even though he was pressing his lips together in what he must have hoped was a tough-guy look. Bobby's parents seemed bewildered, not quite knowing where they were, and his younger brother devastated. Only his younger sister, probably about twelve, tried to uphold the social niceties, chatting with the people who passed in front of the family members seated in a row of folding chairs.

When Andy walked into the Methodist church on Washington Street the next day, the first person he recognized was Shelley, seated alone. He slipped into the pew beside her and gave her a kiss. Although her eyes were red from crying, she looked wonderful, her skin already touched by the summer sun, her dark hair flowing straight below her shoulders, resting on the simple black sleeveless dress she was wearing. They exchanged a few of the sorts of banalities that Andy had been sharing with his other friends in town, and then when the service began she clutched at his hand and held it tightly until the end. She continued to hang on to him as they filed out into the church cemetery for the brief burial service.

Afterward there had been a modest reception in the church community room, where Shelley and Andy had stuck together while seeking out and greeting friends they had shared with

Bobby in high school. More than a few of them were married, and some had young children either in their arms or at their side. They all greeted Shelley and Andy as the couple they had been throughout high school, and it had felt natural to them both. After a while, as the crowd began to thin, the two of them walked back out to the grave, where the casket had been lowered but the dirt not pushed in yet. They each threw a handful of red, clayey soil onto the casket.

As they were walking out to the street, Andy said, "I could use a real drink. That punch just doesn't handle it today." When Shelley agreed, he suggested that they drive up to Winchester, where they could find a restaurant that would serve a drink with lunch on a Saturday afternoon. She asked him to follow her to her parents' house, since she had driven their car. As they got closer to the house, Andy felt that he could drive these last few streets blindfolded, he had driven them so often at every hour of the day and night. She had held up one finger to him as she walked from the driveway to her house, a brick rancher, and he was pleased to see that she had not decided to change clothes when she emerged only a minute or two later. He liked it that they were both dressed up, and it made the lunch date feel like a continuing observation of Bobby's death. They had both known him since grade school, and had often double-dated with him and whatever girl he was seeing at the time.

His sad reverie was interrupted there, because Andy had reached the foot of Altamont Circle. He and Shelley had been together almost continuously since the moment he saw her walking back out of her house in her black dress. They had been inseparable for the rest of the summer. Andy had known by the following Monday morning that he wanted to stay in Strasburg if she was going to be there for the summer, too, and he found himself a construction job. Although she had left Greensboro and was now in college in Fredericksburg, halfway across the state, they saw each other nearly every weekend their senior year, and attended each other's graduations. After that there had been little doubt that they wanted to be together, and when they both found jobs in Charlottesville, they found and moved into the Spartan cottage in the country.

Jim, so happy in his life there, so loyally awaiting their return each day, had helped them feel like a family, and it was not till they married the following year that there had been any difficulties whatsoever. Marriage was not just different by definition from all that had come before in their years of knowing each other; it required a whole different psychology. Both of them felt the pressure and reacted badly. The part about lifelong commitment, about fidelity, made Andy feel a little claustrophobic when he thought about it too carefully. Shelley, always the more realistic of the two, had not expected some sort of instant happy ending the moment they were married, but neither had she expected Andy to go so skittish on her. It made her grumpy with herself, and also with Andy. Things had gotten so tense that they had told their friends, in jest of course, that they were going to Key West to save their marriage. And in a wholly unexpected way it had.

If Andy had pondered the definition of marriage, had wondered where its limits were in a world that insisted that everything was changed, a world of inconsequential sex, of open marriages, of make-up-your-own wedding vows, if Andy had, in short, been a bit confused, the spear to the groin had been as clear a message, however unintentional, as he could have received. Even Shelley realized that they were both changed by it, so much so that when Jan had come on to him on the balcony that night, it had not really bothered her. It was not Andy's fault, after all, that they lived in a world that did not seem conducive to young marriage. Andy was grateful for her understanding and even though he would not say so to himself, was relieved by whatever limitations the trip to Key West had defined. He was relieved that the tension had drained out of their lives, that they could just be happy together.

Yet he had never thought he would see Susanna again, never thought that, if he had, she would even give him the time of day. As he rode up in the elevator he realized that there was no way he could tell Shelley that he had seen Susanna. And he realized, even as he made it, that this decision did not bode well.

9

THE FOLLOWING WEEK, Andy left a note in Susanna's box as he promised he would do, proposing that they meet that Friday on the steps of Old Cabell, where they had first run into each other the week before. She responded with a note in his box in the English department accepting the offer, and he looked forward to the day with more anticipation than he knew was healthy. He was already feeling guilty about keeping this from Shelley. But for the big day he dressed as he usually did for class, in jeans and a flannel shirt. Susanna was once again dressed neatly and even professionally, this time wearing a dark skirt, and not a long baggy earth-mother skirt, but one that sheathed her figure and was well above the knee. Andy had of course seen her splendid legs before, but he could not remember having seen them in a skirt. Their difference in dress reminded him of their difference in age, although certainly it mattered less now that he was in his mid-twenties than it had at the end of his teens, when they had first known one another. They walked over to the Corner to pick up sandwiches and then back across campus to sit in the amphitheater to eat them. The sun was warm this April day, and there were other lunchers sitting in twos and threes on the concrete seats. After Andy and Susanna sat down and unwrapped their sandwiches, she kicked off her flat shoes and stretched out her legs.

"I've wondered," Susanna began, "although it's none of my business, whether you told Shelley about seeing me."

"Oh, lord, Susanna," Andy said. "I'm already nervous enough. And you ask me this?"

"Didn't tell her, no? You're a naughty boy, Andy. Très méchant. A very bad husband."

"Thank you, Susanna. This makes me feel much better."

"And why were you nervous about seeing me? Am I so frightening, really?" She put her hand on Andy's arm and gave him a heart-melting smile, all white teeth and that coppery skin of hers.

"Yes, you scare me to death, in fact." He gave her hand a little pat. "But help me think what I should tell Shelley. Would saying *I ran into a woman I once knew* be enough, really? *We were friends when I first got to college? We haven't seen each other in many years, so it was odd to see her again?* Would simply leaving it at that be more honest than saying nothing? Or must I say *She's quite beautiful* or *I think I was in love with her once* or *It took me years to get over her* or *She lives alone in the country and says she's very lonely?*"

"Hmmm. No, I don't think either approach would work, actually. Saying too little is at least as bad as saying too much, although less painful for both of you. Perhaps you could say only that you saw me again, that we once meant a lot to each other, that you are of course in love with her and therefore do not plan to see me again, unless you run into me by chance on campus. That would work, I think."

"Yes, you might be right. And yet it would be such a lie and isn't it better to say nothing than to actually lie?"

"What part of it is a lie, Andy? You do love her, yes? After all, you married her not that long ago."

"Of course I love her. I've loved her since I was a little boy, actually. But you know what part is a lie." Andy looked down at his sandwich. He realized that he had not taken a bite of it and did not really want to. He wrapped it up and put it back into the bag.

"I don't want to make trouble for you, Andy. Last week, it was so wonderful to see you, so unexpected, and we fell so happily back into our old rhythms of conversation. I was amazed at how familiar you were, how comfortable I was with you again after so much time. I have been lonely, it's true, and of course the time we had together in Concord has stayed with me as well, has felt more and more, um, special, as the years have passed. But I was too stupefied by the moment of seeing you again to think clearly about what this might mean for you, what it might require of you—do to you. It's very touching, somehow, that you find me so dangerous. But I am not a child; I can't just come back into your life and bust things up. And I won't."

"Are you breaking off with me?" Andy said with a laugh. "Again?" He put his hand on her bare knee. "Shouldn't we at least have something to repent first?" He gave her knee a squeeze to say that he wasn't serious, or perhaps he was only half-serious.

"Mais, oui. We must immediately go make love in the back seat of my car. That will make us both feel so much better about not seeing each other again. We could be quite proud of ourselves and there would be no regret, none at all."

She was laughing, too, but the point had been made. It was a good point.

They sat quietly for a while, not uncomfortably. She was still holding her sandwich, which she had taken the tiniest bite from. She wrapped hers back up, too, and put it in the bag.

"Bien, André. What a lovely lunch. Merci. And now I must really go to class. Let's be friends always, but only passing friends. Au revoir."

Andy stood when she did and grasped her, but it was awkward. He felt uncoordinated, somehow, and she was stiff as a board in his arms. He kissed her cheek and smelled her peppery smell and then she pulled away, stooped for her things, and turned to go up the steps.

"Susanna," he said to her back. "We can't just let this go. We can't pretend we didn't run into each other and don't know how the other one feels."

Susanna had turned back and looked at him. Her expression was not the usual one she wore, that of the jaunty cynic. She looked grim, her lips pressed tightly together.

"No, Andy. We must pretend. Anything else is impossible." And then she turned again and was gone.

He sat back down and tried to absorb how bad it felt to have done the right thing. Or more accurately, to have had the right thing done to him.

As it happened, Andy did not run into Susanna again during the last few weeks of the semester. After a week or so, he put a new note in her box in the French department office, proposing another conversation, another casual meeting, but she did not respond. A second week passed and he put a folded scrap of paper in her box that said only, "Are you sure?" When she did not respond to that one either, Andy stopped sending notes but could not stop thinking about her. He watched for her on campus, sat often on the steps of Old Cabell, found reasons to walk past the French department office in New Cabell. Nothing. He would have thought she was avoiding him but there had been all those months before their paths had finally crossed when they had also not seen each other.

The last weeks of the term were busy weeks, at least, when he had papers to write and when the restaurant was filled with law firms making a last pitch for new law grads by introducing them to the expenses-paid world that they were about to inhabit. Their reckless spending on multiple bottles of Margaux and Château d'Yquem not only helped to distract Andy but helped to line his pockets. Although Shelley's semester ran a month longer than his, she was occupied, too, as the end of the school year approached. Like schoolteachers everywhere, Shelley felt the accumulating effect of the ongoing year, growing more and more exhausted and going to bed early more often than not. She and Jim still walked him to work in the late afternoon, but she was generally asleep by the time he got home from the restaurant. So Andy often found himself alone with Jim after midnight on long walks in the neighborhoods near downtown. These walks gave him what time he had to think about his situation. What did he feel for Susanna anyway? He knew that he was suffering something more than simple lust, although lust was certainly a part of it. No time of his life before or since had been as wholeheartedly devoted to sexual pleasure as the month he had spent with her in Concord. If those days had remained easily accessible to his fantasy life ever since, they were now at the center of more than just his fantasies—of all his idle thoughts. The ache was not only in his groin; it was also farther up, in his stomach, in his chest. His body hurt and, even so, he often felt outside his body, felt that he was dragging his physical self around—an anchor on dry land. Just like Shelley, but with less reason, or at least with a less honorable reason, he was also exhausted.

Then one afternoon about ten days before Shelley's school year ended, she came home from school with her friend Jan in tow. Andy could tell by Jan's eyes, which were red and puffy, that something was wrong. But she put on a good front for him, giving him one of her clingy, lingering hugs followed by a peck on the lips, a pinch of the skin at his waist, and a broad smile.

"You're keeping in shape, Andy. I thought you grad students immediately got all doughy from never leaving the stacks."

"Perhaps I'm not as devoted a scholar as most. Also, walking Jim gives me the occasional gulp of fresh air. Speaking of which, I think I'll take him for a jaunt right now."

Since there was no objection from either woman, and Shelley actually gave him a grateful little smile, he grabbed the leash and he and Jim were in the elevator five seconds later. He didn't have to work at the Five and Dime that night and it was obvious that Jan had a lot on her mind, so he took Jim for a longer walk than usual, up to McIntyre Park, where Andy killed some time throwing a stick, which Jim retrieved with all the enthusiasm he usually reserved for tennis balls.

When they got back to the apartment, an hour had passed and Jan was gone.

"She's really upset, Andy," Shelley began as soon as she saw him. "It's Carlos. She found out he's having another affair. But this time when she confronted him about it he wasn't even apologetic. He basically told her that this is just the way it is. And this one isn't a girl, although it is another student."

"So Hal was right about Carlos, not that it surprises me."

"Yes, I guess he was. But she was probably even more rattled, somehow, by his attitude about it. It's almost as if he's daring her to leave. And they've been together for such a long time."

"So what's she going to do?" He and Shelley had moved to the kitchen and Shelley was petting Jim, who had just had a big sloppy drink of water and was dripping on her shoes.

"She doesn't know. This just blew up last night when the boy left a careless message for Carlos on their answering machine. It was all she could do to hold herself together during school today. But I asked her if she'd like to stay here for a while, and she said yes. I hope that was okay. She seemed so distraught and made it clear she doesn't want to be at home right now."

"Of course it's fine with me if you're comfortable with it."

"She's going to need a certain amount of TLC, you know, but I trust you not to give her the wrong kind, if that's what you mean." She gave him a wry smile.

"I don't know, Shelley, I think a little revenge sex might be just what she needs. Of course to make things equal, you might have to be the victim, not me."

"Yes, I know what a martyr you'd be if I sent you in to console her one night. Like a man going to the guillotine. But girl on girl hasn't been my kind of fun since I was about eight years old."

"If I did take on that duty and you noticed a bounce in my step afterward it would only be because she looks so much like you. And of course for the two of you to get it on would be the worst sort of narcissism. Although pretty to imagine."

"Okay, let's get off her supposed sexual needs and back to her practical ones. She went home to pack some stuff, and plans to stay here until school is over and then go home to California to sort things out."

Andy opened the refrigerator and found the jug wine and poured them each a glass.

"Seriously, that sounds fine. I'm glad she feels close enough to you to want to come here."

"To us, Andy. Close enough to us. She'd never come here unless she thought you were sympathetic."

"Yes, I will be all sympathy, and yet it will be sympathy at a very high pitch, because it will the sympathy of a castrato. You have nothing to fear."

Shelley crossed the kitchen and gave him a hug. "Nothing could make me more fearful than your need to reassure me on that point," she said. And then she unzipped his blue jeans and put her hand in his pants. She was looking deep into his eyes and her breath smelled of the wine and he naturally believed that she had a little preventive medicine in mind. He could only hope that a regular dosage was recommended. But instead she reached for the patch of scar tissue on his thigh. She gave it a harmless pinch that she held for a few seconds while giving him a theatrically dazzling smile. And then she zipped his jeans back up.

EVEN IF ANDY had been reckless enough to make a move on Jan while she was living with them in their apartment, or foolish enough to respond to any move that an obviously confused Jan might make, his emotional life was far too complicated already to add any further note of chaos. He was relieved nonetheless to see over the first few days Jan was there that she and Shelley were obviously growing closer. Whenever Andy returned to the apartment and the two women were together, they were inevitably sitting on the couch, their legs tucked beneath them, drinking a glass of wine and talking confidingly. Jan had gotten all of her overt anger out pretty quickly, or at least the first wave that came before the stage when she just felt numb and hurt. When Andy asked Shelley late at night in bed what in the world they were talking about, she told him that they were telling each other their life stories, talking about their mothers, their sisters, boys, high school, college.

"Boys?"

"Well, she has more experience in that department than I do. You tied up a lot of my best boy-friending years, you know."

"Glad to hear it."

As she got closer to Shelley, Jan treated Andy more and more like a brother, which had one disconcerting aspect. The apartment had a master bedroom and bath and a second bedroom and a second bath for guests. Jan was not overly fond of wearing anything but her panties once she retired for the night, and apparently did not own a robe. On her late-night and early-morning trips down the hallway to the bathroom, then, she was mostly naked. Without making any special effort to be underfoot at these moments, Andy found himself in her presence surprisingly often, including several times when they were walking down the hall from opposite directions and had to do a little jig to get around each other. He was grateful for the view—her breasts were high and shapely if small, and her nipples and quarter-dollar-sized areolas were a rich, chocolate brown. Still, he was careful to stay fully dressed when he was not in his bedroom, if only to hide any signs of arousal that might break the sibling spell.

Even though he was spending more time than usual with a lump in his pants, he was not really distracted from the more urgent problem of Susanna. He had no idea if she was staying in town for the summer, or if she had gone back to New Orleans until classes started again in the fall. One day when he felt more than usually unhinged by the notion that she might be just fifteen miles down the road, with nothing but those miles and her integrity separating them, he looked up her number in the phone book. Wouldn't she be every bit as sad—and as horny—as he was? He persuaded himself that she would be, so he filled his lungs with air and dialed the damned number. It rang and rang. He tried an hour later with the same result and then resolved not to begin obsessively dialing her every hour for the rest of the summer. Surely Susanna was back home and he should go home, emotionally, himself. Shelley had only a few more days of school to survive, and then Jan would be on her way to California, and Shelley herself could begin to recuperate, a process that would inevitably draw them closer together than they had been able to be recently.

That night, when they were in bed, Shelley began, in a tone that seemed ominous to him, "I've got something to talk to you about, Andy." At first he felt caught, but then he realized that all of his misdeeds, at least so far, had been inside his head, and even Shelley could not have intuited them. He turned so that they were face to face.

"Jan has asked me to go back to Sausalito with her when school is out. It would just be for a week or so. She hasn't told her folks that the marriage is breaking up, and she thinks it would be easier if she had me with her. They're Catholic, and she doesn't think they'll take it well."

Andy quickly got over his relief that the subject was not himself. "Do you really need this now? When school's over, you ought to just sleep for a week rather than jump on a long flight."

"I don't know; it might be restful just to get away. I feel more tired emotionally than physically. And although this is going to be hard for Jan, it really won't be for me, I don't think. Jan promises to drive me down to Big Sur, and just staring out at the Pacific might be the best thing I can do for myself right now. Besides, she really does need me, and I want to be a good friend to her."

"It's great that you two have gotten so close. I'm glad for you. But you don't think Jan has any of that revenge sex in mind, do you? Because if she does, I really want to be there to see it."

Shelley laughed and rubbed his head. "Noted. If she makes any moves on me, I'll tell her it just has to wait till we get back to Charlottesville. Because your masturbatory satisfaction is always the most important thing, of course."

"Just glad you recognize that. This will assure us a long and happy marriage, I firmly believe."

"Yes, with an emphasis, I'm sure, on firmly."

This time when she reached below his waist it wasn't to grab the scar tissue. "Well," she said, "good evening, Mr. Firmly. Very pleased to see you. Or at least to shake your hand. Or whatever."

"Very pleased myself," said Andy. "You and Jan just, uh, go wherever you like."

"How agreeable you are, Mr. Firmly," Shelley said. "How very, very agreeable."

THEIR LAST DAY of school was a Monday, and by late Tuesday afternoon Shelley and Jan had left Charlottesville to stay in a motel near Dulles, where they would fly out to San Francisco early the next morning. As it happened, Hal had left for Greece a couple of weeks before, planning to spend most of the summer with friends in Chania on Crete. John was going to meet him there in late July, but for the moment he was at loose ends. He called that Thursday without realizing Shelley was away, hoping to scare up a dinner with them over the weekend. Andy was already bored and lonely after two days of restaurant work and long walks with Jim, so he asked John to come stay with him for a few days if he felt like it.

"Just because Shelley's away doesn't mean you can play with my affections," John said after he'd accepted.

"I think you'll be pretty safe with me," Andy replied. "Who knows what sorts of things Shelley and Jan are up to, but we will remain resolutely ourselves—you the faithful lover and I the helplessly heterosexual spouse."

"That's a deal. I'll focus all my charm on Jim," John said.

"Not that you'll need to. Like the rest of us, he's utterly smitten with you."

John arrived the next afternoon, and since Andy did not have to work that night, they went for cheap Mexican food at La Hacienda on Emmett Street and then to see a couple of old Hitchcocks at Vinegar Hill.

As they were taking the short walk back to Andy's apartment after the movies, Andy asked John why he had not gone to Crete when Hal went.

"I don't know," he began. "I guess I thought we needed a little time apart. Hal gets so restless when we have to spend a few months in Concord without any sort of break. I decided I ought to give him some time alone with his friends in Chania to mellow out and, of course, to fuck his brains out. Next time I see him he'll be tanned, and slim from swimming and eating nothing but fresh fish, and with any luck sufficiently sated on Greek boys so that we can behave like a real couple."

"But you must not be that jealous or this would drive you crazy."

"No, I'm not jealous in the sense that I'm afraid of being displaced by any of the many people Hal has sex with. He loves me and I know it. And I'm not unaware of the effect I have on others. Hal and I both know that if I wanted to replace him there would be sufficient opportunities. But Hal is really all I want, and it's just the slightest bit humiliating that he doesn't feel the same way. Still, I don't think it's personal, if that makes any sense. It isn't like I'm not man enough to hold him. He just isn't built that way. It's some sort of deep-seated psychological need that I simply don't have. I'd be most happy to emulate an old married couple like you and Shelley."

Andy laughed nervously. He knew he could confide in John, that John would not even tell Hal anything that Andy asked him not to. And of course John had been friends with Susanna before he had, and it would be natural to tell him that Susanna was living in Charlottesville. But Andy was reluctant to go down that road, to announce that he had seen Susanna and then try to leave it at that. John would want to see her, and would wonder that Andy had not told him already. And besides, John rarely opened up this way to him, and Andy didn't want to change the subject too quickly from John's concerns to his own. Perhaps he would bring up the subject of Susanna tomorrow.

The next day was a Saturday, and Andy had to work at the Five and Dime that night. Since John was content to spend a quiet evening alone, a book in hand and Jim adoringly at his side, he decided to stay on for at least another couple of days. Shelley called that afternoon and seemed pleased to hear that Andy had some company, and said she had been thinking about hanging on in California till the following Saturday. Things had gone as badly with Jan's parents as Jan had feared they would, so Shelley thought it would be helpful for her to remain a little longer than she had intended. And they were planning that trip down to Big Sur.

John and Jim walked Andy to work that evening, and Andy was already feeling the adrenaline rush of a Saturday night. Even though the university was only in summer session, the tourist season had clicked in, especially in this Bicentennial year, and the restaurant promised to be jammed with people, as the reservations book confirmed. While he was scanning the names in the book for that night, he saw the name *Agincourt* followed by a dash and the numeral three. His heart did a little flip-flop. Surely this was not Susanna. But then Agincourt is not a particularly common name. Just to be safe, Andy asked the hostess to give the party to another waiter.

Susanna appeared at the late seating, about eight forty-five, with two well-dressed and well-tanned older people who were almost certainly her parents. She did not see him when the hostess was seating them, and before they did he asked Sam, who was going to have the table, to serve them three glasses of good champagne on his tab. Andy kept his back to their table as much as possible until the champagne was poured, and he watched for Susanna's reaction when Sam told her who it was from. She looked around in bewilderment until Sam pointed in Andy's direction. Andy gave her a little wave, and she waved back. He waited a minute or two for Susanna to say whatever she would say to her parents about the source of the champagne, and then went over to their table, his heart in his throat.

"But, Andy, you work here?" Susanna began.

"Yes, yes. I must not have mentioned it."

"No. Well, Andy, please meet my parents, Helen and Tom Agincourt. They're visiting me, and I naturally wanted to introduce them to the best restaurant in Charlottesville, so … "

Susanna's father stood up and offered his hand. Her mother raised her glass and said, "How thoughtful of you to send us this champagne. We're so glad to know a friend of Susanna's."

Andy shook Tom Agincourt's hand, noticing that his suit was every bit as expensive looking as those worn by the Washington and New York attorneys who came to woo the law students. Her mother was wearing a sleeveless light blue summer dress and two strands of pearls. Her hair was lighter in color than Susanna's, and looked like it had been done that afternoon at a beauty salon. Susanna was also wearing a sleeveless dress, with spaghetti straps, a rose color that made her complexion glow even in the failing light coming in from the big windows. She looked astonishing, and still somewhat astonished. Andy spoke with them for another minute or two and then wished them an enjoyable meal.

It was a good thing that he was able to do his job without thinking too much about it, because he was deeply distracted for the rest of his shift. He tried to compensate by moving a little faster and being just the slightest bit more unctuous, and his customers seemed as satisfied as ever. Although he shot Susanna a smile from time to time when he happened to catch her eye, he stayed away from their table until they had paid their check and were gathering themselves to leave. Then he went over and shook all of their hands, receiving their expostulations about how much they had enjoyed the meal and their further thanks for the champagne. When he took Susanna's hand, he managed to ask her if she was staying in Charlottesville for the summer.

"Yes, in Scottsville. I'm beginning to do research so I can choose a dissertation topic."

"How great" was all he could think to reply.

Andy had three more tables, but they cleared out within half an hour, and after another quarter hour of straightening up, Andy headed for the stairs. Sam stopped him to ask how in the world he happened to know a woman like Susanna, and then casually mentioned that she was sitting down at the bar.

"You're joking," Andy said. "Are her parents still with her?"

"No, the bartender said her parents left with a driver who had been nursing Diet Cokes at the bar while they ate, and after walking them to the front door, Susanna claimed a barstool herself and ordered a snifter of cognac."

"Jesus, has Randy … ?

"Like a homing pigeon. You'd better get down there and save the poor girl. Although she looks like she can take care of herself."

Andy flew down the stairs and saw Susanna in her rose-colored dress, sitting as promised at the bar.

She was facing straight ahead and Randy, on the far side of her, was turned on his stool to face her. When Andy took the stool to her near side, she saw him in the mirror and turned toward him, careful to swing her head so far that Randy could not see the grimace she shot Andy.

"How're you doing?" Andy asked in as neutral a voice as possible.

"Just great," she said, and mouthed the word "now" to him.

Randy leaned toward the bar to speak around Susanna to Andy. "This r-r-r-avishing lass admits to knowing you, Andrew," he said in his booming voice. "I had not yet asked her if she's acquainted with Shelley as well."

At that, Susanna gave Andy another grimace, and Andy responded in a voice as soft as Randy's was loud, "No, Susanna and I were friends years ago in college and then we lost track of each other until just recently." Then to Susanna he said, "Did Randy mention that he owns this joint?"

Susanna turned back to face the bar, perhaps realizing that she should not be overtly rude to Andy's boss, no matter how big a creep he was.

Randy did not throw in the towel just yet, apparently hoping Andy would head home to Shelley. Still, Randy refrained from saying anything else that was overtly aggressive, and when Andy ordered a cognac, too, Randy's attention began to wander as he sized up other prospects in the room.

Just then, Saint John came through the door. Andy could see out the front windows that he had wrapped Jim's leash around a small tree, and Jim was sitting contentedly.

Andy waved a hand to John and said as he was approaching, "I think this is a face you'll be happy to see, Susanna."

She was off the stool in a second and into John's arms. He was not so shocked to see her that he failed to pull her off her feet and swing her around in a very balletic move. As they always had, the two of them looked beautiful together, a pair that only a casting agent could have imagined. With his wonderful posture and air of self-containment and that blond head of hair, he was like Peter Martins, and Susanna was mostly incomparable, but perhaps some combination of Julie Christie and Vanessa Redgrave.

They exclaimed over each other and patted each other and hugged once again, and then Andy introduced John to Randy, who was gape-mouthed at what he was seeing. "Good lord," he said, "I've wandered into a college r-r-r-eunion." He suggested that they take a booth so the three of them could more easily talk, and after leading them to one he said his goodbyes.

As John and Susanna caught up with each other, John avoided the obvious question of how Susanna and Andy happened to be sitting together at the bar. But Susanna explained without being asked that she had brought her parents to the Five and Dime, and that mama et papa had gone back to the Boar's Head for the night. "And don't we all need a drink after an evening with our parents?" Susanna said.

This did not exactly answer the question, and after a brief silence, Andy said, "Was this your first time at the Five and Dime, Susanna? You said you didn't know I worked here."

"No, I'd been here before. But when we ran into each other on campus that day you never mentioned your working here. So I was almost as surprised to see you as I was to see our Saint John here." She gave John's hand an affectionate pat.

But at this point John must have calculated that it would be far more awkward to avoid the subject further than to get it out of the way.

"So you two have been in touch?"

"Not since Concord in 1970," Susanna said. "We saw each other on campus six weeks or so ago and spent some time catching up. Andy told me about his marriage, of course … "

"But I'm so sorry Andy didn't let us know you were nearby, Susanna. And Hal would love to see you again. You were always a particular favorite of his."

"The feeling is mutual—I always loved both of you guys, and I'm so glad you're still together, you and Hal. But don't blame Andy, John. I'm just going to be completely honest here, Andy, d'accord?"

Andy nodded and Susanna continued. "As you'll remember, John, dear Andy and I had fairly robust feelings for each other way back when. And when we saw each other again, we both realized that all the conditions were right for another wildfire. So we decided to avoid each other as much as possible."

"Actually, she was the grownup here, John," Andy said. "I can't take credit for this much strength of character."

"No," John said with an appreciative smile at Susanna. "I shouldn't think you could.

"So, gosh, I guess I'm like the cavalry," he added, "having arrived just in the nick of time. Or more like the fire department."

"Andy's off the hook for this one, John," Susanna said. "I really didn't know he was working here, and he had no idea I was going to hang around after my parents left."

"Look, what you kids do is none of my business. 'Judge not,

lest you be judged'—that's my credo. But I'm just so glad to see you again, Susanna."

Andy thought that this would be a good time to check on Jim. The dog seemed happy to see him, but after Andy had spoken to him for a moment and rubbed his ears, Jim seemed contented to lie back down and watch the few people passing by on the mall at this time of night.

When Andy returned to the table, John said, "I've ordered us all another cognac, but only after extracting a promise from Susanna to come back to your place for the night. She has no business driving home this late after drinking. I explained to her that Shelley is away and offered to sleep on the couch so that she could have my bed. She agreed to come back with us only if she gets the couch. And then I'll be like Tristan's sword, separating the two of you."

"Let's hope this turns out better than Tristan and Isolde," Andy said. "But of course, you mustn't drive home tonight, Susanna. You're very welcome to stay over, given the excellent chaperoning we can expect."

"Great. Saint John was always my moral compass back in Concord—he told me then, for instance, that you were far too young for me and I should leave you alone."

"Glad you didn't follow his lead on that one."

"Me too."

They both looked at John and he held out each arm, palm up, like a priest offering a prayer.

"JIM IS SUCH a slut," Andy said as they were walking up the hill to his apartment. "Five minutes and he's already fallen for Susanna."

"It happened more quickly than that," John said. "I'd call it love at first sight when she walked out of the restaurant."

Jim had greeted Susanna as if she were an old friend, and had insinuated himself between Andy and Susanna as they walked home.

When they got to the apartment and Andy was showing her the view from the balcony, John disappeared and returned with a tall glass of ice water. "I hate to kill the party, friends," he said, "but I started reading a mystery of Shelley's—I assume that Andy the grad student wouldn't be caught dead reading anything this side of T. S. Eliot—and I really want to get back to it."

He put down his glass and took Susanna in his arms again. "This was a lovely surprise. When Hal and I get back from Crete, we're going to have you over to Concord, first thing. Be good, you two."

After he had gone, Andy said, "Well, so much for Tristan's sword."

They both laughed and then stood at the railing in silence, scanning the dark landscape in the cooling evening.

"So you waited for me at the bar," Andy said after a while.

"What makes you believe that I was not picking up your Scottish boss?"

"Just a hunch."

More silence. "I don't know what I was doing. After being with my parents, after watching you all evening as you scurried about doing your job, after good food and a lot of good wine, I just didn't want to get in the car and make that dark drive to an empty house. The bar seemed so inviting, at least until Randy materialized, and I did want to see your face one more time before setting off."

He turned to her and put his hands on either side of her face, holding back the cascades of rich, coppery hair. "I'm so glad you did."

She smiled at him, but it was a frozen smile. She looked as if she might be on the verge of crying. "Maybe I'm as big a slut as Jim," she said, and now there were tears in her eyes. "I haven't been able to get you out of my head, Andy. But of course I really did not know you would be at the restaurant, and even if I had I could not have known that Shelley would be away, that I would end up here, with or without Tristan. And of course I didn't even know where here was."

"It's karma, Susanna. Fate. Kismet. Even the mystery that John picked up turned out to be unputdownable. If he had picked up something crappy, we'd be safe, protected by his sword."

"That's an image I do not wish to pursue," Susanna said.

He kissed her then, very gently on the lips, still holding her face in his hands. And then he pulled her to him, wrapping his arms around her and burying his own face in her hair. There was that faint, peppery smell, not the fragrance of her conditioner or her perfume, but her essential odor. He felt tears coming to his own eyes.

Then she was pushing him away. "Don't think I'm being coy, Andy. But not here, not tonight. You're right, so many unexpected things had to happen to place us here tonight. But this is your home, yours and Shelley's, and we mustn't."

Andy could not respond. He felt as if he might pass out—he was that lightheaded with desire. Nothing could make him agree with her at this moment, and yet the dim awareness that she was right stopped him from disagreeing, from pushing through her logic, either verbally or physically. He could see the intensity of color in her cheeks, even in the dim light from the living room, and knew that she would have relented. He grasped her again and put his face to her neck, and they stood still in the cooling night, their lust cooling too, and contemplated the course on which they were set.

PERHAPS IT WAS the two cognacs, but Andy managed to go to sleep once he had gotten pillows and sheets for Susanna to use on the couch, and a T-shirt of his that she could use as a nightshirt. He even found a new toothbrush, and left it for her in the guest bathroom along with a towel. After he had gotten into his bed he heard her close the bathroom door, but he had fallen asleep while waiting for the sounds that would say she had emerged. He woke up a little after 3 A.M. with a serious case of cotton mouth. The only satisfactory cure, he knew, was the pitcher of orange juice in the refrigerator. He walked in his undershorts as quietly as he could to the kitchen, noticing as he went by the opening to the living room Susanna's form under the white sheets on the couch and the dark mass of Jim, that slut, asleep on the floor beside her. He filled a glass with juice and drank it down, and then filled the glass again to have as a bedside remedy as the night went on. As he walked out of the kitchen Susanna's voice emerged from the darkness.

"Could a girl get a sip of whatever you're having?"

He walked over to her, not thinking to pour her a glass of her own. "Orange juice okay?"

"Perfect," she said. She had sat up on the couch, her back against an armrest and her legs pulled up. His eyes were used to the darkness so he could see her even in the dim light that came in from the night sky. She took a long drink from the glass and then put it down on the coffee table. He could not see her well enough to make out the expression on her face, but he could see that she was smiling. Did he detect a bit of ruefulness in it? Then with one quick motion she pulled the T-shirt he had given her over her head and tossed it on the table as well.

"Come here," she said, and he did as he was told.

10

THE FIREWORKS PROMISED to be the best ever. Shelley, who was not in other ways someone who liked spectacle or high drama, had always had a particular thing for big fireworks displays, and even in an ordinary year she wanted to be on the Mall in Washington for July Fourth if at all possible. For the Bicentennial, there was never any question about whether she and Andy would go. But in a concession to the larger crowds expected this year, she had decided with a friend of hers from Northern Virginia that they should avoid the Mall itself. Instead they would watch from across the river in Arlington, claiming a space on the hillside by the Iwo Jima Memorial. Her friend Mildred Sullivan, with whom Shelley had been close growing up in Strasburg, had preceded her by a year at Mary Washington College, and while in graduate school in Charlottesville she had met and married a medical student. He was now a resident at Georgetown University Hospital, and they lived in a relatively modest house in McLean. Millie and David Copenhaver had one child already and she was pregnant again. She and Shelley had worked out the details for the day, which would involve some barbecuing and beer drinking at the Copenhavers' house with a few of their friends, then an early move to the memorial where they would claim a good spot and drink a few more beers while waiting for the fireworks to begin. That is, if the incongruously hardcore Park Service police would permit them to lug a cooler onto the hallowed grounds. Then Shelley and Andy would spend the night in McLean, saving them the long drive back to Charlottesville at the end of the day of celebration.

In spite of the joint planning that Millie and Shelley had done, the Watsons still felt that they had insinuated themselves into a party that would have happened without them. To assuage their mild guilt, they brought a case of Miller High Life in bottles, already iced in a cooler, several pounds of Italian sausage for the grill, and a potato salad that Shelley had made from a recipe of Andy's mom's. At Shelley's urging, they had set off an hour early from Charlottesville so she could help Millie get ready. Pregnancy suited Millie, who looked ruddy and robustly healthy when she met them at the front door with exclamations about all the stuff they were toting. She was not a petite woman, but round in a way that was not at all fat, which somehow made the small bulge of her stomach barely noticeable. Beneath her short brown hair she had a round face, round arms, round breasts, a round tummy. She was wearing khaki shorts and as she led them into the kitchen Andy noticed that the cheeks of her fanny were also perfectly round. David, who was in the kitchen with their young blond daughter Julia, was himself geometrical looking, an inverted triangle of a thin waist and a broad chest and shoulders, surmounted by another inverted triangle of a sharp chin broadening to a halo of blond curls.

Perhaps because he was not aiming at surgery, David had not yet learned the fine medical art of arrogance. He and Andy had developed a friendship of their own while the two couples had overlapped in Charlottesville, and the two men were genuinely happy to see each other.

"Done any caving lately?" was always one of the first things out of David's mouth when they were reunited. By now it was a friendly joke, but like most enduring sources of amusement it had begun with something that was not very funny at the time. David was referring to a famous, or for Andy infamous, spelunking expedition the two of them had made several years before, when they were first getting to know each other. David, an experienced spelunker, had asked Andy about a series of caves a half-mile west of Concord. Andy had managed to talk to a professor he knew in the geology department at Concordia to get some specifics about the site, but David had in the meantime found far more detail from printed sources in the university library in Charlottesville. So there was no doubt whose expedition this would be, and Andy, who had never been in a cave that you could not walk into standing up, was happy to cede the responsibility. David, it had turned out, was not into equipment. Except for a couple of flashlights and a Thermos of hot coffee, his outfitting consisted of a good pair of hiking boots, blue jeans, and a warm shirt.

They had driven to Concord in Andy's old Fiat on a late-spring Saturday morning, and had no trouble finding the dirt road that would take them within only a few hundred yards of the cave that David had in mind. After consulting a small notebook he had pulled from his shirt pocket, David told Andy where to stop and then poured a cup of coffee from the Thermos, which he offered first to Andy.

"You'll get a chill down there until you work up a sweat," he explained, "and even though the morning is warming up we'll be very happy for the rest of this when we come back to the surface."

The opening to the cave was inconspicuous, just a hole in the ground with a few bushes around it, but when they crawled in, the space opened up a bit as they descended on a rocky path at about the same angle as a stairway. There were a few boulders they needed to scramble over, but otherwise the path seemed reassuringly there, a sign that many others had preceded them and presumably lived to tell about it. Their eyes adjusted to the growing darkness at about the same rate as the light from the cave mouth diminished, so they did not need their flashlights at all as they scuttled down. But then they came to a feature that would introduce Andy to a sensation he had never known before, claustrophobia. The cause was a geological formation that David told him was nicknamed the Chute. This was a vertical passageway about six feet deep and about two feet in diameter. David shone his light down the narrow passage, and they could see that the Chute was hardly a perfect cylinder, given the irregular protuberances in the rock that formed it. But the surfaces of the Chute had been smoothed somewhat, presumably by millennia of water running down from the cave mouth, and perhaps by several generations of wriggling spelunkers.

"Why don't I go first?" David said, and with that he began to work his way down through the space.

Perhaps because Andy had never had any fear of tight spots before this, he followed David without much thought, and although there were a few places requiring a squeeze, he was down in a matter of seconds. Their reward was finding themselves in a huge room—one that was several times their height and perhaps sixty feet long and twenty feet wide. David switched off his light for a minute so they could experience, for the first time in Andy's life that he could recall, utter darkness. It brought to mind one of Andy's grandmother's favorite expressions, how she would describe something as being "black as a pocket." But this was the deepest and blackest pocket imaginable. Standing perfectly still, with the light off, Andy became aware of the atmosphere in the cave, its coolness and dampness and mineral smell. In spite of the rich texture of the air, it felt somehow fresh, as though it had been filtered and purified by all that rock and darkness.

David switched the flashlight on again, and trained it across the ceiling and walls of the cave.

"Just look at all the colors," he said. "I can never get over how brightly decorated these dark spaces can be." He was right; the flashlight picked up streams of iridescence, the trails of minerals leaking down the walls, and patches of flora that clearly did not rely on photosynthesis. Plus the rocks themselves, mostly limestone, were more varied in color and shape than you would notice in the brightly colorful world to which our eyes are accustomed.

"Let's keep moving so we don't get too cold," David suggested, and they made their way across the rocky floor of the room.

The next passage, at the far side of this cavern, was more like the first passage than the second. It sloped gently downward, but its ceiling was lower, requiring that they crawl down feet first, their bellies up. It was the longest passage yet, extending perhaps forty yards, and opened into a tunnel-like cavern that had a streambed in the bottom. The tunnel was about eight feet in circumference and the stream was narrow enough that they could straddle it as they walked. The only way you could tell which direction the stream was moving, because it barely moved at all, was a seeming downward tilt in the direction they were walking. But a thought then struck Andy with a chill more dramatic than the chill the air provoked. "How do we really know if we are moving uphill or downhill this deep in a cave this dark?"

Andy was evidently not just thinking this but asking it, because David said, "The hairs in our ears act as a kind of gyroscope, giving us a pretty accurate sense of the slope as long as typical gravitational forces are at play. Now if we were on a roller coaster or in jet fighter I'd feel less confident."

"Yes, driving a jet in this cave would be pretty scary."

But that slight whiff of disorientation planted a more distressing thought in Andy's brain. And with the thought came a kind of panic that had revisited him ever since, sometimes even in the rumbling elevator that took them up to their apartment in Charlottesville, and especially when he thought back to that moment over the streambed at the bottom of the cave. Here and now, though, the thought was not in any way abstract. It was very specific: "What if I can't wriggle back up the Chute? What if I get stuck there? What if I can't make myself do it?"

Now he actually shuddered, and he managed to say to David, "I think I need to go back."

To his credit, David heard the utter seriousness in Andy's voice, but he treated it lightly, like a timely suggestion.

"Yes, we've really gone far enough. I think we're going to just get more of the same with this tunnel until it reaches a point where we can't go any farther. Besides, we've been down here longer than you think." He shined his light on his wristwatch. "Forty minutes, so it will be well over an hour by the time we get back up."

"If we get back up," Andy thought. Luckily this really was only a thought, not an utterance. What he did say was, "Will you lead the way?"

David did. They walked back up the tunnel—it did feel as much like up as going the other direction had felt like down—and after a few minutes David found the passage that sloped up to the right toward the big cavern. He tucked his flashlight in his pants and began to crawl up the slope on his hands and feet. Andy did the same and soon they were standing again in the big room. While they caught their breath they both explored the walls and ceilings of the cave with the beams of their flashlights, and then they crossed the room again. At the bottom of the Chute, David said to Andy, "Why don't you go first?"

Andy tucked his shirt in tight, to give the walls nothing to grab, and dropped his flashlight down the front of his shirt. There was a boulder just to the side of the Chute on which you could stand and get a head start. Andy climbed onto the rock, took a deep breath and wriggled up into the opening. He had only begun to work his way up when he felt a powerful push on the bottom of one boot from David, who had evidently climbed onto the rock himself to get some leverage. Andy stiffened that leg and David pushed him up through the space till he could get his hands and then his arms above the top of the Chute and pull himself up. Although getting through the passage had not required much of his own exertion, he was drenched in sweat. He fished his flashlight out of his shirt to give David some encouragement, but David was already almost out. Andy reached down and gave him a tug, but it was only ceremonial—David seemingly could have wriggled up a passage five times the height of the Chute. The sweat turned cold on Andy's skin as he thanked David for the boost, and they began to climb in the direction of the light. They could not see the cave opening at first, but the light grew steadily brighter and then they saw a patch of an incredibly rich blue color—could this really be the blue of the sky?—and Andy began to scramble up even faster. As they got within about ten feet of the opening to the cave a sweet smell reached his nostrils. What was it? It grew stronger and the air grew warmer as he emerged from the cave. The light was different, too. Although his eyes had had some time to adjust, so that the light was not overwhelming, it was somehow sharper, and the colors around him seemed brighter, far brighter, than he had ever noticed before. The greens of the bushes were the color of the foliage in a child's painting of trees, and the sky was no less blue than it had been when he first spotted it from underground. Even the orange clay of the Virginia soil was bright, a pure color. And he realized then what his nose had discovered. It was the smell of the spring foliage, a wondrously sweet smell to match the wondrously sweet sight of the world in which we live. Was it his hour or more of deprivation that had made him see and smell the world as if for the first time? Or was it simply the exhilaration that comes on the far side of fear?

"THANKS TO YOU, I'm always caving," Andy told David with a laugh in response to the usual question. "Somehow I can never quite get the memory of that day out of my system."

"Well, at least if you begin to flop-sweat today, I'll know it's the heat and not cold terror."

"You know how we English majors are. Put us astride a stream at the bottom of a dark cave with the prospect that there's no getting out alive and we'll see it as a metaphor every time. At least I'm guessing that's why it still wakes me up in the middle of the night."

"With an existential scream?" David said, giving him a brotherly pat on the shoulder.

"More like a whine. Hello, Julia," Andy said, bending toward the blond child. "Whatcha got?"

Julia held up the soggy remains of a piece of Melba toast, offering it to Andy, and said, "Cookie?"

"No, thank you. And, man, if you think this is a cookie are you in for a pleasant surprise."

"We've tried to keep the definition as broad as possible," Millie said. "It's helpful on a long day like this when a premature sugar high could have some pretty serious consequences for the rest of us."

Shelley lifted Julia from behind and drew the child to her, while Julia wriggled in pleasure and repeated Shelley's name, but dropping the *h* each time, making the word sound just a bit like *Silly*.

"You're silly yourself," Shelley said and put her back down. Julia's legs were moving before she hit the ground and she was out the back door, following her father as he bore a large bag of charcoal to the grill. Andy followed with the cooler of beer, which he managed to wrestle out the screened door without doing any harm either to the screen or to himself. "You want this out here, David?"

"Yes, that's great. Put it beside the porch where the sun won't hit it. And since we're starting the grill work, I think we deserve one now, don't you?"

"Sure do." He fished out two beers and an opener he'd had the unusual foresight to toss into the cooler.

David fiddled with the grill, and the charcoal, and the lighter fluid, until everything was ready for the match, as Andy sat in a deck chair and made small talk about the Georgetown hospital, about summer in Charlottesville, about the crowds expected in Washington on this day. Julia amused herself in the back yard with a variety of toys, including the smallest tricycle Andy had ever seen.

When the flames had stopped and the briquettes were turning white at the edges and the two men were down to the last warm swallow or so of their beers, one of David's colleagues from the hospital came through the screened door. It was possible, Andy thought, that this one was a surgical resident, because he barely gave Andy a glance when they were introduced. He turned immediately to David and in a loud confiding whisper began to tell his host about his date, who was evidently on her own in the kitchen with Millie and Shelley. The man, whose name was Walter, was careful to turn his back to the screened door so that his date wouldn't hear him talking about her, but in doing so he had also cut Andy out of the conversation. Andy couldn't decide if he was more annoyed or amused by Walter's rudeness, but there was something so needy about his eagerness to impress David that Andy decided to cut him a little slack, at least for the moment.

"Channel 7," Walter was saying excitedly. "You've probably seen her doing the weather on weekends. But she's too smart for weather. Wants to be an anchor. Already doing some reporting during the week. And the anatomy on this one. Not in any way gross."

David groaned at the med-school humor. He had smoothed out the charcoal, which by now was white and sprouting small red flames, and put the metal grill over them so the heat could burn off the grill crud.

Andy told himself that it was less his curiosity about the body in question than the feeling that he was now a third wheel that sent him back toward the house. David darted past him and said, "Let me grab us all a beer." Andy paused to receive his, shot David a grateful smile, and said, "I think I'll check out the kitchen staff. Wanna come see Mommy, Julia?" Julia raced over to his outstretched hand and led him up the steps and into the kitchen.

In contrast to Walter, the Channel 7 weathergirl was almost voraciously attentive to the newcomers. She came immediately across the room and squatted before Julia, marveling at the child's beauty, which had been only mildly sullied by the heat and dirt of the back yard. The weathergirl, named Tessa, was herself quite striking, with long raven hair that fell in waves and little flips, and skin that was almost translucent. When she stood to greet Andy she was as tall as he and had impossibly white teeth. She was dressed crisply in an ironed blouse and pleated shorts, and she looked like someone who had not only never been in the sun but had never perspired or even been aware of the heat of day.

"Great to meet you, Andy," she said with what seemed like real feeling, and Andy could detect a slight hint of Texas in her otherwise highly trained voice. He couldn't tell at first exactly what made her so exotic. Yes, Walter was right about her figure, and she had a sort of intensity that undoubtedly grew out of her television fame, however mindless a job she was doing. It was odd, he thought, that doing something embarrassing in public is less embarrassing if the audience is big enough. But then Andy realized the source of her allure: she wore lipstick, and that almost bluish skin was red at the cheek in a way that could only mean the application of rouge, and would her eyes be quite so vivid without the assistance of arts that Andy knew only vaguely, since Shelley rarely made use of them and, as far as he could tell, never needed them? The same was true, he could tell now that he was looking for it, of Millie. If she used any sort of makeup at all, she used it in a way that was undetectable.

But Tessa had asked him a question and Shelley was helping him to a response.

"Yes, you like fireworks, don't you Andy?"

"Of course. It's just that I'm a distant second to Shelley in my love of them. I could actually survive a Fourth of July without seeing them, and I wonder if she could."

Tessa laughed as though he had said something wonderfully witty, and then the doorbell rang.

In came two couples with three young children between them. Andy knew it would be hopeless to sort out who belonged to whom, and the three kids looked so much alike in a certain way—perhaps it was that their clothes were so consciously matched; probably they had been bought in sets—that he almost wondered if the parents themselves could tell who was who. All four of the adults exuded a well-scrubbed athleticism and had light tans that looked expensively acquired. Andy's world was still so much that of the graduate student, or of people in their twenties still just scraping by, and of a carelessness of dress and general appearance left over from what could no longer be called the counterculture, that people this, well, affluent were somewhat rare in his experience, and people who didn't mind looking affluent were even rarer.

The names went in one ear and out the other when Millie introduced them to Andy and Shelley and Tessa, but he understood that the men were also residents at Georgetown.

The wives, more interestingly to Andy, were lovely, lithe, and self-confident, and had that way of women who are used to being admired of seeming both to be paying attention and not; it wasn't quite as though they were only tolerating their surroundings, including the people in their presence, but that they were able to imply something better was just around the corner. And yet even though they were more understated than Tessa, say, in their looks and their guardedness, they seemed somehow hungrier than even the professionally ambitious weatherwoman. Perhaps it was because, unlike her, they were not quite certain what they were hungry for. What was it about these doctors that they all got the best-looking women? Was it that they skimmed off the cream of each nursing crop? Or was it merely Darwinian, their career path proving that they would be the most desirable providers, whatever their deficiencies of personality or character?

But then Andy realized with a start that Shelley was by far the most attractive woman in the room, was always the most attractive woman in any room she was in. Clearly this was not Darwinism at work, given Andy's prospects, now and for all the years she'd known him. And it wasn't only Shelley's dark-haired good looks and the brightness of her smile; she exuded a state of happiness that went beyond joie de vivre or even animal contentment. She seemed, unlike any of these other women or their men, with the distinct exception of Millie, to be at peace with her place in the world. Yes, Shelley liked it that men admired her, and was as vain as anyone about her looks, which she was able to maintain with almost no effort. And she was an accomplished flirt, even if her flirting was, to Andy's eye, more a matter of verbal jousting than of real passion or promise of passion—the flirting of an older woman that is amusing but lacks the small element of doubt about whether there might be a lurking hint of actual lust. No, Shelley's contentment seemed to extend even to Andy himself, to suggest that he was all she needed or would ever need.

This thought filled him with the most agonizing if hypocritical sort of guilt and sadness and shame. Because, much as he did not deserve Shelley from a Darwinian perspective, much as he fell short of her in looks and certainly in character, she was now not the only beautiful woman in his life. Susanna's middle of the night invitation at his apartment ten days earlier had not triggered in Andy even a moment's hesitation. He figuratively and almost literally dove in. And given the pent-up desire on both sides, given the years during which each of them had remembered and perhaps idealized their first outbreaks of mutual fondness and attraction, the first recoupling had gone surprisingly well, a sweet but strong mixture of familiarity, self-deprecating humor, gratitude, and passion. It felt heartbreakingly like love, and caused them to fall back into the madness of that long-ago month of May. They could not even pretend otherwise in front of Saint John the next morning. He accepted his failure as Tristan's sword and knew that any further attempts to reprise the role would be similarly disastrous. So he made an excuse and returned to Concord. Andy and Susanna had spent every possible moment of the next week together, although their one small act of integrity, if that's what it was, was to leave Andy and Shelley's apartment when John did, and not to return there together. They took Jim with them to her cottage above the James, but Andy and Jim went back regularly to the apartment so as to receive Shelley's calls, or to be able to return them quickly enough to arouse no suspicion.

Andy and Susanna's month of May had lasted a week this time, until Shelley returned from California. They did not pretend to break it off then, but they did vow to return to the lives they were leading just eight days before, to see if sanity might also return. They both were miserable, of course, even before the separation began. Susanna knew and accepted the obvious fact that Andy loved Shelley, and he did not pretend otherwise. What could be worse, she said, than to be a person who destroyed love? He was also full of self-contempt, and he was seriously confused. Was it really possible to be so much in love with two people at once? Absurdly, he longed to talk to Shelley about this problem, to talk to her about it as if it did not affect either of them. And the misery that Susanna and Andy felt had only one cure, and that cure was only temporary and led to even greater depths of misery. That cure was the abandonment that came from indulging the passion that regularly welled up during their week together.

Shelley was watching the four children in the kitchen as the three newcomers got oriented to their new surroundings and began to include Julia, whom they seemed to know. The two doctors breezed through the kitchen and out the door in search of David and Walter and beer, and their wives efficiently unpacked the things they had brought to contribute to the meal. Tessa was lavishing her glamorous attention on Millie, taking an unlikely interest in the preparations. Andy crossed the room to Shelley and gave her a kiss.

She accepted it matter-of-factly, apparently unaware of the depth of feeling behind it. In return she flashed one of her high-wattage smiles.

"It really is the Fourth," she said with wonder. "Isn't it?"

IN SPITE OF the vagaries of beer drinking, grilling, and attending to hungry children, Millie kept the party on schedule and got everyone to the Iwo Jima grounds a full two hours before dark. They chose a spot just below the Netherlands Carillion, from which they had a clear view across the Potomac of the Washington Monument, above which the fireworks would deploy. They spread out their quilts on a slight slope of ground, so that anyone sitting in front of them would be below their line of sight, and the Park Police were evidently busy elsewhere, so there was no problem about the cooler. Having claimed their spot, they passed the time watching the grounds fill up with people and taking turns wandering off to check out the big memorial to the flag-raising at Iwo Jima. The memorial was oddly both hokey and affecting, like so many aspects of patriotic display, and it put Andy and Shelley in an even more expectant mood for the fireworks. Walter had not exactly lavished his attention on Tessa, so she went off with them to look up at the memorial, leaving him at the center of the clubby group of doctors, and when the sky finally darkened and people began to settle into their spots for watching the display of pyrotechnics, she eased herself down on the quilt in a tight spot between Shelley and Andy.

"Do you mind if I break y'all up?" she said with a laugh, allowing herself the rare indulgence of using the familiar contraction. She patted Andy's knee and draped an arm across Shelley's shoulders. "We single folks need to stick together amid all this wedded bliss. Besides, I want to watch you watching the fireworks, Shelley. Andy tells me that's half the fun."

"Yes, of course, Tessa," Shelley said. "I'm sure Andy won't mind in the least." And looking over at Andy, she said with mock sternness, "Hey, give her a little more space there, pardner."

"But why do you think we're single, Tessa?" Andy said, wriggling away. "We're oh so married, in fact."

"Really?" Tessa said. She seemed genuinely surprised. "I'm so sorry. You just acted so, I don't know, so much in love that I thought you were probably just dating. I saw that sweet kiss in the kitchen."

"Now I don't mean to shock you, Tessa," Andy said. "But in spite of what you've read, sometimes married people really are in love. And we've only been married less than two years."

"Maybe that's it," Tessa said. "Of course I know married people generally do love each other. I think my parents do. But you two seem to like each other, too—you're just so cute together."

"We've known each other almost our whole lives," Shelley said. "Dating and not dating. We've managed to be friends as well as lovers and now spouses. I don't want to sound all gooey. In fact, I think one of the good things about our marriage is that we aren't too gooey; there's a small element of disenchantment there."

Andy was quiet. He thought with chagrin how quickly the truth about his own behavior could enlarge the field of disenchantment, how all-encompassing it could become.

"That's just so interesting," Tessa said. "But ohhhh, look, they've begun."

THE DRIVE BACK to Charlottesville had been routine enough. They had left McLean in the middle of the morning of the fifth of July, hours after David had gone to the hospital to begin a long shift. On the road, Andy had brought up the subject of the fireworks of the night before, and Shelley remembered in detail her favorite combinations of color bursts and the sounds that followed the bursts like thunder following lightning. They both marveled at the length of the display and at its volcanic conclusion, when every piece of the sky seemed to be exploding, even at the mile or so distance from which they watched, and at just how long that final display continued as the crowd around them at Iwo Jima hollered and clapped and stamped their feet, working up a collective sweat in the humid air. Their reaction had built to the edge of pagan frenzy, a cross between a good acid trip and crazed, sweaty, drunken dancing in the basement of a fraternity house back in Concord. Even the ever-cool Tessa had gone red-cheeked and after the last burst, as things went dark and silent, had given first Shelley and then Andy clinging, lingering, passionate hugs, far more sensuous than anything Walter was in for, Andy hoped and believed.

Shelley and Andy wondered not only that Tessa could have had the bad luck to be fixed up with the ill-mannered and self-centered Walter but that people as nice as Millie and David should have to put up with David's smug but colorless colleagues and their chilly, efficient wives. As Andy sped them along, they kept going back to Tessa, how strange and flattering it was that she had been so drawn to them, how warm and vulnerable she seemed beneath the polished surface, and how sincerely she had wanted to visit them in Charlottesville and begin a real friendship. But lingering beneath their fascination with Tessa was the oddness of her assumption that they were an unmarried couple.

"Clearly she meant for us to be flattered by her mistake," Andy said. They had run the gauntlet of stoplights in Warrenton and were out in the open countryside that would lead to Culpeper.

"I wonder," Shelley said. "Of course she didn't want to insult us after she realized she'd drawn the wrong conclusion about us. So it was a good save to attribute her confusion to that kiss in the kitchen. What was that kiss about, anyway?"

"What, I can't kiss my wife in public?" There was a tone in Shelley's question that seemed sharper than that of the conversation they'd been having for miles now.

"Yes, you can, of course, but you rarely do. I'm not blaming you for the not-kissing—it isn't really our style. We generally make fun of people who smooch in public. You know, what are they trying to prove, and to whom?"

"I wouldn't call one kiss, however affectionate and sincere, smooching."

"But it was a public display, Andy. Let's see, four other women, and four other kids. You had a big audience."

"Really? None of them were even looking at us. It was a

private moment, even if it happened in public. And when did you get so critical of spontaneity?"

"Tessa was obviously looking."

"No she wasn't obviously doing anything. She was talking to Millie. She might have caught us out of the corner of her eye. You don't think I kissed you for Tessa's sake, do you? Why would I even do that?"

"I don't know why you did it. That was my original question."

"Okay, here's my confession to this criminal act. I was thinking how unfair it was that these dreary doctors had such attractive women and then I realized that the most attractive woman in the room was married to me. I felt a burst of gratitude and since nobody seemed to be paying any attention to us at all, I hazarded a kiss. Didn't you appreciate it?"

"Yes, yes, it was very sweet, and if you mean what you say then your motive was very sweet, too. I'm pleased that you think I was the most attractive woman in that room, although I'd hate to compete in any sort of objective contest with Tessa."

"Tessa's more showy, but you're far more beautiful. And what do you mean, 'If I mean what I say'?"

Perhaps Andy felt that he was on the verge of winning this particular exchange, or perhaps he was distracted by the warm air rushing in the car windows or the uncluttered beauty of the fields they were passing through and the occasional distant view of mountains, but he now discounted the slight note of danger that had lurked in Shelley's original question about the kiss. After all, what was he being accused of? Kissing his wife in public? It wasn't as though he had done it ostentatiously or insincerely. What Andy didn't realize until too late was that this couldn't really be about the kiss itself.

"I don't know, Andy, but you've been different since I got back from California. Distant. You aren't jealous that I spent time with Jan, are you? Or mad that I left you alone?"

"You didn't leave me alone. Jim was with me."

"But what is it, then? My suspicion is that Tessa was reacting not to the kiss at all but to some sort of disconnection between us. We did not seem married in the sense of joined."

"My goodness, you're giving Tessa sensory powers that I just don't think she has. If she's this intuitive she will certainly be the best weather gal in history."

"But there's something, isn't there? You're not denying that something is different, there's some sort of estrangement."

"No, I am denying it. Look, you were gone for ten days. I don't resent your time away; I'm glad for you. But it's the longest we've been apart since we got married, since long before we got married. We just need to find the rhythm again."

"So you admit it then, that we're out of sync?"

"I admit nothing, Shelley. This is all in your mind. If you don't trust me, you should talk to Jim about it."

"If only I could. But he's been acting suspiciously, too. Maybe I should have a chat with Saint John and find out just what the two of you have been up to."

"Do you mean John and me or Jim and me? I don't equate the two, of course, except in that they're equally unlikely. But go right ahead, give John a call," Andy said. "Be my guest." He knew of course that there was no way she would talk to John, even if she really was suspicious about something. Especially if she was suspicious. But he shuddered to think what might happen if she did.

AFTER A RESTLESS night, Andy decided he needed to talk to Susanna right away, to break things off before they got in any deeper, not that they weren't already in deep enough. He did love Susanna in some profound way that went well beyond the carnal. And he would suffer and even mourn the idea that they could not see each other. But he knew they couldn't be friends without some sort of sexual connection, and that the sex put his marriage in the most urgent sort of danger. If he had to choose between the two women, and of course he did have to choose, the choice had to be Shelley. Everything about his relationship with her was deeper—everything they had shared since their childhoods, the intertwining of their friendships and families, and of course the thing that Tessa had seen, their own very real friendship. He couldn't, finally, imagine his life without her.

Because he didn't have class that day, he told Shelley he was going to Alderman to study. During the regular academic year, Andy always biked or walked to campus, or in bad weather took the bus. But in the summer session it was possible to park close to the library, so he took his Fiat, promising to pick up some things at the grocery store on his way home. But when he left Altamont Circle he did not turn right toward campus but left toward Rt. 20, the road that led past Monticello and down to Scottsville. Andy thought about stopping at a gas station to call Susanna and warn her that he was coming, and indeed to see if she was even there, but the thought of getting change for the pay phone and slipping the coins in the slot once the connection had been made just seemed too tawdry somehow. Thinking of Susanna waiting on the other end while the coins jangled into the phone felt unbearable. The sound would be the very sound of his own nervousness, of the illicit way in which they had to communicate, of the impossibility of what they were doing. Much better to just take his chances that she would be there. He knew that if she was there she would be alone and would be glad to see him. And she would not disagree with the case he would make. They both knew that what they were doing was wrong and had to stop.

The miles to Scottsville soared past, the small boxy car almost floating up and down the hills and through the curves. The weather was cloudy and it looked like they might have showers, but he was almost completely focused on what he would say to Susanna when he saw her. As he approached the outskirts of Scottsville he realized that he had been driving unconsciously, that some part of him had been steering and pressing the accelerator and the clutch and the brakes, and had been shifting gears as he'd driven through the landscape, but it was certainly not his conscious mind that had been in control. It was more like sleepwalking. When he got to the bottom of the town he turned left and drove alongside the river till the road curved back up to the east. After a few miles he turned right onto a road that was paved for less than a hundred yards, and at a point where a number of mailboxes gathered, the road split off into three or four dirt or gravel driveways. Susanna's, the second drive from the right, was dirt. Andy drove slowly down it through the woods in the direction of the river until it made a sharp right turn and then rose up to what was a bluff over-looking the James. Andy's heart raced when he saw Susanna's Saab parked beside the small frame cottage, whose front porch faced the river. He parked beside her and went to the back door, which opened directly into the kitchen. When he did not see her there, he knocked.

She did not appear immediately, and he waited long enough to consider opening the door and giving her a call. But then she appeared, looking sleepy and disheveled, but in a most beautiful way. Her long, coppery hair was pulled up loosely with a clip, and she was wearing only a long brown T-shirt with images of beignets over each breast, under which were the words "Eat Me." She smiled when she saw him through the door, and her face seemed a deeper, redder color than usual, perhaps from sleep.

He kissed her lightly on the lips when she opened the door and said with an apologetic look, "Did I wake you?"

"God, no. I've been up for hours. I was upstairs reading, deep into a modern French version of the Chanson de Roland. It took me a moment to realize where I was when I heard you knocking."

"You have that just returned from a long journey look. It suits you."

"You don't look so bad yourself," she said, and now that he had walked past her into the kitchen she embraced him from behind. He could feel the soft pools of her breasts pushing into his back and smell her distinctive smell. She did not smell of sleep, but did feel warm, although there was an air conditioner running in a kitchen window.

"How do you stay awake reading in the warm bedroom of yours? I would be out after fifteen lines of verse."

"It's my iron will, Andy. Also fear. I still have no idea what I'm going to write my dissertation about. One minute I'm reading *Abelard et Héloïse* and the next minute I'm reading Shattuck's *Banquet Years.*"

"Sucking up, eh?"

"Well he is my thesis advisor. Maybe I should write about something he's really interested in. But you didn't come here for academic chitchat, did you?"

"No, not really. I came here to give a speech, in fact."

"Mais non. Please, anything but that. On any particular subject, may I ask?"

"Well, of course. On the subject of us. What else?" They were facing each other, only a foot or two separating them. She seemed to be glowing, and he felt himself flushing as well.

"I like your T-shirt," he said. She pirouetted so he could see that it said Café du Monde on the back. When she was facing him again he put his hands on her beignets and, feeling the nipples pushing against them, gave them a gentle squeeze between each thumb and forefinger. They gazed at each other and the air between them seemed crackly.

"I know what you're going to say, cher. You will be absolutely right. Exactly right. Exactement."

Then she pulled the T-shirt over her head, as she had on his couch that evening when John was there. Could it only have been two weeks before? Her breasts were as coppery brown as her arms and legs. She was not wearing any panties.

"Someone has been sunbathing in the nude," he said.

"There has to be some advantage to living so far from civilization," she replied. Then she pulled his shirt over his head, too. He felt his contrasting paleness as he had those years ago when they had swum at the pool in the mountains and made love on the rocks afterward.

She took his hand and led him upstairs to her warm bedroom.

"Strip," she said with mock gruffness, as she pulled the books and notebooks from her bed.

She pulled back the covers and lay on her back. As she reached for him he could see that there were tears in her eyes. He began to cry, too, and then they began to touch each other patiently, their tears wetting each other's faces even as their skin dampened with sweat in the warm room. They had always joked and laughed as they made love, but now they were in deadly earnest. They both believed that this was the last time they would be together in this way, and indeed the last time they would be together at all.

When they finished they dozed in each other's arms, their fluids intermixing. Andy woke with a start as if from a long sleep. Her eyes fluttered open and he said, "I ought to go."

"I know," she said. "But take a shower first."

He walked into the bathroom and she followed him into the shower, and they washed each other solemnly, as though preparing a body for a funeral. After the shower they dried each other with the same sense of ceremony and as they got dressed

Andy realized that the shower had not refreshed him but put him deeper into a post-coital stupor.

"I feel retarded," he said, and Susanna laughed, a small bark of laughter, like a fox barking.

"You are retarded," she said. "But don't worry about it. It's only sadness. I feel the same way."

"I don't want to be sitting here as you drive away," she said. "So I think I'll follow you into Scottsville, stop at the grocery store, buy some razorblades or something." She gave him a quick smile.

And then they were both out the door and after a brief hug were in their cars and heading up the driveway. It had begun to rain, so his car was not kicking up dust as she followed him. When he turned left onto the main road, which wound back down into Scottsville, she was not behind him. Perhaps she had stopped for her mail. The road was slick with rain and as he checked his rear-view mirror to see if she was catching up to him he crossed the line on a curve and an oncoming pickup truck sideswiped him, sending his small Fiat into a series of three-sixties, as he spun toward the ditch at the side of the road. It was the last thing he remembered until he awoke in the university hospital, where the first face he saw was Shelley's. He did not like the expression he saw there.

PART IV

WASHINGTON, 1980

11

WHEN THE NEWS of John Lennon's shooting came in just after 11 P.M., Andy was sitting on the rim. "John Lennon," the night editor screamed. "He's been shot. Minutes ago. Outside his apartment. Central Park West." The rim was the name for the outer precincts of the copy desk, a large rectangular table near the big windows facing L Street around which the newspaper's copy editors were arranged. If each editor on the rim was not quite in reach of the three people at the center of this nightly operation—the layout editor, his assistant, and the slot, who read all of the other copy editors' work and was sanctimoniously known as "the last line of defense" before it was sent down a pneumatic tube for typesetting—then they were easily within shouting distance and close enough so that layout sheets and raw copy could be shoved across the table at but not quite to them. The night editor, who was more or less in charge, if anyone could be said to be in charge of a group of newspaper people, sat at a desk off to the side, also within shouting distance. Unlike the people working on the copy desk, who were also collectively and dehumanizingly known as "the desk," the night editor was a quiet and serious sort, a man of ambiguous sexuality who always kept his cuffs buttoned and his tie knotted snug against his Adam's apple. This editor, who bore the unlikely name of John Jacob James, but who was known on the desk as Jimmy-John, in fact rarely raised his voice. When he needed to talk to someone, he pushed up out of his chair, walked briskly to his destination, and leaned over to speak in a confiding whisper, showing off the top of a full head of flaming red hair. But tonight he wasted no time making his loud general announcement about the death of this pop icon, an announcement that proved by its girlish high pitch why he so rarely raised his voice. Still, whatever else Jimmy-John might be, he was a newsman first, and when the wire-service bulletin had been dropped in his basket, he naturally wanted to be the one to spread the news.

"Did Yoko do it?" the layout editor asked, introducing the one cynical note into what was otherwise a horrified silence.

"No, but she was there. She screamed out 'Help me,' this says." Even as Jimmy-John was responding he was dialing the phone and talking, apparently, with the Page One editor. Soon after that he was on the phone with Nimrod Brewer, the editor of their own section, Lifestyles, with whom he had only minutes before finished a protracted conversation about the headlines in the first edition, which was always delivered to Brewer at his big house in Cleveland Park by ten-thirty. Andy and several other copy editors had been hard at work fine-tuning some headlines based on this earlier call.

After a few minutes of conversation, which on his side consisted mostly of yups, okays, and we can do thats, Jimmy-John bounced up and strode over to the layout editor. This time he did not speak in a whisper, given the importance of what he was about to say. "Okay, we're going to try to have something for final, so everything stays the way it is for late city." Late city was the second daily edition of the newspaper and final was the fourth, with a starred late city operating as the third edition. "Nim is on the phone with Zion right now."

This last news sent a shiver along the rim. Zion was the paper's rock-music critic, and a more unpleasant fellow would be hard to find. His full name was Jedediah Zion, and he was known far and wide as Jeddy, although closer to home, on the desk itself, in fact, he was known most often as "Shithead," a nickname that was not used affectionately. Jeddy's sole goal in life was to be as notorious as the people he covered, but since his only talent of any sort was for self-promotion, his one strategy for meeting this goal was gaining proximity to those who did have talent. Because of this, he never wrote anything like a critical appraisal of any new rock record, in spite of his job title. All of his pieces were, instead, stream-of-consciousness reports about hanging out with rock stars who had a new album to promote. That the album was the band's latest triumph, and more than worthy of purchase by the average reader—these were the inevitable starting points from which all of his pieces began. However distasteful the rockers themselves might have found Jeddy—for one thing he had a raging cocaine habit, and when he wasn't staunching nosebleeds his nostrils were forever streaming a clear liquid that was presumably itself highly narcotic—the record companies respected the size of his audience and the utter impossibility that he would ever say anything negative about an album going on sale. And so he was admitted into the presence of these performers, making him just another of the brownnosing (or in Jeddy's case, red-nosed) hangers-on with whom the stars were forced to deal.

Jeddy had, as he had managed to mention frequently both in person and in print, once had a one-on-one interview with John Lennon in a hotel suite where John and Yoko and their new son were ensconced. Lennon had been on such a parental high that he had tolerated Jeddy's presence better than most of his subjects did, and had been unguarded in a way that Jeddy had mistaken for intimacy. This same feeling of paternal pride would bring Lennon's career to a screeching halt, doing more damage even than breaking up with the other Liverpool lads had done. He had since devoted himself to fatherhood, to baking bread and being contentedly housebound in their apartment in the

Dakota, where he had been living now for several years. He had just this year released his first album since the one occasioning the famous Jeddy interview, but this time Jeddy was unable to secure a reprise. Even Yoko's publicist would not return Shithead's calls.

"Oh, god!" Jimmy-John was again screeching as a he stood at his desk, a new piece of wire copy in his hand. "He was just pronounced dead on arrival at Roosevelt Hospital. John is dead."

Andy thought back to his college years at Concordia, when in the dorms guys could elicit the words "Paul is dead" by making the *White Album* play backwards. That message, if that's what it was, had of course turned out to be false, but this one promised to be all too true. It also made Andy think back to his first weeks in the Lifestyles section, when he was trying out for a job on the copy desk. He remembered the day that Elvis died, more than three years earlier. Jimmy-John's predecessor as night editor had announced that death, too, to a much larger audience given that the news came in well before early deadline. She had delivered it in her brassy Ethel Merman voice. "Elvis just died," she said to general pandemonium. She had waited for the ruckus to die down a bit before offering her only elaboration of the news, serving as both an autopsy and a final word on the human condition: "Straining a stool."

The details in the Lennon case, as they came over the wire almost one by one, were more dignified, but the result was sadly the same. Four shots. Yoko's cry for help. No apparent last words from John. A middle-aged man in the crowd outside the Dakota saying, "I just shot John Lennon." The police describing him as a "local screwball."

Andy felt sadder about the news than he would have expected to, and indeed the level of wisecracks on the rim was well below what might have resulted had the deceased been a flamboyant congressman, for instance, or an over-the-hill starlet. The

Beatles had been for Andy as for every person of his generation a large aspect of the musical accompaniment to his mental life to date, but Andy had not been particularly interested in Lennon in his post-Beatles, Yoko Ono stage. And although Andy did not revile Yoko as some did for being the person who broke up the Beatles, he did wonder how someone so unattractive could have landed one of the world's great catches, and could not understand the attraction even leaving aside her looks. She seemed dull and self-satisfied, a minor talent if that, latched onto a major one, and utterly humorless—altogether not so different from Jeddy. So Andy's sorrow was not for Yoko. And then he realized that it might well be for their son, Sean, or more likely for the years of fatherhood that Lennon had now lost. Andy was a newish father himself, and Shelley was pregnant with a second child. The idea that either the beloved first child—a son not named Jesus as his parents joked that he should have been called, considering the way he and Shelley worshipped him, but Eric—or the already loved if not yet known second child, that either could grow up without him, this created real feelings of pathos in Andy.

Luckily, Andy was on the early shift that night, and would go home at twelve-thirty, just as Jeddy was phoning in his copy for final. He would hear the next afternoon that the copy had come in even more stream-of-consciousness than usual, what one of Andy's colleagues called stream-of-unconsciousness, so that Jimmy-John had had to translate it into something resembling English prose. Whether Jeddy had done a line or two too many upon receiving the assignment from Nim Brewer, or whether he was suffering a deep, personal loss at the death of his close personal friend, or both, Jeddy had produced a piece that Jimmy-John would discreetly characterize to the layout editor as "not written down." It was generally acknowledged that Jimmy-John had in a matter of a quarter hour saved the paper from real humiliation, and not for the first time—most of the freelancers who turned in short late-night concert reviews wrote them in advance, requiring Jimmy-John to pull a lead sentence out of them on deadline in order to prove at least that they had actually attended. But it was also a relief that the Final edition reached, by the estimation of one old hand who knew someone in distribution, fewer than five thousand people. Still, among that tiny fraction of the overall audience were Jeddy's fellow reporters and their editors, who would find the Final on their desks each morning. Jeddy, who was apparently spaced-out enough while dictating his story to believe he had produced another triumph, made a rare long drive in from his isolated house in the West Virginia mountains the next morning so that he could receive the plaudits of his colleagues. When those plaudits were not forthcoming, or came forth only when Jeddy dragged them out of someone, he quickly turned on Jimmy-John, implying to all who would listen that the "flaming tight-ass night editor" had "fucked up my copy, man." All of this had been related by the assistant layout editor, who got to work by noon in order to make the daily eleven o'clock story meeting, which always started exactly an hour late.

All of this, Andy realized from long experience, was far more amusing as an anecdote than as something to live through. He had been grateful the night before not only to miss the Jeddy copy, but also to be on his way home to Shelley and Eric. Once he had walked to the parking lot, greeting the hookers who hung out there, and driven down Fourteenth Street, which at that time of night was so sparsely populated by people that the rats were out in teams, and across the bridge into Virginia, he began to relax and look forward to the warm bodies and dis-tinctive smells of his small family. If Eric was in his crib and not nursing in bed with Shelley, he would smell at his scalp of sweet baby sweat, with perhaps the distant acrid odors of urine or sour milk burped onto his one-piece pajamas, the ones with feet in them. If he was in bed nursing, the milk smell would be fresher and accompanied by greedy sucking sounds.

When Andy got home to their row house in Alexandria, not far from the train station, he went right to the kitchen to pull a beer from the refrigerator, the first step in a ritual of unwinding that would take an hour or so before he could expect to get to sleep. Then he went up the stairs and ducked his head into the nursery, where the crib was empty, and then into his bedroom, where Shelley and Eric were asleep back to back, the nursing having come to an end, clearly, at least for the time being. For Shelley's sake, he took care not to wake Eric, kneeling beside the bed and kissing her on the forehead. She opened her eyes and immediately checked out the bedside clock, presumably to gauge whether or not that beery odor emanating from him was the product of several hours of after-work drinking, a situation that had happened only once or twice but that lingered in her mind.

"John Lennon was killed tonight," he whispered.

"That's horrible," she said. But she had not been fully awake and was immediately back to sleep. In the morning she would not remember having heard the news.

Before going downstairs, Andy ducked into the dark bathroom and peered out across the alley to the row house immediately behind theirs. Two young women lived there together, presumably as lovers. For some reason that Andy did not understand or question, they tended to spend a lot of time at night walking around the apartment with their clothes off, with very little concern for whether the blinds were open or shut. Andy ritualistically checked them out, but they had apparently retired for the night, and their windows were dark.

He went back down the stairs to finish his beer, sitting at the small kitchen table and reading the first edition of the paper, which he had brought home with him. Everything he read felt more trivial than usual because of the event that had eclipsed all of it, the murder in New York that was so utterly unforetold in anything they had worked so hard to put together that day, the hundreds of reporters and editors who had created the first edition. Now it all seemed like a lie, a willful withholding of the story everyone would want to read. Andy decided just this once to have another beer before turning on the TV to see if any station had not yet played the "Star-Spangled Banner" and gone to static.

His graduation with a master's in English had not done much to answer the question that his parents' friends had asked back in Strasburg two years earlier: what would Andy actually *do* with such a degree? The Bicentennial summer marital crisis, which had both culminated in and grown out of his accident and stay in the hospital, had settled one thing in Shelley's mind—they would not be living in Charlottesville once he had graduated and she had finished her second year of teaching. And they still agreed that returning to Strasburg was not what either of them wanted. So almost without discussing it they began to focus on moving to Washington. Many people they'd known in college and since then had gravitated there: if you lived anyplace in Virginia and were not so deeply alienated by it as to want to move to New York City, then Washington was the logical destination. Plus, for whatever as-yet-unspecified sort of work Andy would aspire to, Washington was likely to offer more opportunities than anywhere else nearby.

Of course a graduate degree in English, on top of a couple of years of experience as a reporter, did suggest that a job and even a career that involved writing or editing was a good possibility. So starting a few months before his May 1977 graduation, Andy had begun to follow up on editing jobs that he found either in the newspaper or posted in the placement office at the university. He made several trips to Washington for interviews with journals published by academic groups—the American Sociology Association, the American Chemical Engineering Society, the American Association of Teachers of English. He somehow could not bring himself to answer the ad for the National Association of Associations. It turned out that most of the ads were for production editors—the sort of editor who really had no connection to language, except for entering corrections and perhaps doing some proofreading. Reading proof was not all that Andy hoped for in a job. And these potential employers were apparently looking for someone with actual editing experience. The truth was that for each of his interviews the mutual dissatisfaction—Andy's with the dreariness of the prospect of doing such a job, the interviewer's at the prospect of talking with another shaggy-haired graduate student who really had no idea what he wanted to do with himself—was pretty immediately apparent, and so the meetings soon became exercises in going through the motions. Andy stayed with the Copenhavers several times while he was in town for such interviews, and after the third one, when David happened to be home from the hospital one afternoon when Andy stopped by for his stuff, had gently asked him if he was feeling just a bit blue.

"A bit?" Andy replied. "How about blue-black? How about no light at the end of the tunnel—or the cave, as the case may be?" Andy had said this jocularly, and David had also kept the tone from being too serious.

"Of course," he said at one point, "if you have a good reason to be depressed—your inability to convince anyone that you really want a job, say—then it isn't actually depression. That's what I recall from my psychiatry rotation, at any rate."

But as Andy drove back to Charlottesville he realized that, with or without cause, he was indeed, for the first time in his life, really, going through an extended period of uncertainty, absence of confidence, ambivalence, and, yes, depression. It was not immobilizing but it did scare him, because he couldn't imagine a way out. He would be graduating soon, he had a wife who clearly loved him, given what they had gotten through together, and they were both reaching an age when the possibility of having children was beginning to come up. What was missing was his ability to support the next step in their lives together, or to deserve it. Had his life till now, not any particular sort of triumph but still one filled with a momentum that seemed to be directed at something—had all this been preparation only for a dull and stultifying office job in Washington? He was starting to lose his nerve. The feeling that sometimes came over him was the same one he had felt at the bottom of that chilly cavern. Claustrophobia. Fear. A whiff of panic. The need to escape as quickly as possible. Thank god there was no possibility of his going on for a PhD, or else he would have been sorely tempted, just as a further delay mechanism, a chance to gird his loins, however ridiculous such a thing might look if not taken figuratively. He imagined shuffling into an interview with a large rubber band stretched across his thighs, tight enough to keep him from fleeing from the room, the job, the future.

Just ahead of him as he approached the outskirts of Charlottesville a car slammed on its brakes and Andy had to hit his so hard it caused Shelley's Datsun to skid for just a moment or two. Before he realized that he was going to stop in time, the adrenaline poured into his bloodstream, causing his heart to drum in his chest, the blood to thrum in his ears. Wrecking a second car in less than a year, especially when they had not been able to afford to replace the totaled first one, would not have been at all desirable. So, one disaster averted. Perhaps his luck was changing?

If so, it was changing only slowly, because he would spend

the next few months in jobless purgatory, well past graduation and into the summer. Then two things happened almost simultaneously. The first was that he was offered the chance to teach a course at the university. Given Watergate and the appearance of the Woodward and Bernstein book about it, followed only recently by the film, students at the university were clamoring to be journalists, a suddenly glamorous profession. Since the university offered no courses in the subject and didn't particularly want to take one more step toward turning itself into a trade school (nor did it particularly want students dictating what courses they should be offered, with its overtones of the student strikes of 1970), the English department reluctantly agreed to put on a few courses that it primly called "Nonfiction Writing." Andy was one of the only people in any way associated with the department who had actually sullied himself with journalism, and his writing was generally acknowledged to be pretty fair, if woefully lacking in academic jargon. So he was called in by the department chairman and offered the job. Although Andy agreed immediately, the offer presented two problems. The first was the pay, which was about as low as you could go and still be called four figures. It was not only too little to live on, but it barely justified the expense of commuting from Washington to do it. The second and bigger problem was Shelley, who was not likely to want him teaching in Charlottesville a couple of days a week while she was living in Washington. Neither of them would have to explore the reason for that, given that Susanna Agincourt was still in town writing her dissertation.

The other thing that happened was even more unexpected than the first. A professor Andy had gotten to know, one who had a rare for the department dual career as a respected scholar of Victorian poetry and a glowingly reviewed if non-selling novelist, happened to come to the Five and Dime one summer evening with his showy wife. Andy got the table and while waiting on them, the professor, Douglas Winters, asked Andy about his plans. It was a Tuesday night and the restaurant was not busy, so Andy gave him a longish answer, one that described the growing number of fruitless interviews he had endured for jobs he did not really want.

"So you want to be an editor in Washington, eh?" Prof. Winters said. "And you were once a newspaperman, weren't you?"

When Andy agreed that he had that stain on his record, the professor mentioned a former student of his who was now the editor of the Lifestyles section of the *Post*.

"Give him a call and use my name," he said. "It can't hurt and it might even help. His name is Nim Brewer, Nimrod Brewer."

The next day Andy did just that. When he got through to Brewer's secretary and there was the inevitable long pause after he asked to speak to her boss, Andy had added weakly, "Could you tell him that Douglas Winters suggested I call?"

Brewer had been on the line almost instantly then, and after a brief exchange had asked Andy when he could come in for an interview.

"How about tomorrow?" Andy had said.

"Great," Brewer answered. "Show up at eleven-thirty; I'll see you right after the morning meeting."

Andy had risen early the next day after only a few hours of sleep, since he'd returned home from the restaurant after midnight. Because Shelley was on summer vacation, she decided to accompany him as far as Millie Copenhaver's house in McLean, where she would visit her friend while Andy went downtown for the interview. As Andy had driven past the massive Washington Post building on Fifteenth Street looking for a parking lot, his stomach began to flutter with anticipation, a feeling that located itself further down his torso from the chest-tightening one of dread he had developed before his other Washington interviews. The Post façade was familiar from the Watergate movie, and once the blazer-wearing man at the reception desk had called up to Brewer's secretary and Andy had been sent by elevator to the fifth floor, he also felt a sense of familiarity with the interior surroundings. The place looked unsurprisingly like the version of it that had been constructed in California for the movie, and was acres bigger than the newsroom at the Charlottesville paper. As Brewer's secretary, Meredith something, led him past the main newsroom, he could look to his right, across rows and rows of desks mostly unoccupied by journalists at this hour, and see in one of the glass-walled offices along the wall a barrel-chested man standing and gesticulating who looked suspiciously like the paper's famous editor.

Once they got to Brewer's office there was no place to sit, so Meredith put him at the empty copy desk by the tall bright windows and told him the morning meeting had, predictably, not started yet, so there would be a bit of a wait. The wait would turn out to be an hour and a half, but the time went by quickly as Andy pretended to read the paper and surreptitiously watched the activity going on around him, including a steady stream of people in and out of Brewer's office even after the meeting finally started. The combination of excitement, curiosity, and nervousness made him forget how tired he had a right to be. Meredith did not seem at all surprised or apologetic about the length of the wait, but when after about forty-five minutes he needed to use the bathroom, she did let her face unfreeze momentarily in sympathy. Clearly although she would not have acknowledged in a million years that she herself might have any sort of bodily needs or even functions, she did get it that others might once in a while need to pee.

Eventually a clump of editors filed out of Brewer's office and although they gathered at his doorway, Meredith pushed her way through to remind her boss that Andy was still waiting. The group of editors remained oblivious to how much in the way they were as Meredith squeezed back through them to grab Andy and then lead him into the pack again. They took no notice of him, as indeed nobody else from the section had, although the people passing through the Lifestyles newsroom on their way to what Andy would later learn was the lunchroom would stare at him as if he represented some newly discovered race of being. Once Meredith got him into the office and introduced him to Brewer, her boss asked if she would shut the door on her way out.

"And please tell those hyenas to take the party elsewhere," he said as the door closed behind her.

Andy handed Nim Brewer a copy of his résumé and Brewer studied it as if it contained a hidden code. Here was a man who was comfortable with silence, or was perhaps simply enjoying it while he could, given the chaos Andy had been observing. When Brewer looked up, he had a stare that seemed capable of penetrating concrete.

"So Doug Winters sent you," he began. "How is he?"

"Seems fine," Andy said. "Working on another novel, he says."

"Maybe this one will be the one," Brewer said. "Still got that hot wife?"

"She's probably not as hot as she once was, but she's still pretty warm," Andy said, haltingly. What does that even mean, he wondered. That she's merely alive?

"So you've been a reporter, been to graduate school. What do you want to be when you grow up?"

Although Brewer said this unsmilingly, it made Andy laugh and relaxed him, but not so much that he was willing to tell the truth, which was that he didn't know and never wanted to grow up.

"Your job looks pretty desirable," Andy said. "But I get it that it's taken at the moment and I might have to start a few rungs down the ladder."

Brewer almost smiled, and then after a few uncomfortably silent moments did smile. "I love this job, honestly, but I can't imagine that any sane person would. It's a bit like running a nursery for seventy-five adults.

"Look, here's the situation. I'm trying to fill my copy desk with the smartest people I can find. Not just people with the most journalism experience, but people with a breadth of knowledge. You can learn the journalism part in about three weeks on the job. Smart can't be taught.

"As I remember it, Doug Winters doesn't have much use for people who aren't pretty smart, so I'm willing to take a chance on you. But I only have part-time slots available right now. I'll introduce you to the guy who runs the copy desk in a minute, he'll get you on the schedule, and we'll give you a two-week tryout. If you're smart, you've got a job. Okay?"

Andy was stunned. Not only was this the first job he'd been offered in a spring and summer of trying, but this was a job he could not possibly have hoped for—working at what was arguably the most famous or at least the most notorious newspaper in the country. He got to his feet and stuck out his hand. "This is great. Thanks so much, Mr. Brewer."

Brewer stood up and gave Andy's hand a cursory shake as he headed toward the door. "Call me Nim," he said. "And thank me when you have the job."

As it would turn out, the occasion to offer those thanks never arose again, not because Andy didn't get the job but because nobody ever told him that he had it. The layout editor, a big taciturn fellow from New Hampshire who only got excited when talking about his son's hockey team, which he coached, just kept putting him on the schedule. Some weeks Andy would only get two days, some weeks as many as four. He had filled out the paperwork from personnel even before the tryout, so there was no tipoff from that quarter that he was now permanently employed. Although the work was part time, this job did pay well enough for him to live on, and since his hours averaged out at more than twenty a week he got full benefits. Andy did pretty soon have to tell Mike, the layout editor, about his other job in Charlottesville, which meant he couldn't work on Tuesday or Thursday nights, but Mike only grunted and started giving Andy a lot of Fridays and Sundays.

After the meeting with Nim Brewer, as Andy and Shelley had headed home down Rt. 29, Shelley again brought up a subject that they had of necessity been talking about all summer.

"I really do think I should keep my job, at least for one more semester, Andy. This thing at the *Post* sounds great, if it works out, but by the time we know if it does it will be too late for me to tell the people at Belmont. Millie said you can stay with them while you try out for the job and then depending on how much it actually pays, you can figure out where you'll live when you're working up here."

They had already heard from their Peace Corps friend that he would not be getting back to Charlottesville until the end of the year, so the apartment on Altamont Circle was theirs if they wanted it, at least until then.

"Okay, this works for me," Andy said. "Since my class at the university isn't until the afternoon, I might even be able to drive home after I get off at the *Post* on nights before I teach, and then sleep all morning before class. When I work up there more than one night at a time, though—we have to figure something out about that."

"It means being apart some," Shelley said, "but it won't be for that long and I'll have Jim for company and with two jobs in different cities you'll be too tired to get in trouble, or at least I hope you will."

Andy gave her what he believed was a reassuring smile. He wasn't worried about getting in trouble, but he was still on probation with Shelley, of course, and the need to appear reliable made him feel theatrically so when he looked at her. But she seemed to appreciate the effort, whether or not she felt reassured.

"Too bad Jan isn't still living with us," he offered.

"I think our lives are complicated enough right now without adding her complications to the mix." Jan had begun to have a few dates, but the results had not been good. Although Andy was astonished that one woman could attract so many feckless men, he did think that each of Jan's wild stories made him, even with his glaring imperfections, look just a bit more reliable to Shelley.

"We'll need to find you a reliable car," Shelley said, almost as if she had picked that word out of his thoughts. "One with a good radio, if you really do intend to drive home in the middle of the night sometimes."

He was tired but in the late afternoon light she looked as desirable as he could ever remember her looking. She was brown from the summer sun, and wearing a short denim skirt and a sleeveless top. He loved the subtle curves of her legs and arms, and they were especially alluring when she was tan. The slanting sunlight picked up a pattern of fuzz on her upper arm, invisible normally but now just visible because it had been bleached blond by the summer sun in contrast with her dark skin.

"Scootch over," he said softly and she knew immediately by his tone just what car-trip pastime he had in mind. She kicked off her flip-flops and slid as close as she could get to him in her bucket seat. His right hand slipped between her thighs, where the skin was as soft as anything he could think of. She shifted in her seat, creating just a bit of space between her legs, and he tugged her skirt up a little higher. By the time he worked his way up her thigh, the skin getting ever softer, it seemed, and reached his destination, he could feel that she was ready and waiting. He checked his rear-view mirror and then gazed down the road in front of them. Good, he thought, not a truck in sight. They could expect as much privacy as they would need. He glanced over at Shelley and she already had her eyes closed and her head pitched back. This was not going to take long.

ONE FINAL PIECE of luck came their way that summer. Soon after it became clear that Andy would be working regularly for the Lifestyles section, their new friend Tessa, the weather person for Channel 7, whom they'd met the day of the big fireworks display, offered Andy a place to stay when he was in Washington. She had come to visit them several times in Charlottesville in the past year, and they had been to Washington to visit her. She had a big, airy apartment in an old building just a couple of blocks northeast of Dupont Circle, and because her own trouble with men had not ended on the Bicentennial, she would be happy for the company, especially because she and Andy would both be getting off work late. She had not escaped from covering the weather but had been promoted from weekends to doing the weeknight news shows, so she was making more money than she had ever thought possible, and insisted to Shelley that she did not need Andy to help with the rent.

Tessa and Shelley had grown close in the last year. The only person besides Tessa in whom Shelley had confided about the story behind Andy's accident was Jan, whom she had told right away, both because Jan was still living with them at the time of the accident and because she had suffered through Carlos's infidelities, and so could be counted on to be sympathetic. But Jan had not been very helpful to Shelley, given her permanent estrangement from Carlos and the bitterness that remained, which she found easy to transfer to Andy. By the time he had been released from the hospital, Shelley had known that she herself wanted to work things out with him, and so Jan's anger was not only irritating to Andy, given that she was always there underfoot, with or without her clothes on, but increasingly irritating to Shelley as well. Before school had started at the end of the Bicentennial summer, and much to the relief of all three of them, Jan had moved into her own place. It was at about this time that Tessa had made her first visit to Charlottesville. She and Shelley had driven west of town together on Saturday afternoon to look at junk shops so that Tessa could find stuff for the big new apartment she had only recently moved into. Shelley had felt so comfortable with Tessa, she would tell Andy later, that she had spilled out all their problems to her. Tessa's reaction had been diametrically opposed to Jan's.

"From the second I saw you two together," Tessa said, "I thought you were just the best couple. Andy's so lovable, and any fool can see that he adores you. Maybe it's my Italian blood"—Tessa's last name was Livorno—"but if Andy's truly sorry and he's really finished with the other woman, then I say get over it. These things happen. Of course I have terrible luck with men myself, so I'm probably not the best person to listen to about this."

But Shelley did listen to her, not so much to her easygoing notions about the infidelities of men—this was definitely not ever going to be Shelley's attitude—but more to her big-hearted, romantic sense of who Shelley and Andy ultimately were as a couple. And to her strong sense that Andy was, in spite of all, that rare thing, a good guy. "Trust me," Tessa said. "A man like Andy is not easy to find." Although Shelley herself had never had trouble attracting men, and had never had Tessa's habit of attracting the wrong sorts of men, she was reassured by how much Tessa liked and respected Andy. Besides, as Jan's negativity had proven already, Shelley did not want to hear what was wrong with Andy but what was right. In a way the Watsons' friendship with Tessa grew because she became a sturdy bridge between the two of them, one on which they both could rely. They felt less awkward together if Tessa was there, too, and just being in Tessa's presence, with her almost animal sense of well-being, her energy and carefully tended beauty and confidence, the latter tempered only by her own romantic missteps, simply made them feel better. So they sought out her company and she became a sort of sister to both of them. Perhaps it was this that made Tessa feel comfortable suggesting to Shelley that Andy could stay with her, this and her own sense of honor, which made any possibility of betraying Shelley inconceivable to her—and to Shelley herself. So she never felt any need to reassure Shelley that Andy's spending nights at her place was perfectly safe, and this was the best sort of reassurance. Of course nothing was now inconceivable to Shelley where Andy was concerned—even, given the notion of his brotherly feelings for Tessa, incest—but she did trust Tessa absolutely. And so Shelley was enthusiastic about the idea. This, too, might keep Andy out of other sorts of trouble.

LATE ONE MORNING, soon after he had begun to stay at Tessa's, Andy and she walked to Dupont Circle to go to the bank and the drugstore. Andy was always managing to forget something he needed to bring for his overnight stays—toothpaste, shaving cream—and Tessa had convinced him that he ought to just buy one of everything he needed and leave it all in her guest bathroom.

"Are you sure?" he had asked. "I don't want you to feel trapped in this arrangement."

She had laughed in a way that told him she had no idea what he was talking about. "You just be sure to take all your dirty laundry home to Shelley and we'll be fine," she said.

They had approached the circle from New Hampshire Avenue and were walking around its perimeter toward the bank when who should Andy spot walking in their direction but Saint John, hand in hand with another tall handsome fellow of about his age.

"John, my god, how are you?" Andy said, and gave him a bear hug. "I haven't seen you in months, and now here you are in Washington, too."

"I'm here visiting my friend, Mark," John said. He seemed genuinely happy to see Andy, but the same could not be said for Mark. Andy put out his hand and Mark took it as though his mother had just instructed him to do so. Then Andy turned to Tessa.

"This is my friend, um, actually our friend, Shelley's and mine; this is Tessa Livorno."

"I know you from the tube," Mark said, offering a hand with much more enthusiasm than he had shown for Andy.

As she and Mark exchanged a few words about her local celebrity, and John waited for his turn to greet Tessa, Andy caught a brief look at her through John's eyes. Andy and Tessa had each slept in, having worked late the night before, and even she had that just-out-of-bed rumpled look—her dark hair pulled back in a loose ponytail, no makeup to speak of, the sunglasses she had pulled off while greeting Mark revealing a slight puffiness around the eyes. Wearing a black T-shirt, silvery running shorts, and jogging shoes, she oozed an unselfconscious sensuality. What must John be thinking?

Whatever he was thinking about Andy, and its implications for his marriage, it was clear that Tessa had gotten John's attention. The two of them instantly recognized in the other the magnetism each of them possessed. It was as if they were members of the same exclusive club. When they shook hands it was almost as though they were the old friends, and Andy the newcomer.

"Do you live in this neighborhood, Tessa?" John asked.

"Yes, just up New Hampshire a few blocks on R Street."

"Oh, Mark lives on Church. Not far at all." Then he turned back to Andy. "Are you around later? Let's meet for coffee. It sounds as if we have a lot to catch up on."

In the end they agreed to meet for a burger at Childe Harold. They sat out front in the small courtyard, finding a table with an umbrella to protect them from the late August sun.

"What is it with you and beautiful women, Andy?" John began. "I'm not saying that you aren't reasonably attractive your-self but, mercy, how do you always get so far out of your league? Tessa is just stunning. She's like a beauty pageant contestant."

"I think she actually was in the Miss Texas pageant at some point, as Miss Tyler, so good call. But lovely as she is to see and be seen with, she really is just a friend. She and Shelley are very close, in fact, so close that I'm trusted to stay with her regularly."

"Why regularly? What are you up to?"

"I'm working part time for the *Post*. Nights. And also teaching a course at the university, so we're still living in Charlottesville and Shelley's back teaching at Belmont for at least this semester."

The waiter approached them and, as Andy had observed so often when he was with John at a restaurant, soon found that he could barely tear himself away from John. He introduced himself with a slight curtsy, gave the specials, gave the weather report, and might well have begun telling John the plot of the film he had seen the night before, but John courteously cut him off.

"Would you bring me some extra lemon for that iced tea?" he said with his brightest smile, and the man scurried away, eager for the opportunity to please.

"Okay," Andy began, "let's see if you can explain away Mark as easily as I could Tessa. Where's Hal, anyway? Don't tell me you two have split up."

"No, we're still together. He's back in Chania for the summer. In fact he's supposed to fly into Dulles in a couple of days. I'm picking him up and we'll be going back to Concord so he can begin the semester, reluctant as he is to do that.

"I just couldn't face Chania again. Last summer was not fun for me. When I arrived, Hal had a young Cretan 'houseboy' living in our apartment, but the chores he performed did not involve any cooking or cleaning. He did do some errands in town, probably as a way to get away from Hal. Who was completely smitten. Theo, the boy himself, could not have been more than seventeen, and acted completely bored at all times. This was just a summer job for him. Which somehow made Hal even madder for him. The boy just ignored me—and Hal wasn't much better. As you know, I'm not particularly jealous, but neither do I have any great yearning to fly halfway around the world to be treated like a third wheel. When we got home, things were fine, except for a persistent wistfulness in Hal. But I had no interest in subjecting myself to that again this summer."

"Which brings us to Mark?" Andy asked. The iced teas had arrived along with a small white dish of lemon chunks. The waiter was lingering again, so Andy told him they'd need a few more minutes. When John gave him a concurring look, the waiter reluctantly withdrew.

"Mark is, let's see. Mark is my ego-repair serviceman. He's my reminder that, much as I love Hal and our life together, I have options. And pretty damned attractive ones."

"Yes, he's a very handsome guy. Looks like he works out, too. Does he know about Hal?"

"Yes, of course. In fact I met him through Hal. Mark had been in a relationship with an English professor at Georgetown, a friend of Hal's. We had been up here to visit them, but they've since broken up. Mark and I stayed in touch."

"Yes, I noticed that," Andy said with a little smile. "Mark was holding on like he was afraid you'd step into oncoming traffic."

"You'd be surprised at how chaste it really is. But I'm guessing that you don't really want to hear the details any more than I want to relate them."

"Still, Mark looked pretty smitten. And possessive. He would have vaporized me with a look if he could have, and given the presence of Tessa he should have assumed he hadn't much to fear from me. Or do I send out a different vibe than I think I do?"

"No, don't worry, Andy. You're every inch a breeder, as Hal likes to call your kind. Mark is too clingy, to tell the truth. When we have time together he doesn't like to share me. And anyone from the past just reminds him of Hal and how unlikely it is that he and I will be anything more than friends. It's all very good for the ego when taken in small doses, and I'm already beginning to think that it will be a long two days till Hal arrives at Dulles."

"Seems rather hard on Mark, if you don't mind my saying so. Of course everyone who meets you falls for you, but generally you don't give us much encouragement."

"I wouldn't worry about Mark," John said with a rueful smile. "He's much more like Hal than like me. In the end, I'm more of a bauble to him than someone he's seriously in love with. He can show me off in certain circles and get a lot more action when I'm not around. Which is pretty much always."

The burgers arrived and John let the waiter linger for a few moments before saying, "Well, this looks splendid, and I know you have other tables waiting, so please don't let us detain you." The man backed away like a subject before his king.

"Now you really need to tell me more about Tessa," John said as he fussed with his burger. "She's like an expensive filly. Surely the story is more complicated than you've let on. And what about Susanna? How did that frightening reconnection turn out? Since you and Shelley are still together, it must not have been as dangerous as it looked. Come on, Andy, tell me about all your beautiful women."

Andy's mouth was full as this little speech fell out of John's, and when John stopped talking Andy finished chewing and took a swallow of tea before answering.

"We really have been out of touch for a long time, John. It's a story that just might turn your hair white. I'm surprised that mine didn't fall out."

12

THAT NIGHT YOU met Susanna at the Five and Dime and then did such a poor job of playing Tristan's sword, that was the beginning of a pretty torrid patch for Susanna and me."

"Yes, I thought things were heading in that direction," John said, "which is why I skedaddled."

"You did act a bit like someone running from a flaming house."

The waiter approached but John waved him off.

"Shelley stayed on in California for another week or more, and Susanna and I were together almost all the time. The way we just dove in had to have been due to how things ended between us back at Concordia after Kent State. One day she just vanished, and neither of us had played out the feelings we had for each other. Nor, clearly, had we burned out all the passion."

John's handsome face was wonderfully blank. It was obvious that he wanted to hear this, to encourage Andy to say what he needed to say, but he didn't want to seem too eager or too approving or in any way disloyal to Shelley. And so he managed to keep every sign of expression at a distance, but his eyes were bright with what seemed to Andy to be genuine interest.

"I never really got over losing her like that, John. Yes, I found my way back to Shelley, and that was also a renewal, a return to another sort of love, really, passionate too, but more familiar, more like a return to my real life. Shelley is perfect; she's complete. I never look at her and wish she were more like somebody else, or in any way less like herself. And yet there was this empty place that I had pushed way, way down. It would never have been a problem had I not run into Susanna again. Just one of those things I would carry with me my whole life. A dull ache when I even thought about it. But I did run into her. And although we had been in Charlottesville at the same time for months, going in and out of the same university building even, and Susanna had not made any attempt at all to get in touch with me, still it was hard to believe that her being there was purely accidental, even if she believed it herself."

"But hadn't you two been out of touch? How would she even have known you were in Charlottesville?"

"She said she didn't know. But I'm not sure I believe her. She's as honest as the rest of us, which means pretty honest unless there's a good reason not to be. She might have said she didn't know I was there not out of pride but out of a concern for me, so I wouldn't be too overwhelmed by the idea that she had utterly changed the course of her life on the chance that we might run into one another again. And even if she hadn't heard some rumor that I was in Charlottesville, and checked it out with directory assistance, say, to see that it was true, it might have been just what she said, a vague pull back to college life in Virginia, which might or might not have meant the time we had together. Not to be too egotistical about this, but when things started up again it became clear that she was also satisfying some hunger that went down pretty far."

John and Andy had both finished their burgers. "Should we get some coffee?" John asked as the waiter approached again.

"I know you never sweat, John, but it's too hot here for me. Let's walk over to the circle and find a bench in a shady spot. There ought to be more air moving there, if only from the traffic."

The waiter left the bill with John, but Andy snatched it. "Now that I'm actually employed again, let me pay. Hmm. There's a phone number on the back of the bill, and somehow I don't think it was meant for me."

"Not interested," John said. "But let me pay the tip. I'll give him a little extra to ease the pain."

They walked down Connecticut and into the circle. Perhaps because of the heat and because lunch hour was over for the workers from nearby offices, there were plenty of benches under the trees in the outer ring. They could find a spot well away from the small clumps of lost souls, drunk and probably homeless, who seemed to be permanent inhabitants of Dupont Circle.

When they sat, John said, "And then Shelley came back from California."

"Yes, and Susanna and I were not proud of ourselves. We had treated this as an interlude, a gift of time together, something that would end when Shelley came back. We both felt guilty, me for obvious reasons and Susanna because, well, her reasons were also pretty obvious. No woman likes to think of herself as the type who messes around with another woman's husband. In some ways Susanna's pride is such that she isn't really touched by what she would call petit bourgeois standards of behavior. But this aversion to busting up a relationship is somehow pre-moral, something atavistic, and even if she were immune to such feelings, she knew how much pain I was in.

"So we of course vowed to break it off, to stop cold when Shelley came home. And of course it was not as easy to do as we had thought."

"Did Shelley suspect anything?"

"She knew something was different. But she'd been so caught up in Jan's problems—remember that her husband Carlos had left her to play for your team—and Shelley might have thought I felt abandoned for a sort of infatuation she had with Jan. Not that she had a crush on her, really, but that she was flattered to be needed by her, liked being in the position of displaying her own emotional strength, sharing it with Jan. And Shelley and I had been together for so long without any sort of separation that even a break of two or three weeks felt like an estrangement, especially when it was a separation of choice and not necessity. I confess that this is what I encouraged her to believe."

A woman came up to them to beg. Her clothes were filthy and when she asked for money spittle came out of her mouth along with her words. She had a round waxy face, a sort of brownish-orange, and surprisingly beautiful skin. Andy ignored her but John gave her a five-dollar bill from his wallet.

She mumbled her thanks and then said to John, "You oughtn't be fucking this one. He mean."

John laughed and she shuffled off. "I wouldn't have given her anything if I thought she was a druggie, but it must just be booze, given how plump she is."

Andy didn't say anything. The conventional wisdom was you shouldn't give money to beggars, that it just encouraged them to do more of what got them into trouble in the first place. But clearly nobody else was doing anything for these people, or if anyone was trying it was the sort of help the vagrants would not accept. Andy did indeed feel mean.

"After Shelley got back, I went to see Susanna several times—she lives outside Scottsville, you might remember, on the James—and the visits all had the same rhythm. We fell into each other's arms and made love as if for the last time, and then we'd spend the next hour or so trying to convince each other it really was the last time. But the truth is there was a stretch there, a fairly short stretch, when I wasn't sure I could live without her, if you'll forgive the cliché. I felt guilty, I knew what we were doing was wrong, I had no interest in leaving Shelley for Susanna, but it was like an addiction. I couldn't stop. It was hell, really, although I don't expect much sympathy. The idea of being in love with two women at once doesn't merit any, and I suspect most people probably don't even believe it's possible. But I did love them both. And I suppose I always will."

John rubbed Andy's shoulder. "You don't have to do this if you don't want to. If it's too upsetting."

Andy gave John a weak smile. "No, I want to tell you. I think I've been waiting to tell someone, and I didn't realize that that someone was you until we sat down to lunch together. How in the world did we fall out of touch with you guys for so long?"

"Sounds as if we were all having our own problems. But remember when you and Shelley did come to see us in Concord last fall? Something seemed strained in your relationship then and I didn't have much doubt about what it was. After some time went by and we didn't hear anything, I was reluctant to get in touch. I was afraid the news would be bad."

"Yes, and I guess we got self-absorbed. For some reason Tessa was a sort of balm to our marriage, so we spent a lot of time visiting her up here or having her down to see us. And we saw a lot of our friends the Copenhavers. Seeing a marriage that worked, seeing a family, that was helpful, too."

Andy worried that he seemed to be implying that John's relationship with Hal was somehow not natural enough to be comforting to them, that he had ignored them because they weren't sufficiently useful. But John's expression was all sympathetic agreement.

"Yes, whenever I have a problem, I flee back to Richmond and the family," he said. "They don't provide quite the ego rush of a weekend with Mark, but they do help you remember what's important, and remind you who you really are."

"Do you have any idea just how blessed you are with that family of yours, John? Even if you'd become a banker, married the girl down the street, and joined the Country Club of

Virginia, getting the sustenance you get from your family would have been remarkable."

"And here I am a poofter, and they love me nonetheless." John laughed when he said this. "The reason it's so sustaining is that they never think of me in any way beyond son, brother, uncle—I'm John first, a Brockenbrough, and everything else, my orientation, my careerlessness, is way down the list. It's the source of my reputed saintliness, or at least of my sanity."

"My parents are loving people," Andy said, "and lovable. But they're so utterly middle class, so contentedly conventional, that there's no way I could go to them with a problem like Susanna. Or, if the truth be told, with any sort of serious problem. They're great with the trivial—giving us a small loan, say, or coming up with ideas for presents for Shelley—but any problem of any magnitude deeply embarrasses them. People like them don't have serious problems. Except of course they do—they just don't talk about them or acknowledge them in any way."

The sun had moved enough since they sat down to put them in direct sunlight, and Andy felt his skin beginning to burn. They slid a dozen feet to their left along the continuous circle of benches, stopping just short of a fairly fresh deposit of bird poop.

"In any case, I realized I had to choose, I couldn't keep deceiving Shelley, and Susanna and I couldn't keep deceiving ourselves. It sounds like this went on for months, probably, but it was really a matter of days, hours even. Still, it did feel like months. Everything was in slow motion. As it happens, I made my decision on the actual day of the Bicentennial."

"A patriotic choice, then?"

"What I eventually understood was that it really wasn't a choice after all. It was just a matter of accepting reality, of embracing reality. Shelley is my whole life. I couldn't imagine, and still can't, any life without her. I know I could be happy with Susanna, even after the passion cooled a bit, but only in some sort of desert island scenario. I could never choose to exist without Shelley and be happy for very long.

"But, yes, I suppose the occasion itself had some sort of effect. We were at the Copenhavers', and their happiness as a family, contrasting with the evident loneliness of Tessa, whom we first met that very day, and the way she seemed to be drawn to Shelley and me as a couple, and the back-yard barbecue, the fireworks, the whole swirl of the afternoon and evening, made me realize that what I wanted was to belong to my life, not to be some sort of outlaw from it. And so I decided. Or at least I believe I did.

"When we got back to Charlottesville I went to see Susanna to break it off. It was a morning when I was supposed to be at the library, a rainy day as it turns out. When I arrived at her house we fell immediately into the old pattern, meaning we fell immediately into bed. But we really believed that this was the last time. We were crying, and we'd never done that before, and we didn't have a big conversation afterward, in which we tried to convince each other that we had to stop. We accepted that we had stopped, that this was it. I left her house pretty soon, and she followed me in her car into Scottsville, planning to run an errand—the grocery store, I think. But my car slid on a slick curve, I was clipped by a pickup truck and spun into a ditch. Susanna came right up behind me and thought I was dead. There was a lot of blood from a gash on my head and I had been knocked unconscious. The pickup truck stopped and Susanna told the driver to go call an ambulance. When it came, she rode with me in the back to the university hospital and although the medic told her I was stable, that I wasn't going to die, she must have felt she had to call Shelley herself and tell her about the accident, and stay in the emergency room till Shelley got there. Which was of course the right thing to do, however painful the consequences."

"My god," John said softly.

"I've never spoken to Susanna again, although I did eventually leave a note in her box at school telling her I was okay, so what I know about the meeting is partly surmise and partly what Shelley told me later. Clearly, however worried she was about me, Shelley had time between the call and when she arrived in the emergency room to wonder who the hell Susanna was and why she had been at the scene of the accident. Apparently Susanna had identified herself simply as a friend.

"Anyway, Susanna did wait in the emergency room until Shelley arrived—she must have recognized Shelley from photos in the apartment. Susanna approached her, introduced herself, and told her what the doctors had said—I was going to live but I was still unconscious from a concussion, they were monitoring for the possibility of bleeding in my brain, and I had shattered a hip, and would need surgery to rebuild or replace it. Shelley thanked her and asked where I was. Susanna pointed her to a nursing station beyond the ER waiting room. And then she left, presumably catching a cab back to Scottsville."

"This is almost too painful to hear, Andy," John said, and his face was contorted with concern. "And I'm not even thinking of the head gash and the broken hip."

"Well, those two things did heal. Luckily the gash bled outside and not inside my brain. They needed to give me a pint or two of blood, but there was no swelling to speak of, so I retained however many or few IQ points I had before the accident. And the hip didn't need to be replaced. They went in and were able to put it back together with pins and things, and although I'll never play rugby again I can do almost anything that isn't likely to result in a crushing blow."

"Like drive a car, you mean?"

"Well, like drive a car into a ditch.

"But the other wounds had barely even been inflicted yet,

and they are still healing. And might never heal entirely.

"Anyway, I did come to after a few more hours, and although the pain was pretty intense because they didn't give me any narcotics until I awoke and they could see whether I had my marbles or not, still the physical pain was nothing compared to the look on Shelley's face when my eyes opened.

"She gave me a kiss and asked me how I was feeling, but it was as if she were on another continent, as if she were looking down from space—she was that far away. That look told me everything, and fortunately or unfortunately I had had no memory loss of any kind, so in the time it took her to buzz the nurse I knew that my physical condition was the least of my troubles.

"I'm sorry," I whispered to her.

"There'll be plenty of time for that," she responded. It felt more like a threat than a reassurance. And then the nurse arrived and soon after that a doctor and then a neurological resident, and it was decided that it was safe to operate on the hip, so they put me back under. I've never been so relieved to lose consciousness, although I was of course not conscious of it at the time."

"They must have done a good job with the hip. You seem to walk normally."

"Yes, I was pretty lucky. It aches sometimes, and I have an ugly scar right about here, just in front of my butt cheek, but since I'm not a naturist and am unlikely to be a porn star, it really shouldn't matter much. Shelley sees it as a sort of stigmata, another one to go with the scar from the spear gun."

"You do carry your sins with you, Andy."

"Anyway, I woke up in the recovery room after the surgery at around supper time, and they called her in to see me. The distance was still there in her eyes, of course, but she grasped my hand and asked how I felt.

"'I don't really know,'" I said. "'Pretty doped up.'"

"'The surgeon says you're going to be fine,'" she said, "'and that you have a fairly small bandage on your hip compared to that turban on your head. They were able to fix the hip, so no replacement.'"

"'Good. I can just about feel that I have toes, and I can feel your hand, but I hardly know I have a hip or any other part of my torso.'"

"That was all we had to say for a while, until I began to feel nauseated and she called one of the recovery nurses. She fed some medicine into my IV, but it didn't help much. Once I could feel my body again they took me up to a room. Luckily, perhaps, it was a double room and the bed by the window was occupied. Shelley stayed with me while they got everything checked out. In addition to the drip going into my arm I had a catheter filling a bag down by the side of the bed. Since the nausea was no better, the nurse brought in some ice chips and crackers. Shelley fed me the ice with that looking-down-from-space look. She hadn't sat down since I got back to the room and she seemed ready to leave.

"'Are you worried about Jim?' I asked her.

"'He has been shut in all day,' she said.

"'Then go,' I said. 'I can feed myself these crackers if the ice chips stay down. Just get them out of the package for me, okay?'"

"She did that, and rolled the over-bed table up close so I could reach them, turned on the TV, and put the call button near my hand. Then she kissed me on the forehead just below the bandage and told me to sleep well. What I remember thinking is she wanted me to make a full recovery before she killed me."

"Yes, you're lucky she didn't start pulling things out of you right then, especially the catheter, which would really hurt because of that little balloon they inflate in there to keep it in."

"Is there anything even remotely related to the penis that you gay fellers don't know?" Andy asked.

"Fellers?" John said, scrunching up his face. "Hal had to be catheterized when he had a kidney infection last year. So he got this feller up to speed on all the little details. But I sense we're getting close to the climax of this truly frightening tale."

"Yes, we'd better be. I have to go to work at some point this afternoon."

"SHELLEY VISITED ME in the hospital faithfully several times a day, but she never stayed very long on any visit, and unless I was eating she wouldn't even sit down, but stood by the bed asking questions or giving news of Jim, say, in that by-then-familiar inflectionless voice. They let me out on the fifth day, but I was still confined to the couch or the bed at home for another two weeks, before I could begin to get around on crutches. At first I had a daily visit from a nurse, who would take my temperature and blood pressure, and a physical therapist came in three times a week. My parents had driven down to see me once in the hospital—the third day, I think—and then my mother came alone for a couple of days in my first week home just to give Shelley some freedom. But I suspect that Shelley's emotional chilliness drove her back to Strasburg, since she and Shelley always get along well and my mom certainly wasn't wearing out her welcome.

"I tried to raise the subject with Shelley several times, both in the hospital and when I got home.

"'Not yet,' she'd say each time, at first fiercely and then in the flat, distant way she said everything else. She cooked our meals, helped me in and out of the shower, even shared the bed, although she always slept so close to her edge that I was afraid she'd tumble off during the night. She and Jim went for long walks, but whatever she said to him at those times, he always treated me just the same, coming right to the couch when they got home, licking my face if I was sleeping, or nuzzling up to get his ears scratched if I was awake."

"The tension," John said. "It must have been unbearable. I can hardly stand it now."

"Yes, I kept waiting for her to stick a cooking fork in my neck, or perhaps pour boiling water on my face while I was sleeping. But the silent treatment was punishment enough. She wasn't silent, of course, but the flatness in her voice was a version of that.

"Finally, one morning after I'd been home from the hospital for about a week, she helped me to the couch from the bed, and brought me a tray with coffee and cereal and apple juice. She walked over to the glass doors leading to the balcony and stood there looking out. 'Do you love her?' She said it so softly that at first I wasn't sure she had said anything at all. But even at that low volume I could tell that the flatness had left her voice.

"'We had a thing, a passionate thing, years ago in Concord. I thought I was in love with her then. But it ended abruptly.'

"'Do you love her now?'

"'We had no contact at all for, what, six years, and then she turned up in Charlottesville this spring. She'd moved here a year ago, actually, but neither of us knew the other was around. We just ran into each other on campus. She's studying French literature.'

"'Answer me, Andy, for god's sake.' She still had not turned around, but her voice was no longer soft, and her posture, which had been uncharacteristically slumped at first, was now coiled, her shoulders thrown back."

"'It's over, Shelley. I never sought her out, and it was a huge mistake, but it's over. I was driving back from telling her so when the accident happened.'

"Shelley turned then, and her hands were in fists, her face was red and twisted with anger, and tears were coming down her cheeks. She started at me as though she was going to pummel me, and I managed to tip over my tray as I was trying to get into a defensive position. Fortunately I had moved the hot coffee off the tray already, or I would have had another stigmata even closer to my groin than the others."

John didn't even smile, and neither had Andy. John looked terrified.

"For a moment she hesitated as her instinct to clean up the mess lost out to her anger. She hovered over me, her clenched fists up by her shoulders.

"'Goddamn it, you fucker. If you don't answer my question I'll walk out that door and never come back.'"

"I didn't wait for even a moment, never even considered whether or not I should tell her the truth. 'Of course I'm not in love with her,' I said. 'I'm in love with you. I've always been in love with you.'"

"'Then how could you, Andy? I'm just so embarrassed for you. Much more than for myself.' She was crying freely now, but the tears seemed less from her anger than from real grief. 'We were never going to be like that. It's just so ordinary. So Strasburg. You've ruined everything we believed in, everything we are and were going to be.'

"Then she put her fists over her eyes and wept, her shoulders heaving, as she might have wept upon hearing of my death—or might have, at least, before the crash.

"I started to cry, too. The milk and apple juice had soaked through the quilt that was covering me and felt wet on my legs, but I barely noticed. 'I know, I know. I'm just so sorry.' I said this again and again, a mantra, as she continued to cry.

"She kept on crying for several more minutes, but then she stopped. She wiped her eyes on the sleeve of the sweatshirt she was wearing, and then said: 'I'm going to take Jim for a walk. It might be a long one. When I come back I won't have forgiven you. I'll never forgive you for this, Andy. But we won't ever talk about it again—ever. And if you ever see her again, except by accident, I'll leave you and that will be the end of us. Got it?'

"I said I got it and then she and Jim were out the door. It was the first time I had tried to get up by myself, but I got myself off the couch and managed to clean up the mess, drag the quilt to the washing machine, and even change my clothes. She and Jim were indeed gone for a very long time."

AFTER ANDY FINISHED his story, he walked with John to the corner of 18th and Church streets, where they promised to see each other again soon.

"I don't know how you two survived this," John said. "But I'm glad you have. I hope Shelley doesn't know that Susanna and I were friends, or that I stayed over with the two of you that first night."

"No, let's just keep that to ourselves."

John gave Andy a hug, and Andy felt inexplicably lonely as he walked up 18th toward Tessa's place. He wanted to be home with Shelley.

It was several weeks before he and Shelley could arrange to have John and Hal to Charlottesville. If Andy was working both Friday and Sunday at the *Post*, he usually got up early on Saturday to drive home, giving him almost exactly twenty-four hours in Charlottesville before he had to head back. This time Tessa rode with him to see Shelley and to help with a dinner party they were having for Hal and John. They had decided to invite Jan and the man she was now seeing, and one of Sam's former professors, a youngish film scholar who was originally from Texas. They hoped he and Tessa might hit it off. Several people from the Five and Dime would join them later in the evening, after they got off work. Andy had given up his job there, but said he'd be willing to come back on a Saturday night if they were ever shorthanded, given how lucrative Saturdays could be. So far that hadn't happened, and he wanted to keep in touch with the people he liked there, especially Sam and a couple of the downstairs waitresses.

Although it was late October, they lucked out with an Indian summer day, so it was warm enough in the early evening to leave the doors to the balcony open. The trees were just beginning to turn color in town, but the mountains visible from the balcony already had a reddish-orange tint, which the light itself seemed to pick up as the sun began to set. Everyone upon arriving would make a beeline for the balcony, drawn by the amber light and the clear views in the rapidly cooling air.

They had asked Hal and John to come a bit early, so they could have time alone with them. Hal was still wearing his Greek summer tan and as always was energized by the prospect of a party. He gave Shelley an exuberant kiss on the lips and then pulled her to him in a hug that lingered just long enough to say he knew what she had been through and was glad that it was over. John also gave Shelley a warm hug, opting for a cheek rather than the lips, and hugged Tessa as well. Shelley and Tessa had already gotten into the white wine, and Shelley glowed from that and the warmth of the greetings. Even Tessa had a little color in her porcelain cheeks as she was introduced to Hal.

"Where's Jim?" John asked. "I've missed him almost as much as I've missed the two of you."

"We put him in our room to protect the arriving guests from a lickathon," Shelley said. "Especially Hal."

"So kind, my dear," Hal said, and petted Shelley as though she herself were the dog.

"I've got to go see him," John said, and was off.

Hal explained that the bag he was carrying contained the fixings for Campari and soda, which he had grown fond of in Chania that summer. "I even brought my own lemon." He convinced the ladies to try one, too, so the three of them went to the kitchen for ice and Andy went to check on John and Jim.

Jim was sprawled on his back on their bed, and John was sitting on the bed's edge, rubbing his stomach. Clearly Jim was in ecstasy, and didn't even look up when Andy entered the room.

"God, Jim, you'd leave us in a second and never look back, wouldn't you?"

"Ah, well," John said, "you're still probably well ahead of the game as far as loyalty goes. Shelley looks wonderful."

"Yes, this is a big night for her. Our first party in a long time. She's excited to see you two and to have Tessa here."

John said he would be in charge of keeping Jim off the guests, so the three of them went back to the living room just as Jan and her date were arriving. Jan was dressed as usual in tight black jeans, and when she took her jacket off she had on a tight white T-shirt through which her brown nipples, so familiar to Andy from their hallway encounters when she lived with them, showed clearly. She gave Andy a kiss and one of her full-body hugs, implying, he supposed, that all was forgiven now that she had her own man and was no longer furious at Carlos. Unlike Carlos, the new fellow, Michael something or other, was taller than she was and had straight brown hair pulled back in a tight ponytail. He ran a travel agency on the downtown mall, one that specialized in adventure trips to obscure places. He was younger than Carlos, too, probably in his thirties, and although he lacked Carlos' squat, weightlifter build, he looked athletic, with the long muscles of a swimmer, perhaps. He was carrying a large bundle wrapped in clear plastic of what looked like Hawaiian flowers, including at least one bird of paradise, the only flower from the islands that Andy could name.

Andy shook his hand after Jan had introduced them and given a rushed mini-biography, which included that he had been a student at the university and was himself divorced. "Let me take those, Michael," Andy said. "Thank you. They're amazing." He met Shelley coming out from the kitchen and a brief discussion ensued about where they might find a vase large enough to accommodate the flowers. Andy made a haphazard search while Shelley was greeting Jan and Michael, and then settled for a pasta pot, which he filled with water at the sink. Hal and Tessa were still fiddling with the drinks and seemed to be getting on well. What man, straight or gay, could resist her sweet Texas manner?

By the time everyone had a drink and was out on the balcony admiring the view, Andy's former professor arrived, carrying both a bottle of wine and some sort of fancy chocolates for Shelley. His name was Tom Kellogg, and although he had developed a specialty in film he was a member of the English department, a full professor, in fact, and in his early forties. Andy knew him well enough to know that he had two kids not yet in high school, and that his wife had died of cancer several years before. He had come to the Five and Dime now and then with dates, but it was never the same woman twice. An air of sadness seemed to surround him, but he was smiling broadly now, his white teeth showing from within a carefully tended graying beard.

"My goodness, Andy, graduate students live a lot better than they did in my day. What a place you have."

"It belongs to a friend who is unfortunately about to return from overseas, so I fear we won't be living the high life much longer. Also, I have a hardworking wife."

Tom was a careful amalgam of hip and tweedy, wearing light-colored jeans and a sports coat, under which was a dress shirt with several buttons unbuttoned. It gave off just a whiff of the film world, but not desperately so. When the introductions were made on the balcony, it turned out that Tom had published in Hal's quarterly and had frequented Michael's travel business, mainly for cross-country skiing trips for his kids and himself. When he met Tessa, the Texas seemed to come out just a bit more in each of their accents, and neither of them seemed in any way abashed by the obvious but unmentioned attempt to fix them up.

Because the new men in the group seemed to Hal not to have any non-hetero potential, he showered his attention on Shelley, plying her with Campari, following her into the kitchen when she checked on dinner, and found the large vase for the flowers. Hal emerged first with the vase, which he ostentatiously placed on a table in the living room, drawing attention both to them and to himself. Then he came back from the kitchen with a platter of cheese and crackers and olives and nuts, which he dutifully offered to each of the guests. Hal liked being served better than he liked being the server, and when he got to Andy he acknowledged as much.

"My hands are shaking, Andy, holding this for a professional waiter like yourself."

"Maybe it's just the onset of age," Andy offered brightly.

"Hmm. I bet I could still beat you at handball without much trouble. Next time you're in Concord I want a match."

"But you play all the time," Andy said. "Still, you don't scare me."

"I love this Tessa," Hal said. She and Tom were talking animatedly about things Texan at the far end of the balcony. "Is it true you stay with her when you're in Washington? Is this wise?"

"Some of us can keep it in our pants, Hal," Andy said.

"That's not what I hear, old friend," Hal countered softly.

"Ouch, that really isn't playing fair. But I've learned my lesson. Learned it in the hardest possible way."

"That's good, I guess," Hal said. "You seem as if you almost believe it."

"I do, Hal. I really do."

Just then Shelley came through the open doorway and said, "Do what?"

"He wants to take me on at handball, Shelley," Hal said. "He thinks I'm losing it and he wants to prove it. He probably has his eye on John, wants to displace me."

"Don't we all," Shelley said. John was talking to Jan and Michael. It was the tall people group. "Let's hope Andy looks half as good as you do when he's your age."

Michael had pulled out a joint and lit it. It was interesting as he walked it around like another hors d'oeuvre to see that, unlike the old days, when everyone would eagerly smoke or snort or swallow anything they were offered, half of them declined. Tom and Tessa gave friendly shakes of the head and continued talking. John said no and so did Shelley. Hal and Andy took deep drafts and then Michael returned the joint to Jan, who had begun. Hal and Andy edged over to where they were standing and the four of them passed the joint until it was finished. John and Shelley went back to the kitchen, and although Andy was now slightly stoned, he eventually realized that they had been together in there a longish while.

But just then Shelley came through the doors and gave Andy a little pat on the shoulder. Her eyes looked as if she had been crying, but then the eyes of those who had been smoking the joint didn't look much better. Still she was smiling when she announced to everyone that dinner was ready. Andy could see John carrying a large, clearly very hot Dutch oven to the table.

When everyone had found a seat and been served—Shelley had made paella, using saffron Andy had found at an affordable price at a Hispanic grocery in Adams Morgan—John toasted her, not just as the chef but as a person he and Hal adored. Shelley beamed. Andy looked around at the other guests at the table, each of them digging into the aromatic dish in front of them. They weren't seated in pairs, but Andy thought of them that way: Hal and John, Jan and Michael, Tessa and Tom, and of course Shelley and himself. He realized as he gazed around that they all had one thing very much in common, that they'd each been battered by love, and enthralled by it, and that nobody was even remotely ready to give it up. He raised his own glass—the good Pouilly-Fumé that Tom had brought, which they were serving before the more Spartan soave they had in ample reserve—and waited till each one of them had looked his way.

"To romance," Andy said. "May our lives always be ruled by love." Everyone seconded him, clinked glasses, and drank heartily. Even Shelley, after giving him a quizzical look, joined in.

13

AFTER MORE THAN a year of taking things day by day, Andy and Shelley began to find a rhythm in their relationship again that fall. Andy's schedule at the *Post* settled down to Fridays, Sundays, and Mondays during the weeks he was teaching, and he generally spent those nights at Tessa's. Which gave him four nights at home in Charlottesville. Tessa and Tom had hit it off as well as the Watsons had hoped they would, so before long Tessa began to accompany Andy to Charlottesville on Saturday mornings, often offering to drive them in her large BMW, which was newer and a lot more comfortable than the very used Volvo sedan the Watsons had bought to replace Andy's car. Because of Tom's kids, Tessa always stayed with them on these visits, and Tom rarely went to Washington to visit her. The two couples often did things together, even if it was only going out for bad Chinese food, which was the only sort of Chinese food available in Charlottesville. Toward the end of these evenings, Andy and Shelley would take Jim on long walks, giving the new couple what Tessa would refer to as "cuddle time" and what Andy would call "the copulation hour."

The many non-copulation hours that Andy and Tessa spent together, either on the road or in her apartment before or after work, were remarkably free of any sort of sexual tension. This might have seemed more remarkable to Andy than to Tessa, in part because it wasn't wholly true that Andy saw her only as a sister. He was well aware of her natural beauty, her expensive grooming, her confident femininity, and her killer body.

She never dressed provocatively and unlike Jan, was genuinely modest, taking care to be well wrapped up when Andy was in her apartment. But it wasn't as though she were wearing a suit of armor. She often went running in the mornings, and even though she would be sturdily undergirded, her running attire made it pretty easy to imagine the exact contours of her form. And given the creamy whiteness of the flesh that was visible … well, he could not avoid fleeting thoughts of this sort, but he made a determined effort not to dwell on them. Part of Tessa's confidence was physical, and that along with the as-yet unsuppressed aspects of her southern upbringing, made her unselfconscious about touching. She didn't hesitate to muss Andy's hair when she was making a point, or to squeeze his shoulder in the morning when she approached him seated at her kitchen countertop, reading the paper and drinking coffee. He never shrank from her touch, but he tried not to seem to welcome it too much, and he was careful never to reciprocate. So they were aware of each other physically, but it always felt natural and safe. It was unlike any relationship he had ever had, and it made it possible for him and for Shelley to grower fonder and fonder of her.

If Shelley had had any doubts about Tessa, she would never have permitted Andy to stay with her in Washington. But even so, this clearly qualified in Shelley's eyes as a test for Andy. And Shelley could be confident that if he wasn't coming on to Tessa he didn't have time to be coming on to anyone else, given that he was always either working or with Tessa or on his way to or from Charlottesville. The more evidence Shelley had of Andy's good behavior, the more reconciled she became to him, if not to his infidelity. Or so it seemed to Andy.

When they were together in Charlottesville, he and Shelley also had a sort of professional bond now, as he began to teach undergraduates at the university. He often relied on Shelley's experience as a teacher, and she helped him draw up his first syllabus and answered his questions as he prepared for class. Grading papers was something he thought he knew how to do, given its similarity to editing a piece of newspaper copy. She helped him get into the habit of marking his students' work the day it came in, so that it wasn't always hanging over him. Sometimes on Tuesdays he would be too tired to finish, having worked late in Washington the night before, driven home, and taught a class. But he and Shelley sat down together at the dining-room table each Tuesday, Wednesday, and Thursday night for at least a couple of hours after dinner, something she had always done each weeknight while she was teaching. Sitting elbow to elbow for so many hours while concentrating on their work was reassuring to them both. With her help he settled into teaching, and the fact of his needing her help helped to settle their marriage as well.

Oddly enough, Shelley had been less reluctant to allow their sexual relationship to return to normal than she had been about other aspects of the marriage. Within only a few months of his accident she gave up her position at the edge of the bed, and although there was a brief period involving nothing more than cuddle time, it wasn't long before they resumed their own copulation hours with the old regularity. It was all very serious at first, Shelley approaching him with a certain fierceness that didn't quite seem like anger and didn't quite seem not like anger, and for his part Andy could not escape feelings of guilt and shame and sorrow. But they had always been good together physically, and somehow these emotions that had never entered into their lovemaking before only heightened their pleasure in each other now. As the months went by, the strangeness subsided and if the urgency subsided with it, their returning confidence in each other allowed them, at least, to appreciate again the many comic possibilities built into the act of sex. The return of their old repertoire of jokes that were reliably funny to them—jokes that would not only be unfunny but meaningless to others—was the surest sign yet that the trust was returning to their marriage, not only Shelley's trust in Andy but his own trust in himself.

BECAUSE THEY DID not yet have children (Eric was not yet "a gleam in his old man's eye," as Hal would have put it) and because he was still one of the newer copy editors in the Lifestyles section, Andy volunteered to work on Thanksgiving night. Andy's parents had agreed to have an early dinner in Strasburg so that he and Shelley could be there before he headed to Washington for work. Shelley would eat with her family later in the day and spend Thursday and Friday nights with them, and she and Andy would meet back in Charlottesville on Saturday. The layout editor showed his gratitude to Andy by giving him an earlier shift on the Monday of Thanksgiving week, one that would be over at 11 P.M. Since he would have a short week at home anyway, Andy decided to surprise Shelley by driving to Charlottesville after work that night, something he had talked about doing in the past but not yet actually done, given how easy it was to go back to Tessa's and then drive home in the morning after a reasonably good night's sleep.

When he got off from work that Monday night, he walked up to Tessa's and left her a note, since she would be doing the weather for the 11 P.M. news at just about that time and would not be back at her place until after midnight. He was able to remember where he'd parked the Volvo and to get out of the city in record time. With any luck he'd be slipping into bed with Shelley before two. They'd picked out this Volvo not only because it was a good price, since it was a 1970 and it was now 1977, meaning the 1978 models were already for sale, but because it had a good radio and speakers. In that odd way that happens sometimes at night, Andy was able for a while on the way home to pick up a radio station from Chicago that played just the sort of music he could bellow out, keeping himself wide awake. There was some old Dylan, some newish Randy Newman, even the Rolling Stones doing "Sweet Virginia," as if whoever was playing records so far away could imagine him speeding through the dark Virginia countryside. When he lost the station he just kept on singing other songs whose lyrics he mostly knew: "Brown Sugar," "Rednecks," "House of the Rising Sun," some Beatles and James Taylor and Simon and Garfunkle songs. By the time he got to the outskirts of Charlottesville he was more than wide awake, his adrenaline pumping, and he worried that he might have trouble falling asleep. When he turned in to Altamont Circle he glanced up to the top of their building and saw that there was light coming from the living room, something he would not have expected. Shelley was usually good about turning off the lights, and unless Tessa had called to tell her that Andy was coming, she would not have known to leave them on for him.

The sound of Andy's key in the lock brought Jim running and he met Andy at the door with barks and licks. When Andy looked up, there was Shelley who was following behind Jim. Her look was not one of welcome, or of any sort of greeting. He wasn't sure what the expression on her face meant until he walked toward her and saw, seated on the living-room couch behind her, none other than Randy McRogers, the horny red-headed Scotsman who owned the Five and Dime. He was wearing the same look of astonishment and fear that Andy now recognized as having been on Shelley's face. Before Andy could say anything, Randy was on his feet, grabbing his coat, which had been flung over a chair, and slipping past him, saying only "You have a very loyal wife, Andrew." He had not bothered to burr either of the r's in the sentence and went out the door without bothering, either, to put on his coat.

"My god, Shelley. Randy? Randy, of all people?"

"Nothing happened, Andy. Nothing was going to happen. I know this looks bad …"

Although Andy was flabbergasted, he had not yet had time to get angry, and one thought that went through his head immediately was that it could have been worse, a lot worse. Shelley's clothes were not in any way disheveled and they seemed to have been drinking Cokes, for goodness sake. He picked up a glass from the coffee table and gave it a sniff. No rum.

"I don't guess there's a very good explanation for why you would be sitting in our living room at 2 A.M. with any man, much less Randy. My god, Randy. Did you pick him up at the Five and Dime? Sit at the bar and wait for him to come to you?"

"God no, Andy. I wasn't sleepy so I took Jim out for a walk at about eleven. We walked through the downtown mall and, at the far end, there was Randy in his pickup truck. Probably he had just dropped off one of his 'dates.' He tooted at me and when I walked over to the truck he offered to give Jim and me a ride. When I explained that we were out for a walk he offered to join us. Since it was a time of night when I wouldn't have been comfortable going too far from the mall, I agreed. So he parked his truck and came along and you know how ingratiating he can be when he wants to be. He was all courtly charm and rolling r's."

"Yes, because he wanted to get into your pants."

"I knew that, and I knew it wasn't going to happen, but I suppose I was curious about what it would feel like to have a man come on to me. I mean plenty of men flirt with me, but I haven't been given the full treatment in quite a while."

They were both still standing in the living room, facing each other. Andy hadn't even taken off his coat, and neither of them had moved a muscle. Jim was lying down between them, occasionally looking up when he heard his name.

"So it was an ego thing? But with Randy? Randy will fuck anyone, for god's sake. How does that feed your ego?"

"No, not ego, just curiosity. I wondered, Andy, what it would feel like to be just a little disloyal, to keep a real secret, something you seem to be so good at."

Andy didn't know what to say. Of course he deserved this, deserved even more, if the truth were told. But the timing just seemed so inexplicable, so mean, somehow, given how much progress they had been making.

"Have you done this sort of thing before? How many Cokes at 2 A.M. will settle the debt?"

"Oh, it would take many, many Cokes, Andy, if that's what I'm doing. But this isn't about arithmetic. It isn't about infidelity, at least not about mine. It's about trying to understand what it can possibly be like to be you."

With that she started to cry, and before Andy could really register that she was crying, she'd turned and gone to the bedroom, shutting the door without quite slamming it.

Andy took off his coat, went to the cabinet in the living room where they kept the hard liquor, and poured about three fingers of Virginia Gentleman. He and Jim stood on the balcony in the cold air for a long time while he drank the bourbon. Because Shelley never came out of the bedroom, he went to the guest room and pulled a pillow and quilt off the bed, and settled himself on the couch, Jim on the floor beside him. If the adrenaline had already been pumping when he arrived home, it had gushed during his brief fight with Shelley. The liquor had not done much to counteract it, and he slept fitfully if at all. After what seemed like a couple of hours he heard the bedroom door open and the sound of Shelley's footsteps in the hallway. As she approached the couch he could see in the dim light the ample white globes of her breasts and the dark triangle of her pubic hair. She slipped in under the quilt with him, and neither of them said anything. When he buried his face in her neck he could tell that she had brushed her long dark hair, which felt fluffy and soft. Then she straddled him and helped him off first with his T-shirt and then with his undershorts. They made love on the couch slowly and tenderly. They did not talk at all, and steered well clear of the comic repertoire. Andy never thought even once that this had been the very place where he had first made love to Susanna after all those years apart.

AFTERWARD, THEY DOZED for a while on the couch and then went back to their bedroom, where they slept in each other's arms until the alarm when off at seven so Shelley could get ready for school. Andy fell back to sleep while she was showering and drying her hair, and when she woke him to kiss him goodbye she was dressed in a wool skirt and thin, round-necked white sweater that clung to her figure in a way that would make the boys in her classes a little crazy, he suspected.

"Are we okay for now?" she asked him and offered a wan smile.

"We're okay period," he said.

His last class before Thanksgiving was that afternoon and Shelley had a half-day on Wednesday. They didn't talk again about Randy or about anything else touching on their marriage, but they were careful and courteous with each other when they were together. When Shelley got home from school Wednesday afternoon, she suggested that they take a bath and then they spent the hours until suppertime in bed, cuddling and love-making and snoozing. When they arose and dressed and took Jim out for a walk before dinner, they both could tell that things were right again, and they were able to drop the elaborate courtesy and be together as they always had been.

THE FIRST CHANCE she got on Thanksgiving Day, Andy's mom

asked him how things were between Shelley and him. Andy overcame his immediate impulse to feel that the question was a not-so-subtle attempt to pry. Things had gone wrong often enough at these family gatherings that he had begun to prepare mentally before they began, reminding himself that they were hard for everyone in the family to negotiate, and trying to remember that these were the people who were, more than anyone else in life, on his side. As he and Shelley had driven over in separate cars, so that he could go on to Washington to work, he had tried to think back on the many times he had been oversensitive and too quick to misinterpret a question that later seemed harmless enough. He told himself, almost like a mantra, that the first hour was the most dangerous, that if he could keep from blowing up and hurting his parents' feelings during that time then the visit had a good chance of being emotionally uneventful.

So he took a deep breath and said, "We're great, Mom. We really are."

"That's how it seemed to me the minute you walked through the door together, or else I would never have asked."

Right, he thought.

Instead he said, "And I know the question you want to ask next is whether we're thinking about getting pregnant."

"Andrew, I would never …"

"No, of course you wouldn't, Mom. But just in case you're curious, the answer is 'Soon.'"

The two of them were standing in the kitchen of the postwar colonial house in which he'd grown up. The house itself was not anything special, but the lots in this subdivision had been large, almost an acre, and the foliage had matured over the decades, so that it all felt a little grander than it was. His parents had slowly added to the house as they could afford it, most conspicuously putting on a wing with a new master bedroom and bath upstairs and a family room with a fireplace downstairs. The family room was where Shelley was now, with his father, his older sister, Ellen, and her husband, Joe, and their younger brother, Danny, who was halfway through college at Virginia Tech. His parents already had drawings for a small swimming pool with some sort of pool building that they would do once Danny graduated. Andy's dad was an attorney with a practice specializing in a little bit of everything, and his income was directly tied to the local economy. In good times he did well; in bad times he did a lot of criminal work and often received payment in the form of venison steaks or yard work or a tune-up for his car.

Andy's sister was an attorney like their dad, an assistant prosecutor for the county. She and her husband had been married for a year or so longer than Andy and Shelley, but she had managed to make the conversation about children off limits with their mother, something she could somehow enforce because of her innate bossiness. This transferred the burden to Andy to supply the much-desired first grandchild.

"So once you two get settled in Washington, I can begin to hope?"

Andy's mom had gone to college, at Longwood, where she trained to be a schoolteacher, and she'd met Andy's father at a fraternity party at Hampden-Sydney College, and they dated while he went to law school in Richmond, where he was from. When he graduated they got married and he decided to practice in Strasburg, where she was from and had returned to, teaching in the local elementary school. She got pregnant with Ellen during their first year of marriage, and after that she never went back to teaching. In recent years, with Ellen and Andy long gone, and once Danny had gotten old enough to get his driver's license so that she didn't need to be available to drive him places, she had begun to work in the law office, doing research and helping with the bookkeeping, cutting down on the expenses for his dad's practice.

Andy knew that this was not all she'd hoped to do with her life, and she was still young, in her late fifties. She looked good, having put on only a little weight over the years, and she evidently colored her hair to keep it the same cinnamon brown it had been as long as he could remember, in contrast to his father's head of close-cropped silvery hair. Her family had been deeply sustaining for most of her adult life, but now her own parents were gone, her siblings had either moved away or grown resentful of her comparative affluence, or both, and she was lonely. Ellen was nearby but was so focused on her career that she didn't offer his mother much in the way of support. Now his mother had just finished peeling potatoes and cutting them up to boil, meaning she was more than halfway through her Thanksgiving dinner preparations, which she had begun at dawn by stuffing the turkey and getting it in the oven.

In a sudden burst of sympathy, Andy crossed the kitchen to the sink, and leaned over her shoulder to give her a kiss on the cheek. This discombobulated her, and she said something about not surprising her when she was holding a knife, but he knew she was pleased.

"We'll see what we can do about that baby, Mom. As you say, once we get settled in D.C. It's about time I beat Ellen at something."

"It's not a race, Andy," she said, but not very convincingly. "Pour yourself some coffee and go visit with the rest of the family."

Just then Shelley came into the kitchen. "What can I do, Kate?" she asked. Andy's mom's face lit up.

"Let me get my list," she said.

WHEN ANDY GOT back to Tessa's that night after work, he

found her sitting in the big bay window on the main floor of her apartment, staring out into R Street. There was a bottle of tequila on the table beside her, along with what was left of a lime and a bowl of what he assumed was salt. She held a glass in her hand, and it was pretty obvious that she was loaded. For one thing, she was dressed only in a man's white shirt, white panties, and furry pink slippers. Her long dark hair was not combed or teased or pulled back in a tight ponytail as it usually was, but looked more mussed than it did even when he sometimes caught a glimpse of her first thing in the morning. And she had on no makeup whatsoever, which made her look appealingly girlish and somehow unformed.

"Come have a drink, Andy," she said, unselfconscious about how much leg she was showing and how little else the shirt was covering up. "Happy Thanksgiving!"

"You didn't have to work tonight?" he asked.

"No, that dumbass who does weekend weather also does holidays. I'd have been glad to do it, since I didn't have anything else to do—Tom and his girls went to spend Thanksgiving with his dead wife's family. But it's a contract thing. Not enough time to go back to Texas, since I work again tomorrow night."

"You should have come to my parents' house with us."

"Oh, you two lovebirds deserve a little time without me hanging around."

"Still, you don't seem to have had the best Thanksgiving."

"Me? I'm fine. Went out to dinner with some friends from work, and then I got into the cactus juice. Have some with me?"

She swung her legs off the window seat cushions and was facing him, holding out the bottle. "Grab a glass and come sit beside me here. It's okay, I won't bite."

He went to get a glass and although he was dazed and not a little stimulated by this side of her that he had never known before, still he had the presence of mind to tell himself that this was Tessa and this was definitely off limits.

She poured the tequila into the glass he brought her until it was half filled. He took a slow sip, declining her offer of lime and salt, and felt the burn as it went down.

"Come sit by me, Andy. You know I'm a good girl. I wouldn't do anything to hurt Shelley or cause any stress in that perfect marriage of yours. I'm just a little drunk and I feel a little abandoned by Tom. It's like I'm the other woman even though the wife is dead. Long dead. Sucks."

Andy put down his glass and sat beside Tessa, careful to leave a foot or more of space between them. "I'm not scared of you, Tessa. It's just I've never seen you like this."

"I know; I look like a tramp."

"Not at all. You look wonderful. The real you is even more beautiful than the TV you."

She reached over and mussed Andy's hair. "You be careful, Andrew, I'm feeling just a bit vulnerable right now. I never do take holidays well."

Tessa asked him how his day had gone, and he told her about dinner with his family, how they'd all managed to get along, how having to leave right after dinner for work had been a good thing, how stopping by Shelley's parents' for only twenty minutes had been an even better thing—how all in all it had been a really good day.

"God, your lives are so perfect, Andy. I love you both but man it kills me how perfect you two are."

"Really? You're the one with the glamorous life. We're just struggling along, trying to get our lives started."

"But you're so good together. It isn't fair. Even when you fucked your old girlfriend—sorry, did you know that Shelley told me all about that?—it was just a blip on the screen."

"It was a lot more than a blip, Tess. We're still getting over it."

Tessa poured herself another drink, sucked on a slice of lime, licked her finger, stuck it in the salt, sucked on that, too, and then downed about a third of a glass of tequila in one gulp. Then she started to cry.

He rubbed her shoulder and when she didn't stop crying he told her about finding Shelley and Randy McRogers together earlier in the week.

That made her stop crying. "No!" she said. "D'you think anything happened? And Shelley told me the thing she hates most is sneaking around. Here I believed everything she says."

Andy told Tessa Shelley's side of what happened, and how willing he was to accept it and forgive her, how he was only angry for a little while.

"Really?" Tess said. "You're some kind of angel, aren't you, Andy? You really need some sort of reward for so much good behavior."

With that she swung one leg over so that she was straddling him. She looked at him for a moment and then pulled his face to her chest and cradled his head in her arms. As she held him pressed against her breasts and he held her, his arms around the middle of her back, he could feel her begin to cry again, her emotions building until her chest was heaving against the side of his face. Andy stayed very still and waited until she had cried herself out. When she stopped he thought about how much he would like to undo the last few buttons of her shirt and slip off her panties and just feast his eyes on all of that extraordinarily porcelain flesh. His dick was hard against her crotch. But he just held her tight while her breathing slowed and she continued to hold him, too. He thought she might have dozed a bit and still he didn't move a muscle, but just absorbed the rhythm of her breathing. Finally he mustered all of his willpower, knowing that part of him would regret this for the rest of his days, and also knowing that this was in some ways the first moment of his marriage to Shelley.

"Let's get you to bed, Tessa," he said. He held her hand and she followed him like a little girl. He tucked her in and she was asleep before he left the room. His one hope was that she would be too drunk to remember any of it.

WHETHER SHE REMEMBERED it or not Andy would never know. The next morning they both slept in, and when she found him seated at the kitchen counter she had showered and was dressed in her usual running outfit. She tousled his hair as she generally did. "I seem to have drunk a bit more tequila than was absolutely necessary," she said as she poured herself some coffee. And that was the closest she came to any sort of recognition of the events of the night before. Both of them worked that Friday night, came home, and went directly to bed so they could get an early start to Charlottesville the next morning. She and Tom and he and Shelley went to La Hacienda that night and afterward they all went to Tom's house for a drink, the first time they had done that. Tom's kids had stayed on for the weekend with their grandparents, which meant that Tessa, also for the first time, would be sleeping over with Tom. Andy could see on Tessa's face as he and Shelley hugged her after the drink that however disappointed she had been about being shut out of his Thanksgiving celebration, and whether in any case that had just been the tequila talking, she was happy to be where she was right now.

As they rode home in the car, Shelley said, "Tessa told me after dinner that she and Tom had a serious talk about their relationship today. He wants her to get to know his kids. He thinks she should start staying over with him when she visits, and that the kids will just have to get used to it."

"That's real progress," Andy said. "I thought she looked especially pleased with things tonight. But I wonder what the next step could be. I can't imagine her leaving her TV job for life as a professor's wife in Charlottesville. And he's got tenure. Unless he can wangle a job at one of the Washington universities, he's not going anywhere."

"Maybe this will be enough for her for now. And you never know what people will do for love."

He thought about Tessa just two nights before, what she was on the verge of doing not for love but because of love. He knew Tessa liked him, and would have been comfortable with him had they succumbed, but she would have been acting out of misery, the disappointment she felt in her relationship with Tom. How awful would they both have felt now, she given the sudden turn in that relationship, he because he had allowed the prospect of a moment's pleasure to undermine all the progress he had been making with Shelley. Even if Shelley had never found out, he and Tessa would have shared the shame and regret for a very long time.

"No," he said to Shelley now. "You never do know."

14

TWO DAYS AFTER John Lennon's death, Andy met Tessa in the early afternoon before both of them had to go to work. She was accompanying him to Garfinckel's on a special mission. Shelley was turning thirty in a few days and he had already planned a party for her for Saturday night. Millie Copenhaver was helping him with that, but Tessa was helping him with a more delicate problem. Shelley was now sufficiently pregnant with their second child that her underwear was on the verge of no longer fitting her. If she took the same approach to the clothing problem as she had with her first pregnancy, anything new she might buy would be strictly utilitarian. She probably wouldn't buy anything new for herself in the way of underwear, but dig out the same garments she had worn when she was pregnant with Eric, what Andy liked to call her orthopedic underwear. He didn't think he could face that industrial-strength stuff again, but more important, of course, he didn't think she should have to. He wanted to buy her things that would help her feel as beautiful as she was during the last months of her pregnancy. When he explained the problem to Tessa, she had immediately volunteered to meet him in the foundations department of Garfinckel's.

He entered the store from F Street, wondering whether this had been a good idea. As embarrassing as it was to shop for women's underwear alone, might it be that much worse to do it with Tessa? But when he saw Tessa, wearing sunglasses and a scarf, a look she had increasingly adopted as her TV fame had grown in Washington, he could tell immediately by the brisk way she approached him and kissed him on the cheek that she was going to be in charge and it was going to be fine.

"Not sure if we can find what we want here," Tessa said. "But if we can it will be so much better than the maternity department. At least that's my guess, since I've never been knocked up myself."

Given that they were there after the lunch hour and that downtown shopping was a dying habit, the store was not crowded, so an elegantly dressed saleswoman soon latched on to them. She was tall and a very dark shade of black, with dramatic cheekbones and the carriage of a queen. Had he been alone, Andy would not have been able to speak at all in her presence. But perhaps because she and Tessa shone with something like the same wattage, they seemed to form a team immediately, Tessa saying only a few confidential words before the saleswoman set off in a purposeful way, Tessa matching her stride for stride and Andy hanging back. Already overcome with that deep feeling of malaise that shopping always triggered in him, he was content to let the two women work things out. He paused at a case filled with plastic eggs and began touching them idly, his mind already far away from anything in the store.

"André? C'est toi?" He looked up to see a black beret and that rust-colored hair that could belong to only one person.

"Susanna!" He could hardly believe it.

"What are you touching there, Andy? Stockings? Not for yourself, I hope."

He quickly put down the plastic egg he held in one hand. "No, I'm here with my friend Tessa buying, um, some things for Shelley for her birthday."

He thought he should give her a kiss but decided not to. She was wearing a long black wool coat to go with her beret and black leather gloves. In her hands were what appeared to be half a dozen pairs of panties.

"But, Susanna," he said, looking at the objects she held.

"I know, I know. But I have a real job now, Andy, as an analyst at the World Bank, and well, you know, we must put aside childish things."

"Or in your case put on girlish things."

"Yes, exactement. How are you, Andy? Did you recover fully?"

He felt stupid with the surprise of seeing Susanna again after another jump of years. At first he thought she was speaking of his heart, but then he realized she meant the accident. They had not seen each other again since that day.

"Yes, they had to put my hip back together, but it mended fine and it never bothers me. A full recovery, yes."

They stood looking at each other, not eighteen inches separating their faces. Neither said anything for a long few moments.

He saw Tessa and the sales clerk making their way in his direction. Susanna put the panties down on the egg display and dug in her wallet. "Here's my card, Andy. Perhaps we can have a drink sometime and catch up. I want to know what you're doing, but now's not the time or place."

He didn't say anything but he leaned over and gave her a kiss on the cheek and smelled her familiar peppery smell. And then she gathered up her things and was gone.

"You shouldn't let strange women pick you up in department stores, Andy," Tessa said when she reached him. "Although that was a very beautiful girl. Way out of your league, I'd guess."

"I'm sure you're right, Tess," he said, relieved that she had either missed the kiss on the cheek or was only pretending to misunderstand the situation. "Here," he said, handing her Susanna's card. "Destroy the evidence, won't you?"

She took the card and looked at it and said, "You can throw

this away, Andy, but the World Bank is only a ten-minute walk from here."

When neither of them said anything for a moment, the sales clerk turned to a glass-topped counter and began to spread out the panties and bras that she and Tessa had chosen. "I think you'll find some things to like here, Mr. Watson," she said.

THEY HAD MANAGED to fill their admittedly small row house with friends for Shelley's party. The Copenhavers were there, of course, and Tom had come up from Charlottesville to join Tessa. Saint John and Hal had driven from Concord and would be staying with Mark, who had had other plans for the evening. ("Doesn't want to encourage breeders," was Hal's assessment.) Even Andy's odd friend Rick the super-rationalist, who was now a corporate lawyer in Washington and no less cynical or socially awkward for all the wealth he had already accumulated, had come, armed with a magnum of Taittinger no less. There were other friends from his college days and Shelley's, people who had also been drawn to Washington and were beginning families and settling in. And there were friends that Andy had made on the copy desk at work. In the early part of the evening, Shelley drifted among the guests with Eric in her arms, Jim padding closely behind them like a Secret Service agent. She was wearing the embroidered denim maternity jumper that had been her uniform when she was pregnant with Eric, somewhat dressed up tonight with a white silk turtleneck. Because her actual birthday had been the day before, Andy had given her the several elaborately wrapped (by Tessa) gifts in the Garfinckel's boxes, so he knew she was looking crisp and frilly beneath the jumper. Her skin was glowing even more brightly than usual, and her dark hair was even shinier, perhaps because of the hormones the pregnancy had triggered. Eric was himself looking snazzy as well as snug, wearing a new pair of blue Dr

Denton's that Tessa, his godmother, had bought him. He was playing peekaboo with the guests, now shyly burying his face in his mother's neck, now squealing and laughing at people he knew, his face turning red with pleasure in the warming room. Ellen, a high-school girl who lived two houses down, was coming at eight-thirty to put Eric to sleep after Shelley nursed him. She would sit with him upstairs in case the festivities woke him up. Millie was in the small kitchen warming the gallons of chili she had made, and was opening containers of condiments she had sliced or chopped or grated earlier in the day. David Copenhaver was wandering between the kitchen and the back porch, where there were several cases of Rolling Rock on ice, plus the miscellaneous six-packs of beer the guests brought, and jugs of Inglenook white and red. Tessa, the only bona-fide celebrity at the party, was meeting her fans, charming them with her natural modesty and self-deprecating humor. Tom stood alongside her, beaming with pleasure. Andy was also greeting the guests and tending to their needs, waiting for the call from Millie to get their balky oven going when she wanted to heat the loaves of French bread she had found somewhere in McLean that day. One of his friends from work had agreed to man the stereo and had come in with a large box of his own albums, "just in case." As the noise level rose in the room, Andy got a glimpse of Shelley and Eric and whoever that was growing under her jumper. Her face had gone as rosy as Eric's. She was flanked by Hal and John, Jim on guard behind her, as Hal was making all of them laugh, undoubtedly recounting some new outrage in the Concordia English department. Andy could not think of a time when he had been happier.